ALEX KAVA

BLACK FRIDAY

A MAGGIE O'DELL NOVEL

MIRA®

MIRA®

ISBN-13: 978-0-7783-2800-1

Recycling programs
for this product may
not exist in your area.

BLACK FRIDAY

For questions and comments about the quality of this book please contact us at
Customer_eCare@Harlequin.ca.

www.MIRABooks.com

Printed in U.S.A.

Walter Platt Carlin
November 13, 1922, to September 6, 2008
Husband, father, officer, gentleman, friend—
You were definitely one of a kind.
We miss you every single day.

CHAPTER
1

Friday morning, November 23
Mall of America
Bloomington, Minnesota

Rebecca Cory stood her ground despite another elbow shoved into her shoulder blades. She'd let the first two shoves go. A quick glance back at the tattooed man convinced her to ignore this one, too. The man towered over her, wearing camouflage pants and a muscle T-shirt. No signs of a coat. Quite a strange fashion statement considering it was twenty degrees outside and snowing, but not a bad idea in the crowded mall.

Even with a glance it would have been hard for Rebecca not to notice the purple-and-green dragon that snaked down the man's arm, its tail curling up around his neck and its fire-breathing head squeezing out of the T-shirt's tight armhole. The tattoo crawled all the way down past the man's elbow. The same elbow that kept finding its way into the middle of Rebecca's shoulder blades.

She told herself to be patient. She could finally see the

order counter as the line to the mall's coffee bar grew shorter. It wouldn't be much longer. She tried to concentrate on the Christmas music, what she could hear of it through the crowd's chatter and the temper tantrums of impatient toddlers.

"…in a winter wonderland."

She loved that song. But it certainly didn't feel like winter in here. Sweat trickled down her back. She wished she had left her coat back with Dixon and Patrick who were guarding a rare find, a bistro table and four chairs in the mall's overcrowded food court.

Rebecca hummed with the music. She knew all the words. They had sung Christmas songs on their long road trip. Connecticut to Minnesota. Twenty-one hours. Thirteen hundred miles. Surviving on Red Bull, convenience-store coffee and McDonalds. She hadn't caught up yet on sleep although yesterday they all crashed after Thanksgiving dinner at Dixon's grandparents' house. The first holiday meal she'd had in years—turkey, dressing, real mashed potatoes and all the trimmings. Granddad said a blessing. Nanna served seconds whether you asked for them or not. Dixon had no clue how lucky he was. Family, tradition, stability, unconditional love. It gave Rebecca hope to see those things still existed despite being absent from her family's life.

Another elbow.

Damn!

She resisted looking back this time.

What in the world was she doing here?

She hated malls and yet here she was on the day after Thanksgiving, the busiest shopping day and craziest shopping crowd of the year. She'd let Dixon talk her into it, just like this whole trip, convincing her it'd be an adventure she'd never forget. He'd been doing crap like that since they were in kindergarten and he convinced her paste tasted like cotton candy. You'd think she'd learn by now that Dixon's taste for adventure was pretty much like his taste for cotton candy, tame and sugar-coated, the hype being the most exciting part of anything Dixon did. What did she expect from a guy who quoted Batman and Robin?

And poor Patrick, along for the ride, trying to be the good sport.

Patrick.

He was a whole different story. She should have found Patrick's behavior endearing. Instead, she thought it a bit suspicious that this totally cool and together guy would want to travel 1300 miles to spend Thanksgiving with her and Dixon. Seemed a long way to go just to get inside her pants.

That wasn't fair.

She knew he didn't have any family to keep him in Connecticut over the long holiday weekend. His mom was in Green Bay. He had a stepsister in D.C. He'd asked if they could cut through Wisconsin on the way back, like that was part of his excuse to go along. That maybe they could just drop in and say "hi" to his mom. *But no big deal if it didn't happen.*

That was Patrick. Low-key, mature, steady as a rock. Dixon called it "boring." Rebecca called it dependable and she liked that about Patrick even if she wasn't so sure about his intentions. Dependable felt good. Having Patrick along felt good, though she didn't like admitting that even to herself.

They'd become friends working at Champs across from the University of New Haven. Patrick tended bar and Rebecca waited tables. She wasn't old enough to serve drinks to the table and if there wasn't another "of age" waitress working then Patrick did it for her, always so patient about it even when he was swamped behind the bar.

Patient, kind, gentle...very suspicious.

Pretty weird, or maybe just sad and pathetic, that she found all that suspicious. Mostly in the beginning. Not so much anymore. Next to Dixon, Patrick was her best friend. Her mom didn't think it was normal for Rebecca to have boys as best friends.

"Are you having sex with these boys?" her mom wanted to know. Then when Rebecca told her "absolutely not," her mom seemed even more perplexed.

"You're not a lesbian, are you?" her mom had asked and quickly added, "Not that there's anything wrong with that."

In the last three years Rebecca had watched her mom and dad yell their way through a divorce. Her dad immediately married the coworker he claimed to have just met. Her mother reciprocated with her own stream of men. After watching the two of them, Rebecca had long ago made the decision to concentrate on her future, to use their love life catastrophes as inspiration. Her future was her escape and she wouldn't allow someone, dysfunctional parents or a boyfriend, to screw that up for her.

Besides, her love for animals, especially dogs, was the one thing Rebecca knew without question. Taking care of them, healing them would save her. She looked to it as her salvation from an otherwise dreary, miserable life. She knew veterinary school would be a long haul, but she was willing to put in the tough hours. Maybe someday have her own clinic. That and a pack of dogs, a couple of horses, some cats, too. Her mom wouldn't even let her have a small dog in their post-divorce condo. It was just as well. Not having someone she was obligated to, had made it easier to leave for college and live on campus. Same theory went for not having someone to hold her back, distract her from her dream.

When her mom asked if she was coming home for Thanksgiving, Rebecca's first inclination was to blurt out that she didn't have a home. But her mom wouldn't have understood. And she certainly wouldn't have allowed Rebecca to travel halfway across the country with Dixon and Patrick, so Rebecca lied.

No, not really a lie.

She simply told her mom that her dad had asked her to spend Thanksgiving with his new family. That was actually true. He had asked her to join them on their extravagant Thanksgiving trip to Jamaica. It wasn't Rebecca's fault that her mom hadn't checked it out, that she would rather swallow fire than talk to her ex-husband.

By the time Rebecca made her way back to the table, Patrick had gotten a Cinnabon for each of them. From the look on Dixon's face she knew Patrick was making him wait for her.

Add dependable and courteous to that list.

It made Rebecca smile just as Andy Williams started singing, "I'll be Home for Christmas." The mall must have the same Christmas CD collection that Dixon owned.

Dixon was singing the words to "I'll be Home for Christmas" as she set down his Red Bull and coffees for her and Patrick.

She barely sat down and he bit off a mouthful of cinnamon roll while popping the tab on his drink. Her friend was charming and talented and witty and totally oblivious to anyone else when he was obsessed. Which was the reason they were here at the mall on the day after Thanksgiving. His latest obsession involved the red backpack at his feet.

"Chad and Tyler are already here."

He waved at them across the food court but they even didn't look his way. Typical, but Rebecca didn't point out to Dixon that the two jocks still treated him like an elementary school tag-along. The four of them had gone to school together up until Rebecca's mom dragged her away to Connecticut. Dixon chose West Haven for college partly to be with Rebecca but as soon as he came home to Minnesota, Chad and Tyler could draw him into their escapades with a simple phone call.

Rebecca noticed they both carried red backpacks identical to Dixon's. What did he get himself into this time? She pulled off her coat and let it hang over the back of her chair. She usually stayed away from Dixon's adventures. She wiped at her bangs that were pasted to her forehead and stretched her back expecting it to ache from the tattooed man's elbow.

"We agreed to start on the third floor and work our way down."

"What exactly is it you guys are doing?" Patrick asked.

Rebecca wanted to kick him under the table. Dixon took on causes like they were T-shirts with slogans that he changed every other week. Most likely this was Chad and Tyler's idea. Dixon read Vince Flynn novels and superhero comic books—Batman was currently his favorite. He did a cool imitation of Homer Simpson and knew all the characters from *Lord of the Rings*. Not only could he find Venus, and sometimes Mars, in the night sky, he could name all three stars in Orion's Belt. When he told Rebecca he had decided to major in cyber-crime, she couldn't imagine him stepping out of his fantasy world long enough to deal with real life criminals. He was a smart, quirky guy and Rebecca hoped he'd realize soon that he didn't need Chad and Tyler.

"Do you realize that eighty percent of toys sold in the U.S.A. are made in China?" Dixon told Patrick as he stuffed another piece of cinnamon roll into his mouth. "And that's just toys. Don't even get me started about other products. Like those cute little patriotic flag pins everyone puts on their lapels...made in China." He drew out the phrase like it was all the proof he needed to substantiate his argument. Never mind that it sounded like he had memorized it from some pamphlet.

Patrick glanced at Rebecca as he sipped his coffee. She winced, wanting to tell him it was too late.

"Over a half million production jobs were outsourced to other countries last year," Dixon continued. "Just to make everyday products that we can't live without."

"Like your new iPhone," Rebecca said pointing to the gadget in Dixon's shirt pocket, the earbuds a constant fixture dangling around his neck. "Made in China but you can't live without it."

"These are different." He rolled his eyes for Patrick as if saying she didn't know what she was talking about. "Besides, this was a gift, a reward, in exchange for lugging around this backpack all day."

"Ahh," Rebecca said and didn't have to add that she knew there had to be a catch.

"And I can live without it, Miss Smartypants," he added.

"Really?" Rebecca raised an eyebrow to challenge him.

"Of course."

She put out her hand. "Then loan it to me for the day. You owe me for losing my cell phone."

"I didn't lose it. I just haven't remembered where I placed it."

But already Dixon's smile disappeared as if he was

trying to contemplate life without immediate access and communication to the world. Just when she thought he couldn't bear to relinquish it, he pulled the cord from around his neck and slid the cord and the iPhone across the table to her. The smile reappeared.

"Don't break it. I just got it."

"What about the backpack?" Patrick asked.

Both Rebecca and Dixon looked at him as though they completely forgot what they had been talking about. Patrick pointed to the pack at Dixon's feet.

"What's the deal with the backpack?" he asked again.

"That, my friend, contains the secret weapon." Dixon was back to his infomercial. "Inside is an ingenious contraption that will emit a wireless signal. Completely harmless," he waved his hand, "but enough interference to mess up a few computer systems. Wake up a few of these retailers. Last time I was home Chad and Tyler took me to a rally with this cool professor at UMN, drives a Harley, one of the big ones."

Rebecca couldn't help but smile. Dixon wouldn't know a Harley from a Yamaha, but she didn't say anything.

"This is a guy who's been in the trenches, knows what he's talking about. You know, he's been to the Middle East, Afghanistan, Russia, China. Professor Ryan says that until we hit people in the almighty pocketbook nobody's gonna care that we outsource hundreds of thousands of jobs every year or that the southern invasion is stealing twice that many jobs right here, right out from under us."

"Southern invasion?" It was Rebecca's turn to roll her eyes at Dixon. She'd lived through many of his obsessions and humored him by listening to all of his rants, but once in a while she had to let him know she couldn't take him seriously. Next week Dixon would probably move on to saving beached whales.

"So why the padlock?" Patrick asked, still interested.

Dixon shrugged like it didn't matter, that the padlock was a minor point and besides, he was finished with his spiel. Rebecca recognized the look. He was ready and impatient, looking over his shoulder, concerned with finding Chad and Tyler. That's when she knew this idea was probably theirs. Not Dixon's. But he'd go along, wanting to be friends with the cool guys, the high school jocks he grew up following around. They were always getting Dixon in trouble and she didn't understand why he kept going back for more. Maybe another semester away at college, away from them, would help.

One thing about Dixon, he was there for his friends. Rebecca could account for that. In the early days of her mom and dad's divorce Dixon was always there for her, just a phone call away, telling her it had absolutely nothing to do with her, reassuring her, making her laugh when it was the last thing she thought she'd ever do again.

Dixon's iPhone started playing the theme song from *Batman* and she slid it back over.

"It hasn't even been five minutes—" she started.

"Hey, I can't help it, I'm a popular guy."

But within seconds of answering Dixon's face went from cocky and confident to panic.

"I'll be there as soon as I can."

"What's wrong?" Rebecca sat forward. The mall noise had amplified. Somewhere behind them a PA system was announcing Santa's arrival.

"That was my granddad." Dixon's face had gone white. "They just took Nanna to the hospital. She may have had a heart attack."

"Oh my God, Dixon."

"You want us to go with you?" Patrick was already pulling on his jacket.

"Yeah, I guess," Dixon said, trying to stand but stumbling over the backpack at his feet. "Oh crap." He pivoted around trying to look beyond the crowd. "I promised Chad and Tyler." He picked up the backpack with a pained look and dropped it on the table as if the weight of it was suddenly too much.

"Don't worry about it," Rebecca said, grabbing the pack, surprised at how heavy it was but sliding it up over her shoulder as if it were no problem. "I just need to walk around with it, right?"

"I can't ask you to do that."

"You're not asking. I'm offering. Now go."

"How will you get home?"

"Patrick and I will figure it out." She gave Dixon a one-armed hug, all she could manage with the awkward weight of the backpack.

He handed her the iPhone and she tried to wave him off, but he insisted, "No, a deal is a deal."

They watched him disappear into the crowd as a family of four took over their bistro table. She and Patrick made plans to meet by the Gap in an hour. Rebecca's mind was on Dixon's grandmother while she stopped at the restroom. She had known Mrs. Lee since she was a little girl. She always treated Rebecca as though she were a member of the family, this time even giving Rebecca their daughter's old bedroom.

"I know it's a bit outdated, but I couldn't bear to change out the wallpaper," Mrs. Lee had told Rebecca as she showed her around the room, explaining that daisies had been her daughter's favorite.

Rebecca was clear across the food court by the time she realized she had forgotten Dixon's backpack hanging on the restroom door. She swore under her breath as she turned around, hurrying back to retrieve it.

She saw Chad and hoped he didn't notice her. He was headed in the opposite direction. She was watching him when the explosion happened. Everything moved in slow motion. She was paralyzed by a flash of red-and-white light engulfing Chad's body. The sound of the blast reached her ears just as glass shattered and fire erupted.

An invisible force knocked her completely off her feet. She felt hot air lift her. Pressure crushed against her chest. She slammed back down to the floor with a rain of metal and glass and wet debris showering over her, stinging her skin and scorching her lungs. She couldn't move. Something heavy lay on top of her. Pinning her down. It hurt to breathe. She could smell singed hair.

When she opened her eyes the first thing she saw was an arm ripped apart and lying within a foot of her. For a panicked second she thought it was her own until she saw the green dragon tattoo splattered with blood.

It looked like it was snowing, glittery pieces floating down. Rebecca closed her eyes again. Through the moans she recognized Doris Day's voice, singing, *"Let it snow…"*

And then the screams began.

CHAPTER 2

Newburgh Heights, Virginia

Maggie O'Dell slid a pan of stuffed mushroom caps into the oven then stopped to watch out her kitchen window. In the backyard Harvey entertained their guests, leaping into the air to catch his Frisbee. The white Labrador retriever was showing off. And her guests were humoring the big dog, laughing and chasing him through the fallen leaves. Three adult professionals acting like kids. Maggie smiled. Nothing like a dog to bring out the inner child in everyone.

"This is all quite an accomplishment," her friend, Gwen Patterson said, trying to point with her chin while her hands stayed busy chopping onion.

At first Maggie thought her friend meant the spread of munchies the two of them had prepared. It was a feast that looked more like a cocktail reception than a college football big-screen marathon. But Gwen wasn't talking about the food.

"I mean getting us all here together," Gwen explained.

"All of us in one place without a crime scene…or a corpse."

"Yes, but there's free food and beer," Maggie said. "That's usually enough."

"True." Gwen smiled. "You never did tell me why your brother couldn't make it."

"Guess he got a better offer," Maggie said, relieved that her back was to her friend. She didn't want Gwen to see the disappointment. It was best to keep things light. No big deal. Her psychologist friend would poke and probe if Maggie wasn't careful. "Hey, I can't expect to drop into his life and have an instant relationship."

She risked a glance over her shoulder only to see that her instinct was right. Gwen had stopped chopping and was watching her.

"There's always Christmas," Maggie added, trying to sound positive when she knew it was a long shot. She hadn't even brought up the subject with him. One rejection per phone call seemed sufficient.

"Do you think we have enough food?" Maggie wanted off the subject. This was supposed to be a day for relaxation. No stress. Just watching college football with friends, sharing a beer and some killer salsa.

"This is plenty," Gwen reassured her and went back to chopping.

Maggie stood with hands on her hips, assessing the island countertop that showed off trays and platters of finger foods. She had never thrown a party before. She didn't attend many either. In fact, she rarely invited guests to her house. Funny how getting an extended warranty on life had a way of making a person do things she thought she'd never do. Less than two months ago Maggie and her boss, FBI assistant director Kyle Cunningham had been exposed to the Ebola virus. Maggie had survived. Cunningham hadn't been so lucky.

"I don't know if we have enough. I've done a couple of road trips with Racine," Maggie said, trying to ward off the memories of being confined to an isolation ward and the helplessness of watching her boss go from a vibrant leader and mentor to a skeletal invalid sprouting tubes and lifelines. She closed her eyes, again keeping her back to Gwen as she grabbed onto the counter, pretending to survey their spread.

Keep it light, she reminded herself. *Relax. Breathe. Enjoy.*

"You'd never guess by looking at Racine but she can put away a pile of food."

As if summoned, Julia Racine came in the back door, her short spiky blond hair tousled, her sweatshirt sporting a few dry leaves, a smudge of dirt on the knee of her blue jeans. The scent of fall trailed in with her. She looked more like a punk rock star than a D.C. homicide detective.

"Your dog cheats," Racine announced, running her fingers through her hair as her eyes took in the kitchen activities. "He knows all the shortcuts," she said but the carefree frolic in her voice disappeared as she glanced from Maggie rinsing celery at the sink to Gwen chopping onion at the island counter.

Maggie could tell in an instant Racine wasn't comfortable, not just in Maggie's kitchen, but in any kitchen. The tall, lean detective crossed her arms and stayed pressed in a corner. She'd probably rather be back outside with Harvey, Ben and Tully. Racine wasn't a woman used to the company of other women. Maggie understood that. Too many hours spent with male colleagues. In many ways Julia Racine reminded Maggie of a younger version of herself.

"Back behind you," Maggie said, pointing to the cabinet

Racine leaned against. "There're some white square appe-
tizer plates. Could you pull out a stack and put them on the
counter. Some glasses, too."

Racine seemed startled by the request but Maggie moved
on to her next task without further instruction. Out of the
corner of her eye she saw Racine recover and nonchalantly
get the plates and glasses.

Maggie plopped down the freshly washed bunch of
celery on a paper towel next to Gwen's cutting board. She
pulled out a couple of stalks, handing one to Racine as she
munched on her own. This time when the detective leaned
against the counter she didn't look quite as rigid and out of
place.

"So," Racine said, taking a bite of the celery and letting
the word hang there. Obviously she was more comfortable.
"What's the deal with you and Benjamin Platt?"

Maggie glanced at Gwen.

"That's actually a good question," Gwen said then
shrugged in defense for joining in.

Maggie realized she might regret making Racine feel
comfortable in her kitchen.

"He's quite a hottie," Racine continued without prompting. "I mean if you're into that soldier of fortune type."

"He's a doctor," Maggie found herself countering.

"An army doctor," Gwen added.

Maggie stopped what she was doing, ignoring Gwen
but getting a good look at Racine, making eye contact
briefly before the detective felt it necessary to straighten
the plates and glasses she had put on the counter minutes
ago. Maggie's first impulse was to wonder if the young,
tough-as-nails detective was jealous...of Platt, that is. Not
Maggie. Several years ago when Racine and Maggie first
met, Racine admitted she was attracted to Maggie. She had
even made a pass at her. Somehow the two had gotten past

it all and became friends. Just friends. Though in times like this, Maggie wondered if Racine still hoped for more.

Maybe it was due to a temporary setback in Racine's own love life. Racine hadn't even mentioned her most recent lover, though Maggie had told her to bring a guest. Instead of asking about the elusive lover, who, if Maggie remembered correctly, was an army sergeant and soldier of fortune herself, Maggie simply said, "Ben's good company."

Maggie's cell phone interrupted any further discussion. She found herself relieved.

"This is Maggie O'Dell."

As soon as Maggie heard her new boss's voice, the muscles in her neck went tight. Her holiday weekend off was about to end.

CHAPTER
3

Bloomington, Minnesota

They called him the Project Manager. He didn't mind. It was better than some of the names he'd been called in the past. Like John Doe #2. Project Manager was definitely better than that. He still bristled a bit at the John Doe #2 label. He was always in charge. Never number two. Didn't matter that being mistaken as number two had been to his advantage. Besides, that was almost fifteen years ago.

The name on his new driver's license was Robert Asante and he took time to correct anyone who didn't pronounce it accurately.

"Ah-sontay," he would say. "Sicilian," he would add, like it meant something to him when, in fact, he simply wanted them to believe his olive complexion was from Italian ancestors and not from his Arab father. Though it was his white American mother whom he truly owed for his deadliest disguise, indigo-blue eyes. Anyone who doubted his ancestry usually put all hesitation aside when they looked into his eyes. After all, how many blue-eyed Arab terrorists could there possibly be?

And how many of them would be wearing a gold wedding band on his left ring finger? Everyone who asked to see his ID also got a glance at the photo inserted on the opposite side of his wallet, the photo of him with his family, a beautiful blond woman and two little girls. Even the wireless earbud in Asante's right ear, the leather jacket he wore with jeans, a T-shirt and designer running shoes portrayed him as an all-American businessman. Minor details that he knew made all the difference in the world. Details that had earned him the nickname, the Project Manager.

He retreated to the parking lot and now stayed inside his car, parked across the street, a safe distance from the shopping mall. Close enough to hear only the echoes of the blasts and far enough away to avoid the initial chaos. This particular parking lot was also out of view of any security cameras. He had double-checked during one of his many practice runs. Although it hardly mattered. Already the car's windshield was filled with snow, obscuring the view inside if anyone happened by.

Earlier, he had watched on the small handheld computer monitor as each of his carriers moved into place. Three separate carriers. Three separate bleeps in his ear. Three separate blinks of green light skipping across the computer screen as he tracked them.

Tracking them had been the easy part. Without them realizing it, Asante had planted GPS systems on each carrier. Now he detonated each one with a simple touch of a button. His well-planned mission reduced to nothing more than a touch-screen video game, blowing up each carrier. One after another, leaving only seconds in between.

First CARRIER 1, then CARRIER 2, and finally CARRIER 3.

He could hear the echo of each blast. Each explosion confirmed each detonation. Confirmed success of the mission.

There was nothing like this adrenaline rush. It was better than drugs. Better than sex, better than a well-aged single malt Scotch. His fingertips still tingled. Okay, maybe it was only the frigid weather.

He sat back against the crackling-cold vinyl of the car seat. After hundreds of hours, weeks, months of planning, step one was complete. He took several deep breaths, not bothered by seeing his own breath as he exhaled. Not feeling the cold, conscious of the adrenaline still pumping through his veins.

He was ready to call in confirmation. Then he heard it in his ear. Faint at first.

"Bleep."

A pause. Maybe the monitor had malfunctioned.

Another bleep.

Impossible.

He shot forward in the car seat. Pulled up the computer monitor.

The machine gave another bleep. Then a *bleep, bleep, bleep.*

A green light started blinking across the screen in unison with the annoying sound.

Asante brought the small computer screen close to his face until it was almost touching his nose. And yet he still couldn't believe his eyes.

One of his carriers was still alive.

CHAPTER
4

Mall of America

Patrick Murphy was on the escalator going down when the first explosion rocked the steps beneath him. Shoppers clutched the handrails and looked around, startled and curious, but no one panicked. After all, Santa had been due at any moment. Maybe the mall had some theatrical entrance planned that included fireworks. The place was certainly big enough. Patrick had never been in a four-story mall that had its own amusement park, theater and aquarium. The place was amazing.

No, the first blast went off without any panic. Only curious looks and turns on the escalator. No one panicked. Not until the second blast. Then there was no mistaking, something was wrong.

Without thinking Patrick twisted around. Instinct drove him in the opposite direction. He tried to fight his way up the down escalator, shouldering past shoppers, three thick, who were frantically headed down, shoving their way, using heavy shopping bags to pry through. Patrick tried to climb, pressing forward. He grabbed onto the handrail, almost losing his balance. The handrail was moving in the opposite direction, too. He tried to use his body to push against the crowd. He had a swimmer's build, strong broad shoulders, tapered waist, long legs and a stamina and patience that came from physical discipline. But this was impossible, like swimming against a current, being caught up in a rip tide.

A linebacker of a man dressed in a parka told Patrick to get the hell out of the way while he stiff-armed him in the ribs. A teenaged girl screamed in his face, paralyzed and clutching the handrail, not allowing Patrick to pass.

The third blast was closer, its vibration almost rippling the steps of the escalator. That's when Patrick gave in. He turned back around and allowed the mob to carry him down the escalator. But as soon as they reached the bottom Patrick forced his way to the up escalator, grateful to find it practically empty. He raced up the moving steps. By now he could smell sulfur and smoke but continued to climb. Maybe his training actually had made a difference, taken hold of him without notice. It wouldn't be the first time he relied on gut instinct. Usually he trusted it. Lately he wasn't so sure.

Within the last year he had changed majors and with it his entire future. Not a good idea your senior year of college. It was an expensive undertaking for a guy working and scraping for every credit hour dollar. What started as a vocation and change of major had actually turned into a passion. All thanks to a father he'd never met. But Patrick knew it wasn't the extra classes in Fire Science that now made him race toward smoke. It probably wasn't even all those volunteer hours at the fire department that kicked him into full-throttle instinct, although firefighters were trained to push their way into burning buildings when everyone is clamoring to get out.

But this drive, this urgency, this gut instinct that had taken control of him and propelled him toward the explosions, had little to do with his new training and everything to do with Rebecca. He had left her back on the third floor at the food court, back where it sounded like the explosions had come from. He couldn't leave without her. Had to make sure she was okay. How many times had she checked on him? Made sure he was okay? All those nights working at Champs.

"You don't look so good," she'd say in between orders and refills. Then at the end of the evening after they were finished cleaning up, both tired, dead on their feet and needing to get back to study, she'd hop up onto a bar stool in front of him and say to him, "So tell me what's going on." And she'd sit quietly and listen, really listen, eyes intent and sympathetic. She'd listen like no one else ever had.

Patrick started to feel the spray from the sprinklers above and yet the smoke still stung his eyes. He pulled out his sunglasses then he yanked the hem of his T-shirt up over his nose. He stayed close to the wall. Let a rush of hysterical shoppers race by. Then he pressed forward again, slowly, taking in everything through the gray haze of his sunglasses. He tried not to trip over the debris, some from the explosion, other stuff that people had dropped or left behind: half-eaten food and spilled shopping bags. That's when Patrick thought about the backpacks.

He couldn't forget the bad feeling he had listening to Dixon Lee talk about their innocent prank. The whole time Dixon explained their scheme to send wireless static, some sort of interference that would play havoc with the retail shops' computer systems, Patrick kept thinking something didn't sound right. He should have listened to his gut instinct.

Why would anyone put a padlock on a backpack just to carry it around the mall and mess up a few computers?

CHAPTER
5

Rebecca stumbled and quickly reminded herself to not look down. She didn't want to see what she had bumped into this time. She continued to wipe at her face, each glance at her fingers found blood, some not her own. She tried raking her fingers through her long hair, but kept cutting her fingertips on pieces of glass and metal.

She was cold and shaking, her vision blurred, her heart hammering so hard it hurt to breathe. Her throat felt clogged, her tongue swollen. She must have bitten it. And when she did suck in gasps of air, the sting of acid, mixed with the sickly scent of sulfur and cinnamon, gagged her.

A small gray-haired man slammed into Rebecca, almost toppling her. She looked back to see him holding a hand up to a bloody pulp where his ear once was. Other shoppers pushed and shoved. Some of them also injured and bleeding. All of them in a hurry to flee even if their shock tangled their legs and confused their sense of direction. They dropped everything they didn't need. Rebecca stepped in a puddle she hoped was soda or coffee but knew it could be blood. She tried to sidestep another and instead, skidded on a slice of pizza.

Slow down, she told herself. Not an easy task with all the chaos racing by and bouncing off her.

Toddlers were crying. Mothers scooped them up, leaving behind carriers, strollers, diaper bags and stuffed animals. There were screams of panic, some of pain. Smoke streamed from the blast areas where small fires licked at storefronts despite the sprinkler system misting down from the high ceiling.

The PA system announced a lockdown. Something about "an incident in the mall." And through all the noise and chaos Rebecca could still hear the holiday music.

Was it just in her head?

She found it macabre yet comforting to have Bing Crosby telling her he'd be home for Christmas. It was the only piece of normalcy that she had to hang on to as she stumbled over discarded food, shards of glass, broken tables and puddles of blood. There were bodies, too, some injured and unable to get up. Some not moving at all.

She didn't know what to do, where to go. Shock was taking over. The shivers that overtook her entire body came in uncontrollable waves. Rebecca knew enough from her pre-vet studies to recognize the signs of shock. The symptoms were similar for dogs and human beings—rapid heartbeat, confusion, weak pulse, sudden cold and eventual collapse.

She wrapped her arms around her body. That's when she discovered it. The pain shot up her left arm. How could she not have noticed it before this? A three-to-four-inch piece of glass stuck out of her coat. Without seeing the entry she knew it had pierced into her arm. The sight of it made her nauseated. Her legs threatened to collapse and she caught herself against a handrail so that she didn't tumble to the floor. Still, she slid to her knees.

Don't look at it. Don't panic. Breathe.

She saw a policeman and felt a wave of relief until she recognized the man was mall security. No gun.

Yes, that's right. She knew that.

She'd worked for a pet shop in a local mall her senior year of high school.

He was close enough now that Rebecca could hear his frantic sputters into his handheld walkie-talkie.

"It's bad. It's really bad," he said. He looked young. Probably not much older than Rebecca. "I don't see anyone else with red backpacks."

Even through the shock, it sent a chill through Rebecca.

The backpacks.

She tried to stand, tried to twist around and look toward the direction where she had last seen Chad.

No Chad. Not even a wounded Chad stumbling around like her.

All Rebecca could see was a scorched wall. Smoke. Bits and pieces. A pile that looked like a heap of smoldering black garbage.

Chad?

She felt dizzy. Her throat tightened. The nausea threatened to gag her.

No, she wouldn't think about it. She couldn't think about it.

Rebecca looked in the other direction. Standing now, gripping the handrail with white knuckles and wobbling to her feet. She could see a black hole where the women's restroom used to be. The restroom where she had left Dixon's backpack, hanging on the door of the first stall. The backpack that she was supposed to be carrying.

Oh God. That's what exploded. The backpacks.

She slid back to her knees, the realization hitting her

hard as she eased herself onto the floor. There was something sticky underneath her. She didn't even care. How close had she come to becoming a smoldering pile of garbage?

Somewhere from inside her coat she could hear the theme to *Batman,* and amidst the stampeding feet and the moans surrounding her, the music seemed not at all surprising. In this bizarre version of reality the theme to *Batman* seemed to fit in perfectly.

CHAPTER
6

Newburgh Heights, Virginia

This wasn't at all the day Maggie O'Dell had planned.

R.J. Tully turned on the TV in Maggie's great room but instead of listening to ESPN's pregame predictions Maggie could hear bits of news as her partner flipped from one cable news channel to another.

"There's nothing yet," Tully reported to the others all gathered around the counter that separated the kitchen from the great room.

"A.D. Kunze said it just happened," Maggie told them. "Local police haven't arrived at the scene yet."

"Then how does he already know it was a terrorist attack?" Benjamin Platt asked.

"He doesn't, but the governor's a personal friend." Maggie tried to relay what her new boss had just told her— which wasn't much—while she jotted down a list of what she needed to pack.

"So he calls in the FBI?" Julia Racine joined in.

Maggie shrugged. The nice thing about having friends

who were colleagues was they understood better than anyone else what the job entailed. The bad thing about having friends who were colleagues was that they couldn't shut off being colleagues.

"They think there were at least two explosions inside the mall," Maggie said. "Possibly three. They believe there may be more targets."

"But why send you?" Gwen didn't bother to hide her irritation. "You're a profiler, for God's sake, not a bomb specialist."

"They'll need to draw up a profile immediately, so they know who to start looking for," Tully said, remote in his hand, still pointing it at the TV from across the room. Still flipping channels though he had the TV on MUTE now. "They've got to put pieces together as soon as possible before any eyewitnesses start second-guessing what they saw or heard."

Maggie glanced at Tully, looking for signs that he might be disappointed he wouldn't be going along. They had been a team before budget cuts and before his suspension. Paid suspension. It was protocol anytime an agent used deadly force. Less than two months ago Tully had shot dead a man he had once considered a friend. The agency would find it justified. Maggie knew Tully would, too…eventually. Just not yet.

"Okay, so Kunze needs a profiler on the scene. That doesn't answer why it has to be Maggie." Gwen fidgeted with the knife that had recently been chopping vegetables. Maggie watched her friend stab the knife's tip into the wooden cutting board, then pull it out and stab it again like a person tapping a pen out of nervous energy. "Are you sure you should even be flying?"

This made Maggie smile. There was a fifteen-year age difference between the two women and sometimes Gwen found it difficult to hide her maternal instinct. Although it made Maggie smile, all the others were looking at her now with concern. The same case that had garnered Tully a suspension had landed Maggie in an isolation ward at USAMRIID (the United States Army Medical Research Institute of Infectious Diseases) under the care of Colonel Benjamin Platt.

"I'm fine," Maggie said. "Ask my doctor if you don't believe me," and she pointed at Ben who remained serious, not ready to agree just yet.

"Kunze could send someone else," Gwen insisted. "You know why he's sending you."

Maggie could hear the anger edging around the concern in her friend's voice. Evidently so could everyone else. Harvey even looked up from his corner, dog bone gripped between big paws. The silence was made more awkward by the oven timer that reminded them of what the day had started out to be.

Maggie reached over and tapped several of the oven's digital buttons, shutting off heat and sound.

More silence.

"Okay," Racine finally broke in. "I give up. I seem to be the only one who hasn't gotten the latest news alert. Why is the new assistant director—"

"Interim director," Gwen interrupted to correct.

"Yeah right. Whatever. Why's he sending O'Dell? You make it sound like it's something personal. What have I missed?"

Maggie held Gwen's eyes. She wanted her to see the impatience. This was bordering on embarrassing. People in Minnesota may have lost their lives and Gwen was worried about department politics and imagined grudges.

Tully was the one who finally answered Racine. "Assistant Director Ray Kunze told Maggie and me that we were both negligent on the George Sloane case."

"Negligent?"

"He blames them," Gwen blurted out.

"He didn't say that," Maggie insisted although she remembered the sting of the words he did use.

"He insinuated," Gwen corrected herself. "He insinuated that Maggie and Tully, quote, 'contributed to Cunningham's death.'"

"He told us we have some proving to do," Tully added.

Maggie couldn't believe how calm he was, explaining it over his shoulder as he kept an eye on the TV, as if he was simply updating the scores of the day. The subject did not have the same effect on Maggie and Gwen knew that. Perhaps Gwen had even picked up Maggie's initial anger and carried it for her when Maggie had become weary of the burden. It wouldn't have been so bad had Kunze not triggered a guilt Maggie had already saddled herself with. Some days she still blamed herself for Cunningham's death even without Kunze's accusations of contributable negligence.

Her psychology background should have reassured her that she was experiencing a simple case of survivor's guilt. But sometimes, usually late at night, alone and staring up at her bedroom ceiling, she'd think about Cunningham getting infected, both of them exposed to the same virus. Just the image of his deteriorating body and how quickly he had gone from strong and vital to helpless, caused a sinking hollow feeling in the pit of her stomach, an ache accompanied by nausea. That feeling was very real, physically real. Cunningham was dead. She was alive. How was that possible?

"So he sends you off to Minnesota to appease his friend

the governor," Gwen said. "You. When there's probably someone there in the Minneapolis field office."

"Gwen." Maggie bit her lower lip. She wanted to tell her to stop. This wasn't something to discuss with or in front of Ben and Julia, or even Tully.

"It's just not right."

The sudden volume of the TV drew all their attention as Tully pointed and punched until it was loud enough to hear the FOX news alert:

"There have been reports of a possible explosion from inside Mall of America," an unseen voice announced while on the screen a bird's-eye view appeared of the expansive mall. It was, perhaps, stock film since the parking lot was not full and the trees had green leaves.

"911 operators have experienced a flood of calls," the disembodied voice continued. "Emergency personnel, as well as our news helicopter, are on their way so we have no details as of this moment.

"We can tell you that Mall of America is the largest mall in America. More than 150,000 shoppers were expected to visit the mall today, traditionally called Black Friday, the busiest shopping day of the year."

Inside Maggie's great room there was silence. No more accusations. No more questions. No more arguments.

Ben crossed his arms as he stood beside her, shifting his weight only slightly so that his shoulder brushed against Maggie.

"Forget the politics," he said calmly, quietly, an obvious attempt to reassure her. "Just go do what you do best."

Before Maggie could respond or ask what he meant, he added, "Go get these bastards."

CHAPTER 7

Mall of America

"We've got a problem," Asante growled into his wireless headset. He avoided people in the parking lot, some standing in the frigid cold just staring while others ran to their vehicles.

"What's the problem?"

Asante could barely hear the response.

"We've got one carrier still on the move."

There was silence and Asante thought perhaps the connection had faded out.

"How is that possible?" came the reply.

"You tell me."

"There were three blasts. No one could survive that."

"You watched them?" Asante asked with careful accusation.

"Of course." But the conviction wavered against the hint of Asante's irritation.

"You saw each one?"

"Yes. I saw all three arrive in the food court area." Hesitation, then the admission. "Carrier #3 brought two friends along. I didn't think it was a problem."

Asante stayed silent when he wanted to remind his point man that he didn't get paid to think. No matter how willing, no matter how capable they appeared to be, Asante had learned to trust no one but himself. It was a tough lesson he had learned long before Oklahoma City, one that had taught him to always, always have cutaways like McVeigh and Nichols for each and every project no matter how small or large.

"I'm headed back in."

More silence. Asante knew exactly what the man was thinking. *You must be insane.* But of course, he wouldn't dare question the Project Manager.

"What do you want me to do?" The question came quietly, hesitantly and probably with the hope that Asante would not request that he accompany him.

"Find out who those other two are." He could almost hear the other man's relief.

Asante continued, making his way through the cold and the snow to the back of the mall, toward the same exit he had used earlier to flee. Before he'd left the sanctuary of his getaway car, he'd exchanged his Carolina Panthers baseball cap for a navy blue cap with PARAMEDIC embroidered on the front. He'd also changed his jogging shoes for a pair of hiking boots. On purpose the boots were three sizes too large for him. A shoeprint could be as incriminating as a fingerprint and in the snow the print might be well preserved. He had already prepared the boots with socks in the toes, making them a comfortable enough fit that he could run in them if necessary.

The jogging shoes he'd kept and thrown into a duffel bag with everything else he would need including a syringe filled with a toxic cocktail he always carried for himself. It was one more detail, a safeguard for a project manager who insisted on controlling even the details of his own death if it came to that. Today he'd need to use it on the surviving carrier instead of on himself.

He had never intended to return to the scene but took every precaution if it became necessary. He had researched and studied the mall's routine until he knew it by heart. Within seconds the mall's security would come over the public address system announcing "an incident" and ordering a lockdown. Shops would pull down their storefront grates. Kiosks would close down and secure their merchandise. By now the sprinkler systems on the third floor would have been activated. Escalators and all portions of the amusement park would come to a screeching halt.

The fire department would be alerted as soon as those sprinklers opened. Asante expected their sirens any moment now. In fact, he was surprised he didn't hear them already, but the snow might slow them down. The local police would follow. As soon as a bomb was suspected, a bomb squad and a sniper unit would be sent. Mall security carried no weapons. Asante figured he had ten minutes at least, thirty minutes at the most, before he had to deal with a ground and air mass invasion of armed responders.

As he plodded through the snow he set his diver's watch to count down the seconds. Thirty minutes should be more than enough time to find the errant carrier and terminate him.

CHAPTER
8

Patrick shattered the glass to get the fire extinguisher. Yards away, the explosion had blown out storefronts and ripped open brick walls, yet here it hadn't left even a crack in the glass case that housed the fire extinguisher. He pulled the extinguisher's pin, ready to use it, but found only smoke, no fire. Still, he pushed his way through the gray mist, thick and wet like a fog on a humid summer morning. Again, he was going the wrong direction. He waited until a stream of shoppers shoved by, then he tried to move forward.

Over the intercom he heard the mechanical voice repeating the same calm message, "There's been an incident at the mall. Please remain calm. Walk, don't run, toward the nearest exit." The Muzak system was still playing holiday songs. No one noticed either.

Patrick stopped to help a woman who had gotten shoved to the side. She was wrestling her baby out of a stroller. The infant looked unharmed but was screaming. The mother was wide-eyed and panicked.

"Oh my God, oh my God!" she kept mumbling.

Her hands were shaking and jerking at the blankets and straps that kept the baby restrained inside the stroller. She stumbled and rocked back and forth, losing her balance like someone who had too much to drink. Patrick noticed she didn't have any shoes on. Her feet were already bloodied from the shower of glass that glittered the floor. He looked around and discovered the three-inch heels tossed aside. He scooped them up and offered them to her.

"Your feet," he pointed.

She didn't seem to hear him. She didn't even look up at him. Once she had the baby in her arms she ran for the escalators, leaving behind the stroller, a diaper bag, a purse... and her shoes. She didn't notice the trail of blood her feet left.

Patrick put out one fire, a kiosk of cell phones already charred from the blast. He recognized a couple of stores and knew he was close to the food court. It had to be just around the corner. The smoke was thicker here. Harder to see. He had to feel alongside the wall and watch his feet. Debris littered the floor, slick and crunchy. He worried the rubber soles of his One Star high-tops might not be thick enough to withstand the larger pieces of glass and metal. Through the smoke he saw a sign for the restrooms. It dangled overhead and he realized this was where he had last seen Rebecca.

Finally.

Only Patrick couldn't see the doorway. It was gone, replaced by a huge, ragged hole. The wall was buckled, lopsided and charred. Bricks bulged and hung loose like toy building blocks tossed and shoved out from the other side. Water seeped from one of the holes in the wall and a smell like rotten eggs, maybe sewage, flooded the area. He prayed that Rebecca wasn't still inside the restroom when the blast went off.

That's when Patrick tripped, slamming himself against the sharp bricks, ripping the palm of his hand open, but managing to stay on his feet. When he looked down he saw the long dark hair first and thought he had tripped over a mannequin. After all, the legs were twisted and knotted together like they were made of plastic and were stuffed into a garbage bag. But there was nothing plastic about the eyes that stared up at him through the tangled hair. Her jaw had been torn away, leaving a wide gaping smile. Patrick's first reaction was to reach down to help her up. Then he jerked back when he realized she must be dead.

He took a better look at the twisted pile of legs he had tripped over and for the first time his head began to swim and his knees felt a bit spongy.

The legs were no longer connected to the rest of the woman's body.

CHAPTER 9

Lanoha's Nursery
Omaha, Nebraska

Nick Morrelli pulled out a credit card. He knew his sister Christine was watching him so he tried not to wince, flinch or clear his throat. All signs she would be looking for.

She had already told him that he didn't have to pay for the fresh-cut nine-foot Fraser fir Christmas tree. In fact, she had told him three times, leading him to insist, making him pretend that it was no big deal. And why would it be a big deal? Never mind that he had just left a prominent position with the Suffolk County prosecutor's office in Boston to move back to Omaha. It wasn't like he was fired or let go. The decision had been entirely his choice.

Choice, not impulse.

Impulse was the word his mom and Christine used.

"Your father knows you love him, Nicky," his mom had said when he told her he was moving back to Nebraska. "He doesn't expect you to leave your life and be at his side."

At the time Nick wanted to tell her that the old Antonio

Morrelli would want that exactly. He'd want everyone to
uproot and rearrange their lives to accommodate his sched-
ule especially now when he appeared to be near death. A
massive stroke had left Nick's father paralyzed and bedrid-
den several years ago. Now his only means of communication were his eyes. Maybe it was simply Nick's imagination
but he swore he could still see that same disappointment
and regret in those eyes—now watery blue instead of ice
blue—every single time the man looked at him.

Nick had tried most of his life to do what his father expected, tried to fill the huge shoes. His father had played
quarterback for the Nebraska Huskers, so Nick made sure
he played quarterback for the Nebraska Huskers, but Nick
only played for one season. A disappointment to his father
who had redshirted as a freshman. His father had gone to
law school, so Nick went to law school, only he had no
interest in practicing law or filling the vacancy his father
had left for him in the law firm his father had started.

Nick had even run for and had been elected county sheriff, the position the elder Morrelli retired from as a living
legend. But Nick had embarrassed his father, again, by
tracking down a killer his father had allowed to go unde-
tected under his own watch. It should have made up for all
the rest. Nick had succeeded after all. But that wasn't the
way Antonio Morrelli looked at it. Instead he saw it as his
son embarrassing him, showing him up and making him
look bad publicly.

Nick's move to Boston had probably been the first thing
he had ever done on his own and for himself without the
influence of the elder Morrelli. His father had never been
a district attorney. Had never argued high-profile cases
involving anything close to what Nick found himself a
part of, from drug trafficking to double homicides. These
were the types of cases Nick tackled on a regular basis as

a Deputy County Prosecutor for Suffolk County. And yet it wasn't enough. Apparently it wasn't, because here he was, returning home still searching for something. Hopefully his father's approval didn't remain on that search list.

It must have been what his mother was thinking. She made it sound like Nick was moving back to be close to his father whose deteriorating condition would most likely make this his last Christmas. And his sister, Christine, seemed to think Nick had moved back to play role model to her fatherless teenaged son. That was partly true. He cared about Timmy and wanted to be in the boy's life. But the truth was, at least when Nick admitted it to himself, his reasons were not quite so lofty or noble. In fact, they were fairly selfish.

Yes, he wanted to be close to his family during this last holiday together but he also wanted to be away from the sudden loneliness in his life. There was an emptiness that permeated his Boston apartment and even leaked over into his job. It definitely felt as though he had lost something, but it wasn't his ex-fiancée Jill Campbell. Surprisingly, her absence from his life had little to do with the loneliness he was experiencing. What was worse, leaving Boston didn't help either. The emptiness followed him. This hollowed-out feeling was something that he was carrying around with him. Maybe that wasn't the right way to describe it but it was definitely what it felt like.

His new job at a high-level security corporation kept him distracted. He liked the new challenge. And the position actually paid very well…or at least it would. Eventually. He had only started a month ago.

"I know you're a little miserable," Christine said, interrupting his thoughts.

"I'm not miserable."

"It's okay to admit it."

"I'm not miserable."

She was giving him that look, that "you're so full of crap" look.

Okay, so maybe he was a little miserable. Miserable went well with hollowed out.

"It's understandable." Christine seemed to think they should discuss his life in the middle of Lanoha's Nursery. "You recently broke off your engagement. What's it been? Five months?"

"I'm not miserable because of Jill," Nick insisted through clenched teeth, hoping his sister would get the idea to lay off and at the same time realizing he had probably verified her accusation. If she knew him as well as she thought she did, she'd know it had nothing to do with Jill.

"If it's not Jill," Christine said, pretending to keep it casual by fingering the price tags on some holiday wreaths, "then it must be Maggie."

It was like she stuck a dagger in his side and Nick had to keep from wincing. He had spent the last month convincing himself that Maggie O'Dell had moved on and had no interest in being a part of his life. He had given it his best shot. Anything more and he'd become some psycho stalker. It was over. Time to move on. He told himself this over and over. His head heard him loud and clear. It was his heart that ignored him.

"I know," Christine said, taking his silence as confirmation. "It's complicated."

But it wasn't all that complicated. Nick had met Maggie four years ago, working a case when he was sheriff of Platte City, Nebraska. She dropped into his life as an FBI profiler, smart and witty, tough but beautiful. Nick had known a lot of women—he'd been with a lot of women—but he'd never met anyone quite like Maggie O'Dell. There had been instant chemistry. At least that's how Nick remembered it. But she was married then.

They'd stayed in touch and after her divorce he gave her plenty of opportunity to be charmed by him, even advertised that he was open to a relationship. A real relationship, something Nick Morrelli rarely considered. But Maggie turned him down for whatever reason. Perhaps she just wasn't ready. That's what he wanted to believe. Being rejected was a new concept for him.

But last summer they crossed paths again. Another case with ties to the one four years ago and for Nick it brought back all those memories and some feelings he didn't realize he still harbored. Feelings that slammed him hard. Hard enough that he canceled his wedding engagement.

Then he did the only thing he knew how to do. He pursued Maggie with cards, e-mails, flowers, requests to spend time together despite her living in the D.C. area and him in Boston. Nick thought he was being the proper suitor. That is until he discovered there was someone else in her life. He had let her slip away, blown his chances. This time it was too late.

He'd let her slip away to a guy named Benjamin Platt. Nick had looked up the license plate on a Land Rover he saw parked outside of Maggie's house. Platt was an army colonel, a medical doctor, a scientist, a soldier. He wasn't sure that even a tall, dark and charming quarterback-turned-lawyer stood a chance to compete with that.

"Can we concentrate on Christmas?" he asked after too much silence. He could already see Christine knew she was right. He took no pleasure in the fact that to his big sister he seemed to be an open book.

Before Christine could respond two store clerks interrupted them, coming into the center of the store.

"There's been an explosion at Mall of America," one of them announced. "There may be dozens of people dead."

Customers throughout the store came up the aisles to hear the news.

"That's one of ours," Nick told Christine. He barely got his cell phone out of his jacket pocket when it began to ring.

CHAPTER
10

Mall of America

Asante wasted little time fighting through the wave of hysteria. It was ridiculous. This was why he never stuck around afterwards to watch. There were some he had worked with in the past who enjoyed this chaos—the smell of fear, the clawing and clamoring to survive, the screams and cries of human nature at its most vulnerable. Or, as Asante considered it, human nature at its most pathetic. And from simply a glance, he knew that to be true.

Years ago he learned never to be fooled. Those who bragged that a crisis brought out the best in people would soon have you forget that the exact same crisis would also bring out the very worst in people. Asante stood at the top of the escalator looking down as the wildfire of panic raced through each floor of the mall and he resisted the urge to smile. People shoved each other, stepping over the injured, dropping and leaving behind their precious belongings. If they thought this was bad, wait until they saw what was to come. This was but a distraction.

He followed the GPS signal as he shoved through, keeping close to the walls where he knew any cameras still functioning could not pick up his image as easily. He walked quickly when he wanted to run. Time was slipping by. It had taken him longer than he expected to fight his way through the crowds amassing at the exits. The signal seemed to be taking him right back to where the carriers began—in the food court.

Asante stopped suddenly. He dropped down to the floor, kneeled and doubled over his duffel bag, pretending to be hurt while a security guard ran by. He didn't want security seeing his PARAMEDIC cap and escorting him through to the wounded. He'd find his own wounded.

While on the floor he turned on his wireless headset that fit close and tight over his left ear. He had strapped the small computer, just a fraction bigger than a smartphone, to the inside of his arm so he had both hands free and could still follow the green blinks on the computer screen's map. He poked in a number on the keypad and then turned up the volume on his headset. In seconds he was listening in on the mall's security guards exchange information and curses.

"Where are the cops?"

"On their way."

"How frickin' long does it take?"

This time Asante couldn't help but smile. Their wait was his gain. And now they would warn him when it was time for him to leave.

The food court reminded him of a sidewalk café in Tel Aviv after it had been bombed. It had been in his student days when he was still studying the art of terror. Where better to learn than on the eternal battlefield. Now he looked around at tables and chairs that were strewn and broken like piles of pickup sticks. The walls were splattered with a combination of Chinese dumplings, pizza, coffee, flesh and blood. The floors glittered with glass. The mist from the ceiling sprinklers added to the haze, dampening those who ran away and soaking those who couldn't.

Asante followed the green blinking light on his GPS system, tapping it twice when it malfunctioned and indicated that his target was right in front of him. He pressed several buttons before he realized the computer had not malfunctioned at all. Where he expected to see the young Dixon Lee, he saw instead a young woman. She was curled up behind an overturned table, close to the rail that overlooked the mall's atrium.

She was no longer moving, but she was, indeed, the source of the blinking green light.

Son of a bitch.

This was his errant carrier?

CHAPTER
11

Newburgh Heights, Virginia

Maggie left them to pack. She insisted they stay.

"Please don't let all this food go to waste," she told them. "Gwen and I worked too hard to prepare it." Then with a smile, "Okay? Please stay."

Racine had been the first one to promise though it came out in typical Racine style. "Yeah, no problem. I'm starving. It takes more than a little holiday carnage to keep me from eating."

It was enough to break the ice and make the rest of them laugh.

Still, Maggie wasn't surprised to hear the knock on her bedroom door. She expected Gwen had one last word to get in.

"Come on in."

"You sure?" Benjamin Platt stood in Maggie's doorway looking more like a hesitant schoolboy than an army colonel.

"Yes, of course. Come on in," Maggie told him, trying to hide her surprise.

He showed her the little black doctor's bag he had in his hand. It had become a familiar object over the last two months. Ben had made several house calls after Maggie's quarantine at USAMRIID. Inside the bag she knew he kept a phlebotomist kit for taking blood samples and at least two vials of the vaccine for the Ebola virus.

"Still carrying that around, huh?"

"Ever since I met you," he said.

"I have that effect on guys."

His eyes narrowed. He was serious now, ready to put aside their usual witty repartee.

"You're not due for another shot of the vaccine until late next week, but considering where you're going," he paused, and waited for her eyes, "and what you'll encounter, I think it might be a good idea to give you the dose before you leave."

That he was concerned made Maggie concerned. This was a doctor, who all the while she was quarantined and restless for results, kept telling her to slow down and wait, that they would deal with whatever it was when they found out exactly what it was. The "whatever" they were dealing with ended up being Ebola Zaire, nicknamed "the slate sweeper." Maggie had been exposed but didn't show any signs of the virus. The incubation period for Ebola was up to twenty-one days. It had been fifty-six days since Maggie's exposure. That she knew exactly how many days was a testament to how seriously she still took the threat.

"You don't think—"

"No, of course not," Ben interrupted. "Just a safety precaution. Your immune system has been through a hell of a lot."

"Okay," she said and started to clear a place for him to

set the bag on her dresser. Her Pullman was spread out on the bed, almost packed. She'd learned a long time ago to keep the basic necessities already in the bag. While Ben prepared a syringe Maggie looked for a warm turtleneck sweater. She'd been to the Midwest enough times during this time of year to no longer underestimate the cold.

"It's snowing there," Ben said as if he could read her mind.

"Boot snowing or just snow-snowing?"

This time he stopped his hands and looked up. "There's a difference?"

"Oh, big time. You haven't been to the Midwest in the winter?"

"Chicago, but no. It was spring."

"My first trip I only had leather flats. It snowed like eight or ten inches and the only place nearby to buy boots in the middle of nowhere, Nebraska, was a John Deere implement store."

"Let me guess, you ended up with bright green, size twelves?"

"Something like that."

She rummaged through her closet and pulled out a pair of slipover boots that folded easily. When she turned back to her suitcase Ben was watching her, smiling.

"What?"

"Nothing," he said, shaking his head but still smiling. "You're just pretty incredible, that's all."

She hoped the flush up her neck didn't show in her face. She held up the boots for him to see as she placed them in the suitcase. "I knew eventually I could get your attention with my sexy footwear."

"I hate to disappoint you," he said, setting aside the syringe and coming close enough to touch the back of his hand to her cheek, "but you managed to do that without any footwear at all. The first time I saw those bare feet in oversized athletic socks back at USAMRIID my heart skipped a couple of beats."

Maggie wasn't sure if it was his touch or his rare and surprising admission that caused her own heart to miss a couple of beats.

"A foot fetish, huh?" She tried to keep it light.

"Big time."

Another knock on the door startled both of them. This time it was Gwen.

"Sorry to interrupt. Your ride to Andrews is here."

CHAPTER
12

Mall of America

The glass hadn't plunged in as deep as Rebecca thought it had. It was bleeding but no major gusher. So no major arteries. She still had to pull the chunk of glass out.

She could do this. Of course, she could.

She had cleaned up and taken care of her share of wounds and injuries. Never mind that they were on dogs. Bites from other dogs, rips from barbed wire or abuse from owners. One of the dogs she helped treat had been hit by a car. All of the wounds were gross. No different than this. If anything, it should be easier when it was herself. No sad brown eyes looking up at her. If only her head would stop throbbing and her stomach would stop threatening to shove everything up or down.

The security guard had left and Rebecca felt relieved. Scared and in pain but relieved. *How weird was that?* She couldn't help wondering if the security guards had seen Chad and Tyler and Dixon with the exact backpacks? Had they been watching them on the security cameras? Was that possible on a day like today with the crowds? Or maybe especially on a day like today. How else would they know?

She looked around again and couldn't see any other blue uniforms. Or did some security guards wear plainclothes? If they had been watching the guys and were suspicious of the backpacks that meant they had seen her, too. Would they recognize her now?

Maybe not with this harpoon in her arm.

God, it hurt.

She thought she could hear sirens now. There were shouts from below. Was someone shouting "Police"?

The shouts were drowned out by an ear-piercing electronic buzz. Somewhere an alarm had been set off. No one seemed to pay attention to any of it. There wasn't a sound that could stall the hysteria.

Rebecca stayed put. She tried to assess the damage to her arm. Her coat was shredded on the left side where broken glass must have pummeled her. Funny, she didn't remember.

How could she not remember the pain?

It happened so quickly. She was probably lucky to have just one piece of debris stuck inside her.

She carefully ripped the fabric away from the wound and the sight of her own flesh, purplish-red, raw and torn made her sit back. She leaned her head against the rail, waiting for the nausea to pass. She felt the vibration of the stampede around and under her. She couldn't focus, couldn't hear over that buzz and now there was an annoying whirling sound like bursts of wind through a tunnel. She closed her eyes and that's when she realized it wasn't wind. It was her own raspy breathing.

She had to do better than this.

She needed to get the glass out of her arm.

Come on, Rebecca. Just pull the damned thing out.

One, two, three…like a Band-Aid in one quick jerk.

But she'd need to stop the bleeding when she pulled out the glass. Her eyes flew open. She'd have to shove something into the hole the glass left in her arm. If not, she'd bleed to death. This was actually good. It made her think through the process. It made her focus.

She grabbed pieces of her coat that she had ripped away and began peeling out the lining. It'd be cleaner than the outside of the coat. And it was softer.

"I can help you with that."

Rebecca looked up to find a man standing behind her. He wore a cap that read PARAMEDIC but he was in jeans and hiking boots. No uniform. Although she couldn't really see underneath his winter coat. A duffel bag was slung over his shoulder.

She should have felt saved, rescued. She wouldn't have to do this herself. But there was something about the way he held the already loaded syringe that didn't seem quite right.

CHAPTER
13

Omaha, Nebraska

Nick Morrelli was trying to check flights on his smart-phone while Christine waited to drive them home. Outside the car her son Timmy and his friend Gibson helped the Lanoha Nursery worker load the Christmas tree on top of Christine's SUV. Nick had offered to help, too, but the boys insisted they could do it. He didn't argue. All he could think about was finding a way up to Minneapolis.

His new boss had chosen Nick to represent Mall of America's security company, their security company, United Allied Security. With his experience as a county sheriff he had dealt with homicide scenes and forensic evidence. And as an attorney he had the legal background to protect the company's rights. That's what his boss Al Banoff had told him. Nick guessed it was one of those golden opportunities that shouldn't be questioned. Even if the opportunity would be measured in fatalities.

"How many do they think are dead?" Christine asked him.

Nick gave her a warning look.

"What?"

"Stop being a reporter," he told her.

"I'm just asking," she said, then added, "Out of concern. Nothing more."

"Right."

He waited. He knew she wouldn't give up that easily.

"Seriously, it's bad, isn't it?"

But this time without even glancing at her Nick could tell she was concerned by the catch in her voice. He caught a glimpse of her hand before she hid it in her lap, nervous fingers combing through her blond hair. Explosions going off in a crowded mall the day after Thanksgiving—it was a nightmare that could happen anywhere. That's what grabbed you by the throat and choked your senses for a minute or two.

"Yeah, I think it's bad."

"Reminds me of the Hawkins shooting," she said in almost a whisper.

"It was around this time of year?"

"December 5th."

Nick had been living in Boston at the time but he knew the incident had rattled the state of Nebraska. A nineteen-year-old named Robert Hawkins walked into the Von Maur at Westroads Shopping Mall, took the elevator to the third floor and started shooting. By the time he was finished and turned the gun on himself, eight other people were dead. All of them random and innocent shoppers and store employees.

"That was so hard on the entire community," Christine said, now watching out the SUV windows, as if she wanted to make sure her son couldn't burst in and overhear. "I can't even imagine what this will be like for the families."

Nick operated by getting through life step by step,

prioritizing and keeping focused on what needed to be done immediately. He couldn't think about the victims right now or their families. As heartless as that sounded, he needed to stay focused on his job. For his old job as a Boston prosecutor that meant finding the bad guys and putting them away. This job would be a little trickier. The premise remained the same—find out who did this. Find who cracked their firewall of security. No, not cracked. More like ravaged.

"I'll take you to the airport," Christine said, startling Nick back.

"Looks like there's room on a Delta flight in two hours from now."

"Can you pack and be ready that fast?"

"Sure, why not. If I forget something I'll be at the mall."

She rolled her eyes at him and he thought he saw the beginning of a smile. But just as quickly it disappeared. Her fingers gripped the steering wheel and Nick watched her face transform from sister to mom while Timmy and Gibson opened their doors and piled into the backseat.

"You're gonna miss the Nebraska Colorado game, Uncle Nick."

"You can TiVo it for me, okay?" he told the boys.

Nick caught Christine's eyes and just in that moment they seemed to exchange the same thought: *Oh but to be fifteen again and have the world revolve around only you.*

CHAPTER
14

Mall of America

Patrick saw Rebecca just as he heard the first shouts from down below, "Police, put up your hands." She looked crumpled against the railing that separated the open expanse of the atrium and what used to be the food court. Tables and chairs were tossed and broken, splintered into pieces like a tornado had blown through. She was conscious though hugging her left arm to her body. And there was a man standing over her. Someone trying to help.

But why had he chosen Rebecca?

He remembered trying to help the mother get her baby out of the stroller and wanted to kick himself for being paranoid. Of course, people helped each other.

As Patrick got closer he could see the white type on the man's baseball cap. Paramedic? Strange, he didn't think there was a rescue squad here yet. He looked down over the railing. Two uniformed police officers scrimmaged the mall entrance two floors down. They were the first responders that Patrick had heard or seen though he guessed it was certainly possible for more to be here without him noticing.

Blue jeans, hiking boots, a duffel bag.

Patrick still wasn't satisfied. And there was something in the guy's hand that looked like...*damn, it looked like a needle and syringe.* None of the volunteer rescue and fire units Patrick had ever worked with would approach an injured person with a syringe.

"Hey," Patrick shouted, but his voice was drowned out in the whirl of noises.

"Rebecca," he yelled and saw her body jerk up. But it wasn't in response to his call.

In one swift move she jumped to her feet, kicking at a table leg and sending it into the man's path before sprinting off in the other direction. The man stumbled but only for a second. He pocketed the syringe and bolted after Rebecca, shoving a pair of teenaged girls out of his way. In the chaos no one else noticed.

Patrick took off after both of them.

What the hell was going on?

CHAPTER
15

Washington, D.C.

Andrews Air Force Base disappeared below and Maggie forced herself to not look for it, to stop watching out the airplane window. Killers, she could handle. Being at 38,000 feet and not in control still required conscious effort.

Conscious effort or a Scotch, neat.

It didn't even matter that it was a private jet with comfortable leather lounge chairs. To make matters worse, Assistant Director Ray Kunze sat across from her alongside Allan Foster, the silver-haired senior United States senator from Minnesota. To Maggie's left was the Assistant Deputy Director of Homeland Security, Charlie Wurth. The three men were finally quiet after exchanging pleasantries, a few barbs and then the requisite comments of disbelief and anger. Maggie had simply sat back and tuned them out.

"They warned us," Senator Foster said for a second time.

"We'll know soon enough if this was the work of any organized group or simply one madman." A.D. Kunze looked to Maggie and nodded like it was some secret signal to back him up. "Our Special Agent O'Dell should be able to tell us exactly who to look for as soon as she sees those videotapes."

Instead of agreeing or offering any assurance, Maggie asked the senator, "What exactly were the warnings?"

"We haven't substantiated or authenticated them yet," Kunze answered for the senator. "But I'm certain once we get a look at the terrorists—on the security cameras and from eyewitness reports—we'll be able to determine if the warnings provide an appropriate template."

Maggie found herself staring at Kunze. Did he always talk like this? As if surrounded by TV cameras and reporters?

"I'm just curious," she said and shrugged as though it didn't matter whether or not they shared. "Warnings and threats often reveal more than intended."

Senator Foster met her eyes and nodded, "That's very true." Then as if to squelch any protests, he added, "And the warnings are all we have right now."

"You said security had video," Kunze tossed at Wurth, again reminding Maggie of a politician looking to already place blame if need be.

"Yes, they should have video," Wurth said with a calm that made Kunze's bulging vein in his forehead look manic. "But you know how retail security is. They're more concerned about shoplifting than bombs. We'll be lucky if we caught any of the terrorists on camera. And hopefully the cameras weren't tampered with or destroyed."

Maggie knew Wurth had been awarded his position in Homeland Security for his work investigating the fraud and failures of the federal government after Hurricane Katrina. He had a reputation for pushing the envelope and getting things done. Compared to his FBI counterpart and the senior senator, Wurth would be the one least worried about political correctness or organizational protocol.

Ironic, Maggie thought as she watched the small, wiry black man. Ironic and refreshing to meet someone who didn't premeasure his actions to limit his accountability. In other words, it was refreshing to meet someone in this business whose number one concern wasn't covering his own ass.

Kunze dug a file folder from a bulging leather satchel and handed it to Maggie.

She glanced at the three men as she started to sift through the contents. Each man watched her with different looks that telegraphed their different agendas—looks and agendas as different as were the men.

Maggie guessed Wurth somewhere around her age, middle thirties with a small but athletic frame. He shed his sport jacket as soon as they boarded and rolled up the sleeves of his oxford shirt, a pale pink shirt with a bright red necktie. She immediately liked Wurth who didn't seem to care about putting on airs or hiding his working-class past. He sat on the edge of his chair, nervous energy tapping out with his foot.

In contrast Senator Foster's tall, lanky body lounged back in his chair with legs crossed at the ankles and extending well beyond his personal space. His elbows braced up on the chair arms, hands together creating a steeple of fingers that held up his head and seemed to point out the deep cleft at the bottom of his chin. He reminded Maggie of an academic professor, thoughtful, slow to speak as if he truly were pondering every answer before he responded.

Assistant Director Kunze was physically a direct opposite of both Wurth and Foster. Square head on massive shoulders, Kunze looked more like a well-dressed bouncer at a private nightclub. His stare could easily be mistaken as vacant while, in fact, his mind analyzed and processed every move his opponent made. He used the image of all brawn, no brains to his advantage and had even been rumored to play it up every chance he got.

A.D. Kunze's superiors called him straightforward and quick-thinking. Maggie considered him reactive and impulsive. Colleagues described him as determined, focused and passionate. Maggie saw him as unpredictable, short-tempered and vindictive. In plain English, a petty brute of a man who didn't deserve to walk in Kyle Cunningham's shadow let alone take over his position.

Previous to Kunze being assigned interim assistant director of the Behavioral Science Unit Maggie had never worked with the man, and yet he came to the position loaded with an unshakable perception of her, a preconceived misperception. Evidently her reputation of bending the rules was something Kunze had no patience for. His accusation that Maggie and Agent Tully had contributed to Assistant Director Cunningham's death somehow, by their individual negligence in the case, was absurd. Why Kunze insisted on using it against them puzzled her. It almost seemed ridiculous, except that Maggie knew Kunze might actually be able to pull it off.

Inside the file folder were poor-quality copies of memorandums about several phone calls and e-mails. They seemed standard fare. The group called itself Citizens for American Pride, CAP for short. Maggie was familiar with the group and similar ones. Most of them had gained popularity through the Internet and on college campuses. Their missions weren't all that different from the white supremacist groups of the '80s and '90s, which they disguised with a veil of normalcy and a level of legitimacy.

Instead of holing up in cabins or compounds, the groups—always professing America pride and ideals—held family picnics, sometimes church sponsored, though not affiliated with any one church or Christian denomination. They held rallies on college campuses. From what Maggie remembered, most of the groups preached family values and focused on putting an end to exporting jobs, stopping the floodgate of immigrants coming across the border and encouraging the purchase of American-made products. Maggie remembered recently seeing, as the holiday shopping season began, a full-page ad in *USA Today*, sponsored by Citizens for American Pride, calling for a boycott of electronic games. Their reasoning being that they wanted to prevent the addiction and destruction of American youths.

Picnics, boycotts, rallies, advertising campaigns—none of it sounded like a group capable of bombing a crowded shopping mall.

Maggie was about to ask what basis they had to take these particular threats seriously when a flight attendant interrupted.

"What can I get for the four of you?"

Kunze ordered coffee, black. The other two men nodded in unison for Maggie to go next. Kunze wasn't rattled in the least, nor apologetic.

"A Diet Pepsi," Maggie said.

Wurth asked for the same. Then Senator Foster gave instructions for a gin martini that required a three-step process.

"Do you have anything onboard to eat?" Maggie stopped the attendant before she turned to leave. "I haven't eaten yet today." She thought of the spread of food she had prepared and left for her friends and her stomach felt hollow.

"I'm certain I can find something."

"Yeah, food would be a good idea," Wurth agreed.

This time Maggie saw Kunze scowl at the deputy

director. She kept a smile to herself as she went back to sifting through the file folder. Perhaps she had found an ally in Wurth.

CHAPTER 16

Mall of America

BECCA, DON'T TRUST ANYONE—DIXON

That was the text message that had flashed on the screen of Dixon's iPhone. Rebecca noticed it when she started ripping out the lining of her coat and the phone fell out of her coat pocket. She had forgotten about having the phone. Hadn't even remembered it when she heard the *Batman* theme ring tone earlier.

Without the warning from Dixon, Rebecca still would have run. There was something creepy, something totally wrong about this guy in the PARAMEDIC cap. From her pre-vet experience she knew drugging a wounded animal was best for the animal and the rescuer, but certainly that's not how it worked with people. Was it? And what about the others lying just yards away in much worse shape?

Her instincts had been correct. The guy gave chase, almost grabbing her wounded arm. He was still follow-

ing though now keeping his distance when she managed
to insert herself into a group headed down the escalator.
Rebecca pressed in between an elderly couple and a group
of women with screaming children in their arms. Behind
them were two old women with their arms around each
other, bracing each other up and making it impossible for
anyone to pass by them on the escalator.

Rebecca glanced over her shoulder. He was there at the
top of the escalator, only a dozen or so steps behind. She
avoided eye contact but could feel his stare.

The escalator made it feel like they were moving in slow
motion. There was no way for her to push forward and take
advantage of the temporary barrier between them. No one
dared to rush down the steps. By now all that were left on
the third floor were the trailers, those slowed by shock or
injuries, old age or physical handicaps. The first waves
were already down on the main level of the mall, piling at
the exits.

Rebecca gripped the cell phone in her hand and with
her thumb punched in:

WHAT DID YOU GET ME INTO?

The response chimed back quickly:

THANK GOD U R OK. WHAT ABOUT CHAD &
TYLER?

They were getting to the bottom of the escalator. Her
thumb flew over the miniature keypad:

SOMEONE'S AFTER ME.

WHO IS HE, DIXON???????

They were on the second floor and Rebecca tried to stay
with the safety net group but they were breaking apart,
going separate ways. Another glance back. He was stuck
on the escalator for a few more seconds, looking miserably
impatient, his hand ready to shove the old women out of
his way.

She dashed around the corner, stumbled through a kiosk of sunglasses that had been knocked over. She slipped but kept her balance. Her arm throbbed. Again, she felt light-headed and nauseated. In the reflection of a storefront window she could see him coming, already turning the corner. A brisk walk. Not running. Not yet.

His head swiveled from side to side, watching every-one and taking in everything around them. She kept track of him in the store window reflections as she passed by, avoiding looking back at him and wasting time. All the storefronts were already closed, metal grates across the entrances preventing her from ducking into one of them.

Rebecca kept a steady pace. There was another group approaching the next set of down escalators. She hurried to join them. She wedged herself into the middle just as they started getting on the escalator. A quick glance over her shoulder. He was there at the top, following, not even ten feet behind.

She gripped the moving railing with her left hand and snatched it back.

Blood. And lots of it.

Her hand was wet and sticky with it. The realization that it was her own sent her stomach reeling again. The wound in her arm was bleeding more than she thought.

In her right hand she held the cell phone and began texting again:

WHERE R U? WHICH HOSPITAL?

"Becca."

She heard her name called and twisted around.

Was it possible the man knew who she was?

She saw him looking up and followed his eyes. Leaning over the second floor railing was Patrick waving at her.

Patrick. Steady, reliable Patrick.

Tall, lean, looking strong…and worried. Something

black smeared the side of his face. His hand waved, trailing a bloodstained wrap.

She smiled up at him.

God, it was good to see him.

Something unclenched inside her. It would be okay. She'd be okay. She wasn't alone. They were almost to the bottom of the escalator. She'd hang tight to the group, wait for Patrick to catch up. Another look over her shoulder and she saw him at the top of the escalator. The man in the PARAMEDIC cap saw him, too. He had something in his hand, something that flashed before he pocketed it.

A knife? A gun? The syringe?

The cell phone chimed Dixon's reply:

ST MARY'S. COME HERE.

DON'T TRUST ANYONE.

NOT EVEN PATRICK.

CHAPTER
17

In flight

Maggie set the file folder aside. She was more interested in Homeland Security Deputy Director Wurth's phone call. He took what looked like meticulous notes, while he nodded and inserted "Yes, I understand" several times. For the rest of them seated around him and listening, it was impossible to know what was going on.

FBI Assistant Director Kunze didn't bother to hide his impatience. He waved a beefy hand at Wurth, palm up accompanied by a shoulder shrug. It was as plain as if he were saying, "What the hell's going on?" Wurth ignored him. He continued to take notes in the small leather folio, underlining words and redotting *i*'s in between writing. Maggie saw it as a nervous habit of a man with too much energy. Also a way of controlling information and ignoring the rest of them. Perhaps the deputy director had a few political tricks up his own sleeve.

"Three bombs," Wurth told them even as he was tapping the button on the phone to end his call. "Mall security noticed at least three men with identical red backpacks earlier this morning. They started tracking them just minutes before the blasts."

"Arabs?" Foster made no excuse for his first question.

"Mall security cameras are pretty crappy," Wurth said. "No one seems willing to make that assessment at this stage. They also aren't willing to discount anything either. Right now their focus is making sure there aren't any more bombs in the mall. Some of these sickos get their kicks from waiting for and taking out the first responders."

Maggie remembered all too well. That was exactly the case two months ago when she and Assistant Director Cunningham responded to what they believed was a bomb threat. A quiet suburban neighborhood. An ordinary house. Only the woman and her daughter who lived there had not been the real targets. She didn't want to think about it. Didn't need to relive it again for the hundredth time.

She glanced at A.D. Kunze fingering his too-tight collar and loosening his tie as he shoved into his mouth the last bite of a bagel loaded with cream cheese. Between chews and as he wiped at the corner of his lip he asked, "So how many dead?"

At that very moment, Maggie realized how much she missed Cunningham, his brisk but polite manner, that crinkle of concern indented in his brow, his quiet authority that seemed to enter the room with him. She even missed his nagging. Kyle Cunningham had been Maggie's mentor for over ten years. She'd learned so much from him, taking her cues not only on how to work a case but how to relate to colleagues, when to remain quiet, what to look for, even how to dress. In some ways Cunningham had replaced her father. And losing him felt like losing her father all over again. She didn't need her degree in psychology to understand that was why she was having nightmares again.

Nightmares of going through her father's funeral over and over, still from the eyes of a twelve-year-old.

"It's too early." Wurth brought her back to the inside of their jet and not alongside her father's coffin. He was side-stepping Kunze's question. "You know how these things are in the preliminary stages. We can't rely on mall security to give us an accurate read of what's happening."

"Why not?" Maggie asked and surprised Wurth with her challenge. "You believed their report about three bombs, three men with three red identical backpacks."

Kunze stopped eating and actually sat forward, interested in Wurth's answer.

The deputy director looked from Maggie to Kunze then to Senator Foster who continued to sip his martini but raised an eyebrow to show that he, too, was waiting for the response.

"Right now they think the explosions were confined to the third floor. But the day after Thanksgiving the place was packed. Estimates are anywhere from 150,000 to 200,000 people inside. Depending on the detonation power inside each backpack…" Wurth shrugged—his best guess was as good as theirs. "We don't have a body count, if that's what all of you are looking for. But I will tell you that early reports indicate it's bad, very bad."

CHAPTER
18

Mall of America

Asante had missed his opportunity. He hated loose ends.

He watched the young woman escape his reach and wedge herself even further inside a mob that pressed tight against each other as they swarmed to get out the mall exit closest to them. Asante didn't recognize the young man who waved at her. It wasn't Dixon Lee.

Here on the first floor, cops in uniform with rifles yelled at people to get their hands up. The cops wore Kevlar vests and blue jeans, their badges in plain view, strapped to their arms or thighs. They tried to cut a path through a swarm of shoppers at the side entrance for firefighters and paramedics to enter.

Real paramedics.

Asante resisted the urge to pluck off his own cap and stuff it into the duffel bag. Instead he left it on, parroting the cops, telling people to get out of his way. Only Asante headed the opposite direction. He hurried for the back service exit for a second time in the last hour, walking quickly, not rushing, shouldering past one throng of people and cutting through another. The service exit wasn't marked so no one crowded toward it. He slipped out the heavy door. The alarm that he had dismantled earlier remained silent though it wouldn't have mattered now with the chorus of alarms and whistles and screams.

He dodged behind the set of Dumpsters until he got a good look around. Then he allowed his cap to add confidence to his stride across the parking lot. There was too much chaos for anyone to pay attention to him. The snow came down heavier now. The wind had picked up. The weather became an unexpected bonus.

Before Asante reached the car, he flipped on his headset and punched several numbers into the computer strapped to the inside of his arm.

In seconds came a voice, this time a female voice, calm and ready. "Yes?"

Asante used the computer screen's touchpad to continue his task.

"I'm downloading two photos," Asante said as he ripped off a glove and glided a finger over the computer's touch screen. He had taken quick pictures with his cell phone while on the escalator.

"The woman may have been with Carrier #3 earlier," Asante continued. "That must be how she ended up with his signal."

He tapped the keyboard and touched through the menu to send the photos, his fingers expertly knowing what to do without hesitation. "I want you to tell me who both of them are. Find out everything you can. Start with the woman. I want all the basics: credit cards, driver's license, passport, home mortgage, prescriptions, parents, siblings…all of it."

"No problem."

"I'll let you know when and what photos to release as planned."

"Consider it done. Anything else?"

"I have a flight to catch. I need Danko to continue tracking Carrier #3's GPS signal." A quick stroke brought up that computer screen that showed the GPS signal. It appeared to be stuck back inside the mall. He climbed into his car and took in the scene across the street, wondering if perhaps he could still finish her out here.

"Sir, I may be able to do better than that."

"Excuse me?"

"I have the most recent text messages from that signal right in front of me. I can tell Danko exactly where the subject is headed."

Of course. How could he have forgotten. He smiled. This loose end wouldn't be so difficult to tie up after all.

"Where?"

"Saint Mary's Hospital. She's googling the directions to get there right as we speak. In fact," and she paused, "I can access all the text messages that were made and received from that signal."

CHAPTER
19

Mall of America
Bloomington, Minnesota

Nick Morrelli followed his security escort as they made their way to the front entrance of the mall. He brushed the snow off his trench coat and raked a gloved hand over his hair.

Boots. He should have brought boots.

In his rush to pack he'd forgotten boots. It hadn't been snowing in Omaha.

The escort, who had introduced himself to Nick at the airport as Jerry Yarden, insisted the snow was letting up. Made it sound like the five or six inches on the ground were no big deal to trudge through. This was Minnesota, after all.

"Should be stopping in about an hour," he told Nick.

He followed alongside Yarden, straining to keep up. Nick was almost a head taller but the little man walked briskly through the mall parking lot. That's because Jerry had boots.

Finally Nick slowed and let Yarden go ahead of him to the next police barricade. This was their third one. While Yarden flipped open his ID Nick approached with caution. By now his leather loafers were caked with snow. He was afraid he'd slip and make an ass of himself. Nick waited his turn then without a word he showed his badge and security credentials to yet another police office at the door. This one had his own badge strapped to his thigh. A two-way radio was strapped to his shoulder. He wore a black stocking cap and Kevlar vest, both with POLICE in white letters across the fronts. He held a rifle in one hand and took Nick's ID in the other, lifting it to eye level so that his head never bowed, never lost track of everything going on around him.

He looked at Nick hard, not just comparing the photo to Nick's face but almost as if he wanted to see if he could make him crack, expose any weaknesses, any deceit before Nick made it past his station. Nick wanted to tell the officer he appreciated the tough scrutiny, but to say it would insinuate that he expected something less. Instead, Nick kept quiet, accepted his credentials back with only a nod. As soon as the police officer waved Nick and Yarden through, the man's eyes were somewhere else, ready for the next threat.

Although it was believed that all the bombs had gone off on the third floor, even the first floor showed signs of the explosion. Streamers of debris hung from a huge holiday wreath. The Christmas tree in the center of the atrium was littered with bits and pieces that Nick could tell didn't belong, some shiny, some ragged.

Down here the sprinklers had not been triggered but there was a damp chill. Enough that he caught himself reaching for the lapels of his trench coat and stopping himself before he turned them up.

Off to the side, strung out in front of Macy's, two units of rescue workers barked requests and orders as they handed out blankets and tended to injured shoppers. But Nick's eyes searched above, trying to look up at the four-story atrium. Snipers, dressed in black with Kevlar vests and helmets, were stationed at the tops of the stalled escalators, weapons shouldered and ready. The overpowering smell of smoke and sulfur permeated the air. Shouts echoed down.

"We don't need to go up there," Yarden told him like he was doing Nick a favor.

Nick glanced down at the little man. Removing his stocking cap had released Yarden's large ears and sent his red hair straight up. That, and his ruddy cheeks, made him look almost like an elf. It only added to the bizarre scene.

"Our security office is down this way." Yarden pointed. "County police cordoned it off. Mr. Banoff convinced them to leave everything as is until you arrived."

"No one's looked at the tapes yet?"

Yarden shook his head. "They've had more important things to do." He stopped suddenly, turning to Nick and looking around to see if anyone was watching them. "Mr. Banoff convinced them that it's to their benefit if we sift through the tapes. It'll save time and we understand the equipment so we can pinpoint angles, views, etcetera."

Then Yarden wiggled a long, skinny index finger for Nick to come closer. "You do understand what Mr. Banoff means when he says *sift*, right?"

For the first time since he entered the mall Nick's stomach twisted a bit. He hated to think that his new employer was simply worried about covering his own liability at a time like this. Nick didn't answer Yarden. He simply nodded.

CHAPTER
20

"Keep her still. Can you do that?"

"Yes," Patrick told the large, black woman in the too-tight blue uniform.

He couldn't take his eyes off her purple latex-gloved hands, quick and expert fingers working on the wound in Rebecca's arm.

The wound looked deep. Really deep.

No, he didn't think keeping Rebecca still would be a problem. If anything he thought Rebecca looked too still. He wished she would say something, anything. Open her eyes for longer than a series of unfocused blinks.

"We're gonna need some plasma over here," the woman yelled over her shoulder, making Patrick jump. She noticed him jump, but pretended not to. He appreciated that small gesture. Instead she continued to give him instructions. "And warm. You need to keep her warm," she told him as she pointed with her chin at the blanket.

He immediately pulled it up and started tucking it in along the sides of Rebecca.

"You're doing good," the woman told him. "Real good."

He knew she was giving him things to do to keep him from going into shock, too. He wanted to tell her he was a volunteer with a fire department back home in Connecticut and had some experience with this kind of thing but just as he thought of it, he quickly dismissed it. He realized he didn't have experience with anything at all like this. Not bombs going off. Not friends hurt and unconscious. It was different with Rebecca lying here.

He had barely caught up with her, squeezing and shoving his way through a swarm of people trying to exit the mall. Rebecca had been tapping frantically at Dixon's iPhone while being jostled about. One minute she was trying to tell him something, drowned out by the noise engulfing them and the next minute she was slipping down into the mob, like a swimmer being sucked up under a wave.

He had to pull her up. She was faint and feverish, her eyes rolling back into her head. She grabbed onto his arm and her hand was filled with blood. He had already noticed the wound in her arm. Glass impaled the skin, too deep for him to pluck it out. He knew it would bleed even more if he did that. Somehow he had managed to separate her from the mob and get her to sit down before she collapsed completely.

"You got that plasma?" the woman yelled again, startling Patrick again, but this time, at least, he didn't jump.

He watched her finish the last sutures.

"Is she gonna be okay?" He knew it was a lame question but he needed to ask it anyway.

"Of course she is." But she didn't look up at him, concentrating instead on the rhythm of her fingers. Her right hand sutured while her left hand dabbed at the blood. "Your girlfriend's gonna be just fine."

Patrick opened his mouth to correct her but stopped himself. Rebecca wasn't his girlfriend. She would have been the first one to protest if she could. Not because they didn't like each other. It was an independence thing. At least that's what she called it. She connected independence with being totally on her own. He actually got that. Understood it completely. Or maybe recognized it since it was close to his own philosophy, his own creed.

That fierce independence was probably what connected them in the first place. Although Patrick didn't refer to it as independence so much as a lack of trust. When you grew up without anyone to count on you learned quickly to count on yourself. His mom had done her best but as a single mom she was gone a lot, working long hours. Patrick didn't blame her. It was what it was. Besides, he turned out just fine. Maybe grew up a bit sooner than his classmates. Nothing wrong with that.

He had never felt like he belonged with kids his own age anyway. They were always too immature. Like Dixon Lee, full of unrealistic ideals. Patrick didn't have the time or luxury to worry about and protest things like immigration when it took all his energy just to keep his own job and work full-time so he could pay for his rent and tuition. He didn't make time for guys like Dixon Lee. Didn't let them in. Didn't trust them. Or anyone, for that matter. It was part of the creed. You can only trust yourself. But then came Rebecca messing up his resolve.

She was witty—that dry humor that takes you by surprise—and smart. Not just book smart but capable of debating an issue, reasoning, quipping with a polite sarcasm he found totally charming. Most importantly, she knew how to listen. He'd throw out bits and pieces of himself—the safe stuff, not anything that would reveal his true secrets—expecting her to bat them aside. Only Rebecca absorbed it all. Not just absorbed, but sorted and sifted and tried to put the bits and pieces together. Patrick had never met anyone quite like her.

And oh, by the way, did he mention she was pretty easy on the eyes? Small with an athletic build and enough curves to offset her tomboy attitude. Big brown eyes and creamy skin, although right now, she looked too pale. Her shoulder-length hair was wet with perspiration, the feathery bangs stuck to her forehead. Her normally full lips were now thin and tight from fighting the pain.

Her eyes fluttered open and he reached for her hand underneath the blanket. He decided he liked the sound of her being his girlfriend though he wouldn't admit it out loud. If you let someone in they usually expected to know everything, including all your secrets. Patrick wasn't ready for that.

The plasma arrived and the woman in the blue uniform started preparing the lines and checking Rebecca's other arm for an entry vein. She didn't ask Patrick to let go of Rebecca's hand as she positioned the arm to her liking.

"You're gonna be just fine," she said and Patrick nodded before he realized she was talking to Rebecca now.

Her eyes focused on him and stayed there. She squeezed his hand and he smiled at her. Had he ever told her she had the prettiest eyes he'd ever seen? Of course he hadn't.

He wanted to tell her she could count on him. Right now. For as long as she wanted or needed. She could set aside that fierce independence and lean on him. And it didn't have to mean anything. But instead, he didn't say anything and he knew he would regret it.

CHAPTER
21

Asante lost the GPS signal halfway to the airport. That happened sometimes with control towers and radar from incoming and outgoing airlines. It didn't matter. He needed to let Danko handle the loose ends while he moved on to the next phase. There could be nothing that got in the way.

The snow tapered off. Trucks with blades and sand were already out on the streets. Asante had to slow for them. As soon as he'd speed up again he'd have to hit the brakes and skid around nervous drivers. The first snow of the season and everyone seemed to have forgotten how to drive. He had counted on that fact as being an advantage. Now it was simply annoying.

He caught his eyes in the rearview mirror. The adrenaline had been replaced by anxiety. He told those simmering blue eyes to stay calm, to be patient. Then he took several deep breaths, holding each one before letting it out slow and easy.

He told himself that no project ran completely without flaws. The brilliance of a project manager like himself relied on his ability to react and readjust. And at the same time he had to make it look effortless, to cast the illusion of calm, to let his crew see only confidence, nothing less.

Though handpicked they were followers at heart when you peeled away their individual layers of talent, whether those talents included technosavvy intelligence or physical strength. Asante believed he possessed a gift in reading other people, seeing potential where others saw mediocrity. But he could also detect weakness. Everyone had some vulnerability no matter how well hidden. Asante could find it and, if necessary, exploit it.

From his inner circle, he insisted on perfection. He expected nothing less. Anyone chosen for his crew knew this. Being selected was a commendation as well as a burden. Glitches were unacceptable. A weak link could be quickly removed and the removal was permanent. This is what made him a great project manager.

He set the small computer on the dash to see the screen better. Before he could press any of the preset buttons a call buzzed in. He checked his phone. He didn't recognize the number though he often instructed his crew to use prepaid cell phones to prevent tracking.

"Asante," he answered into his wireless headset.

"You tried to use my grandson," an angry voice came back at him.

Asante knew immediately who it was. He had already been warned that the man might be a problem. "How did you get this number?"

"What the hell did you think you were doing?"

"Once the project has begun no one has control but me. Those are the rules."

"You meant to kill him, didn't you, you asshole."

"Nor are you to have any contact with me." Asante kept his voice calm and steady even as he disconnected the call.

With one hand clenching the steering wheel and the other on the phone's keypad he tapped several keys, ensuring that number would be blocked.

He checked his eyes again in the rearview mirror, disappointed to find the anxiety turning to anger. Calm. He needed to stay calm. He flexed his fingers and stretched his neck from side to side.

Despite the man's fury and accusation, his grandson, Dixon Lee, had not been a mistake or a glitch. Asante allowed himself a smile. Dead or alive, Dixon Lee had been a well-planned insurance policy. Another quick glance in the mirror. Nobody messed with the Project Manager once the project began. Nobody. Not even the assholes who special ordered the project.

Asante turned into the long-term parking lot at the airport and found a space at the far end, close to where he had stolen the car earlier. He gathered up his belongings, stuffing them into the duffel bag. Then he wiped down every single surface inside the car that he had touched. He left the car just as the airport shuttle pulled into the lot. He glanced at his diver's watch. Plenty of time.

He took another deep breath. He hated glitches. In the old days he could predict and ward off every single one. Perhaps it was time to retire. Buy an island somewhere. He had more than enough money stashed safely away in Zurich, even before this project. He deserved the rest. A nice long relaxation, something more substantial than the short escapes that lasted only as long as a box of Cubans and a couple bottles of Chivas.

Instead of focusing on glitches, instead of thinking about Carrier #3 Asante reminded himself of other successes. It calmed him to run past projects through his mind step by step—the early planning, the stages and then the denouement. So when Asante boarded the shuttle bus he nodded to the driver with a brief smile and in his mind he began the playback of Madrid, March 11, 2004…backpacks, the train station at rush hour, bright flashes of light and most of all… success.

CHAPTER 22

Saint Mary's Hospital

Henry Lee paced the hallway, unclenching his fists only long enough to drag nervous fingers over his bristled head and rub the disbelief from his eyes. At sixty-eight he was still vain enough to take pride in his compact, fit and trim physique. He was strong and healthy and unlike his father and grandfather Henry had done everything in his control to prevent hereditary heart disease from shortening his golden years. Everything, that is, except to make sure that his wife, his sweetheart, his Hannah, had also stayed healthy. It was simply inconceivable to him that she was in surgery right here, right now undergoing the emergency triple bypass that Henry thought for certain he had dodged.

He couldn't help wondering if this was some cruel punishment from God though he thought he had given up on the foolishness of His existence years ago. No God Henry could believe in would take away a daughter as murderously as his own had been taken. Hannah was always the one, the believer, the healer, wanting to make sense out of madness. She was Henry's lifeline, his common sense, his sanity. He couldn't bear to lose her. And then to find out that he almost lost his grandson on the very same day. If God did exist He was, indeed, cruel and vindictive.

Henry looked for the boy, again, checking the waiting room and glancing around the corner. Earlier Dixon had come to the hospital when summoned, physically distraught about his grandmother, his eyes red-rimmed, his fingernails bitten to the quick. When he said he had just come from the mall Henry thought his own heart had stopped, realizing what could have happened had he not called the boy.

While the first reports came in about a possible terrorist attack at the mall, the boy remained quiet. The two of them watched the wall-mounted TV while sitting silently side by side in the surgery waiting room. No one else was there, except for a few staff members wandering in and out. No surgeries were planned the day after Thanksgiving other than emergency ones. It took several reports before Dixon—in between gnawing at his poor thumbnail—confessed and explained about his friends and how they had convinced Dixon to help them. The whole time Henry felt the blood drain from his face.

"We were told we were carrying electronic jamming devices," Dixon told him, his eyes darting around, teeth nipping at another fingernail. "I think it might have been something else."

"That's impossible," Henry said but he knew it to be quite the opposite. "I told you to stay away from those two."

"We've been friends since third grade."

"Doesn't matter. They're trouble."

"I've got to find out if they're okay," Dixon told him. "Can I borrow your phone?"

The boy was so distraught Henry handed over his smartphone without hesitating. It was better he make his own calls from the hospital's public phones. They were less likely to be traced. He certainly didn't want the calls immortalized on his monthly statement.

He dialed the second number, this one from memory instead of a crumpled piece of paper, his fingers still shaking from the first call.

"Hello?"

"Allan, it's Henry. We need to have a meeting."

"For what reason?"

"We need to reconsider."

"Reconsider?"

"Yes. We need to stop this."

Henry expected anger. He was prepared for it. He wasn't prepared, however, for laughter.

He held the phone away from his ear and closed his eyes tight against the sudden pain of his clenched jaw muscles, an involuntary reaction from his early days as a boxer preparing for an upper left. This was worse than any punch. When the laughter silenced he brought the phone back to his ear.

"There's no stopping this now. Go home, Henry. Get some sleep."

A dial tone erupted in Henry's ear before he could respond.

CHAPTER
23

It was twilight by the time their motorcade of black SUVs idled at the first set of police barricades surrounding the mall. Maggie couldn't help but notice that the short ride from the airport yielded a breathtakingly beautiful sunset, the sky clear now except for the pink-purple streaks. The only evidence of a recent storm was the glittering snow that blanketed everything in sight. That and the cold, a bitter cold that you could see in breaths that streamed from brief greetings while getting in and out of vehicles.

"Looks like even the national vultures have already arrived," A.D. Kunze said as they passed by a lopsided line of vans and trucks with TV call letters on their sides and satellite receivers on their roofs. A helicopter flew overhead.

"It's all part of the process," Senator Foster told them, looking out at the reporters and cameramen assembling equipment as close to the action as possible.

Maggie noticed the senator straighten his tie in the reflection of the SUV's window. At first she thought she was mistaken. Perhaps it was an absentminded habit. But then he brushed a hand over his silver hair. She glanced at

Deputy Director Wurth, expecting to exchange an eye roll and instead found him doing the same.

"This isn't gonna be pretty," Kunze warned. "I was on the site at Oklahoma City. I'm telling you, nothing smells worse than charred flesh." He pulled out of his pocket a small container of Vicks VapoRub, unscrewed the lid and offered it to the others.

Maggie declined. She had actually smelled charred flesh before.

"I didn't think anything could smell worse than bloated flesh," Wurth said, but dipped his finger in the proffered container and smeared a dab over his lip.

And she'd smelled bloated flesh, too. Maggie remembered without much prompting. She knew Wurth's experience had been with hurricane victims. Her own was from floaters, victims whose killers chose a watery grave hoping to dehumanize and impersonalize them even more.

Senator Foster hesitated at Kunze's offer, watching as the interim director rubbed a generous fingertipful over his own lip and even up into his nostrils.

"I certainly don't want to get in the way of people trying to do their jobs," Senator Foster finally said. "I'm here to show my support."

Kunze and Wurth nodded. Maggie refrained and kept herself from saying, "Sure, why not take advantage of some free reelection publicity without dealing with the gruesome reality." She watched A.D. Kunze and as they all got out of the SUV and made their way to the entrance she couldn't help wondering if that's exactly why Kunze was here. A high-profile case could turn his interim title into a permanent one. But why drag her along?

It was time to find out.

"I'll need someone from security to show me where I

can view the tapes," she told Kunze as she trudged through the snow alongside him.

Maggie was grateful she remembered the slipover boots. Kunze jerked twice trying to keep his balance. It was good timing on her part. He didn't question or challenge her, instead he simply said, "Yeah, yeah, of course."

As soon as they got inside Kunze grabbed Wurth by the elbow, already taking control.

"We need access to those security tapes, Charlie."

"Not a problem." But Wurth's eyes were already upward along with his attention. Maggie realized the man couldn't wait to get to the third floor.

Kunze noticed the distraction, too. "The sooner we connect the bombers the sooner we can get some warrants."

"Of course," Wurth said, tugging off his gloves and stuffing them into his pocket with one hand while the other hand started punching numbers into his cell phone. "I'll get someone down here."

"And Charlie, I sure hope to hell your local guys thought to secure those videos," Kunze said.

"Not to worry. Of course they took care of everything. Just hang on, okay?"

"I'm just saying I better not see videos of those backpacks on the local news."

"We've got it taken care of, Ray."

Maggie stayed back. She'd been a part of these multi-jurisdictional cases before. She knew all the collegial talk from the flight here was over. It was time to let the pissing contest begin.

CHAPTER
24

Nick allowed Yarden to cue up the video for him. He had already tagged several segments from cameras on the third floor, particular instances that had drawn attention before the bombs went off.

"We were watching them," the little man told Nick, as his long fingers flew around the computer keyboard, poking with incredible ease and efficiency. "Shoplifters often use backpacks. And they'll work in teams. That's what we thought was going on."

Yarden sat back and let the first video play. He folded his arms over his chest, shooting glances at Nick, as if anxious for his reaction. Nick leaned forward. The film was grainy, black and white but the angle was decent. The backpacks looked ordinary. Not trendy. Big and bulky and, from the shift in this young man's walk, heavy.

Yarden keyed up another video on a second monitor, but left the first playing.

The second young man was shaggy-headed, a bit shorter and thin. The backpack was identical.

At first glance it bothered Nick that these guys looked

like older versions of his nephew, Timmy and his friend, Gibson. Clean-cut young men, ordinary with confident strides. There were no slumped shoulders. No shifty eyes or heads darting from side to side. They didn't look at all like nerds or social misfits. Nothing like perhaps Klebold or Harris who had been responsible for the Columbine school shootings.

What was even more disturbing to Nick was that they didn't look anything like he expected a suicide bomber to look. Did he expect brown-skinned Arabs? Yeah, he did. And he knew he wasn't alone. Someone suggests suicide bomber and the mind readily conjures up that racial profile.

"They aren't exactly what you'd expect, are they?" Yarden asked as if he could hear Nick's thoughts.

"No. Not exactly." He avoided glancing at Yarden, wanting to at least appear objective. He suspected the security officer was looking for Nick's approval, hoping to bond, confidants taking sides in what could turn into a finger-pointing showdown. "Do you have any decent front facial shots?"

"All of us have been upstairs helping." Yarden suddenly sounded offended. "I only had a few minutes with these before I left to pick you up."

"Sure. I understand."

"I thought that was supposed to be your job."

"Yes, you're absolutely right." Nick could play the diplomat if needed.

"I found a flash. And one of the explosions." Yarden started stabbing at the computer keys again, ready to please and make up for not having what was requested. He fast-forwarded a video clip, shoppers in full-speed animation. Then he stopped and freeze-framed, taking a few more seconds and zooming in before he started the video again.

Nick watched, amazed that even without sound the wall of bricks exploding in front of him made him wince.

"Where is this camera?"

"All of these are third floor. This one is around the corner from the food court."

"Play it again," Nick asked. "Only this time in slow-mode. And zoom out."

"Zoom out?"

"Yes." He didn't even glance at Yarden to acknowledge his skepticism. Instead, Nick leaned forward and waited.

The shot took in the entire stretch of the long hallway, brick walls on both sides. One side had interruptions of doorways. The other was solid. Signs hung above the doorways and in several other locations. Nick watched the wall explode again. It was the side with the interruptions.

"What's on the other side of that brick wall?"

"There's not much down this hallway. Some offices. Restrooms."

"Play it again," he asked.

This time just before the wall exploded, Nick pointed at the monitor. "Stop."

Yarden responded quickly.

"Zoom in on this sign."

Yarden obeyed immediately, no hesitation.

The sign read WOMEN.

"Is the men's restroom next door?" Nick asked.

Yarden quickly consulted a map of the third floor that was spread out across a bulletin board.

"The men's restroom is clear down at the end of this hall and," Yarden said, his voice higher than normal, "on the opposite side."

"So this explosion came from—"

"The women's restroom."

CHAPTER
25

Before he went through the security checkpoint Asante found the airport restroom labeled FAMILY. The single room was larger than he remembered: one toilet, a sink and counter with a changing table and most importantly, a bolted lock on the door. It was perfect. No one would bother him here.

He checked his watch as he hung the garment bag on the door hook. He still had plenty of time to catch his flight. While he unpacked the essentials from his duffel bag he turned on and adjusted his over-the-ear wireless headset. He tapped a number and put aside the phone.

One ring and an answer. "Yes?"

"Give me an update," he said as he dug out of the duffel bag a compact, but expensive and powerful electric shaver, zipping it out of its case and setting both aside for now.

"Text messages indicate Dixon is at the hospital."

"He's okay?" Asante chose his words carefully. But then he already knew the boy was alive. His grandfather had as much as confirmed that in his angry phone call.

"His grandmother is having emergency heart surgery. Rebecca is on her way."

"So they're together?" He punched up the map of the mall's third floor on his computer screen.

"She asked what he got her into."

Asante slid his finger over the small computer screen, zooming in on the map where Carrier #3's bomb had exploded. GPS devices were packed in the backpacks, but every carrier was also given a brand-new iPhone so they could track both carrier and bomb in case one of them decided to leave the backpack behind. He had chosen to keep them all on one floor, the combined blasts close to each other, causing the greatest structural damage as well as creating a larger blast area. That had been his priority. Now he checked to see exactly where Carrier #3's backpack was when it exploded. Zooming in he could see it quite plainly: the women's restroom. The young woman not only had Dixon Lee's iPhone, she had been carrying his backpack.

"Sir?"

"Continue."

"Her name is Rebecca Cory. She's a student at the University of New Haven, a resident of Hartford, Connecticut. Her father is William Cory of—"

"Credit cards? ATM card? Driver's license?" he interrupted as he peeled off his clothes. He didn't need to know the entire portfolio they had amassed. Just those details that mattered.

"ATM card through First Bank of Hartford," the female voice continued, pleasant and soothing as though she were reciting menu items for a special dinner. "She took out a cash withdrawal of fifty dollars two days ago in Toledo. However, a MasterCard looks to be her choice of payment. She uses it for everyday incidentals. Up until two days ago, a daily Starbucks charge in West Haven. Connecticut driver's license."

"Revoke all three. Immediately."

"Yes, sir."

"I want her feeling disabled." He stood before the mirror now in only socks and boxers, thinking this is exactly how he wanted Rebecca Cory—stripped and vulnerable. Figuratively speaking. At least until it was safe to kill her. "Tell Danko that he can find the girl and Dixon Lee at the hospital."

"And if he does?"

"Extract both."

"Yes, sir."

Asante would find another way to use the boy. An extra cutaway when the time was right. A bargaining chip, perhaps.

"What about the other young man?" he asked.

"His name is Patrick Murphy. I'm still working on him."

Asante gave her instructions for what came next, including what to do with Murphy. Before he hung up he gave her a new contact number to use. Then Asante removed the SIM card from the cell phone, destroyed it, and flushed it down the toilet. The portable memory chip held all the traceable data including personal identity information and a record of incoming as well as outgoing calls. From the duffel bag pocket he pulled out a new SIM card and slid it into the cell phone. In seconds he keyed in the password for his wireless headset, punched in a couple of codes and the phone was as good as new and ready to use. He put it and the headset on the sink, safely out of his way.

The shaver indicated that it was fully charged. Within seconds he shaved off his goatee. He reset the shaver's rotating heads so they wouldn't go all the way to the skin but would leave a half inch. Then he started path after path over his head, watching the dark hair, some of it three to four inches long, fall to the sink.

Next came the hair color. The formula was his own special mixture. He squirted it into the palms of his hands and rubbed it over the new stubble, watching his hair turn honey-colored before his eyes. He massaged it into his eyebrows, too.

Cleanup took only a few minutes. Everything he no longer needed, including the syringe, was flushed away or washed down the drain. The hiking boots went into the trash can along with the rest of his clothes. From the garment bag he unzipped an expensive suit, navy blue and tailored to fit him perfectly, as did the white shirt. He left the collar open and stuffed the tie in the duffel bag. He replaced his over-the-ear wireless headset and tucked the cell phone into his breast pocket.

Finished with discarding the Project Manager, he flipped open his wallet to his driver's license and held it up. Once again, he looked like Robert Asante, an ordinary businessman traveling to his next appointment. More importantly, the man in the mirror matched the man in the driver's license photo.

It was time to move on to the next site. Time for the next stage of the project.

CHAPTER
26

"We already have our company investigator reviewing the tapes," the small man named Jerry Yarden told Maggie as he led her through a back hallway.

Maggie couldn't believe it. The security company was reviewing its own tapes? She stopped herself from asking whose authority and what protocol gave them that go-ahead? She'd learned years ago that questioning the locals risked offending them. The result only made her job tougher. It was better if they believed she was on their side. Most people already believed that federal law enforcement would sooner point fingers and place blame than present solutions and share credit.

"I understand someone in security noticed the young men before the bombs went off?"

"Oh yeah, we noticed. Three identical red backpacks." He glanced back at her over his shoulder, not slowing his rapid, almost erratic pace. "You betcha we noticed."

Yarden was Maggie's height, small-framed but long-limbed, arms pumping and swinging loosely as he walked.

He reminded Maggie of a propeller with a thatch of red unruly hair.

"How did you know they were red?"

"Excuse me?"

"Your surveillance cameras are black-and-white, right?"

"Oh sure. We started following them up on the floor," Yarden explained. "We're trained to watch what people bring into the mall with them. We see something suspicious, we follow on the floor. You know, large purses, shopping bags with return items, backpacks, even baby strollers. We had a woman last month sneaking cashmere sweaters under her baby. You'd be surprised what people do."

Maggie smiled to herself. Actually she wouldn't be surprised.

His Midwest manners kept track of her, politely leading the way and holding doors open. Now he pointed to a door at the end of the hall.

"We thought they were shoplifters," he said. "None of us expected those backpacks to have bombs in them."

He beat her by four lengths to the end of the hallway, yanked the door and again held it open for her, his feet spread apart and both arms engaged like the door was a ton of lead. She pushed aside the fact that she could probably bench-press Yarden's weight let alone hold open the door for herself. Instead she thanked him and stepped inside.

He led her through a maze of offices and back to another door. When he opened this one she immediately noticed the room was dim and lit from only the wall of monitors, four rows of ten across with a long control panel of keypads, switches and color-coded buttons.

Sitting at the panel with his back to them was the lone investigator, square-shouldered, dark hair. There was something familiar about the man. Before he swiveled around Maggie recognized Nick Morrelli.

He, however, was not prepared. He did a double take, looking from Yarden to Maggie and back to Maggie.

"Fancy seeing you here," he said with his trademark smile, the one that employed dimples and white teeth in the glow of the computer monitors.

"Hi Nick."

"You two know each other?" Yarden seemed disappointed.

"We've worked together before," Maggie answered, leaving it at that and watching to see if Nick would be compelled to add more. "So you've left the D.A.'s office? You're an investigator now?"

"For United Allied Security."

"Yes, the mall's security company. Do the local authorities know you've been reviewing the videotapes?" Maggie asked Nick but looked back at Yarden who avoided her eyes. Finally Yarden nodded, his head the only part of him in motion now, arms glued to his sides. He reminded her of a bobble-head.

"Yeah, no problem there," Yarden said, still nodding. "They've got their hands full, you know?"

She noticed his cadence grew faster with a slightly higher pitch in relation to his amount of guilt. Even the tips of his ears grew red.

"We're only here to help," Nick told her but Maggie knew from experience that Morrelli's loyalties were sometimes divided, and often resulted in something close to personal quicksand.

Four years ago Nick Morrelli had been county sheriff of a small Nebraska community that was held hostage by a killer—a killer who was targeting young boys. To solve the case Morrelli had struggled to abandon a lifetime of loyalty to his father, the previous sheriff, in order to save his nephew. Maggie and Nick's paths had crossed several times over the years but most recently last summer when, once again, Maggie had been sent to Nebraska to profile another killer. This time Nick's loyalty to a childhood friend had almost jeopardized the case.

"Well then, so you two know each other," Yarden said, anxious to break the silence and ease the tension. "That should make this easier, right?" The little man spun a chair around and held it for Maggie. "Ms. O'Dell—"

"Agent O'Dell," Nick corrected.

"Oh yeah, right. Agent O'Dell."

She sat in the proffered seat, next to Nick, giving him only a glance and focusing her attention instead on the wall of monitors. They had been cueing the tapes, stopping them at important intervals. Over a half dozen of the screens were already freeze-framed.

"As you can see, all we've been doing is tagging segments that might be relevant." Nick waved a hand at the screens. "Isn't that right, Jerry?"

"Right. There's an awful lot of tape to look at. We're just trying to narrow it down. We're not discarding anything. We're just looking and tagging."

Maggie almost felt sorry for the nervous little man. She could hardly tell him to relax, that it was Nick Morrelli she didn't fully trust and not Mr. Yarden whom she had only met moments ago.

"Agent O'Dell will need to see the carriers," Yarden said quickly, grabbing the opportunity to move on. He took the seat on the other side of Maggie. "The tapes are grainy at best." Even before he scooted his chair forward his fingers were flying over the control panel. "We work on a three-second system. That is the camera takes a shot every three seconds. It's not continuous, so it might seem a bit jerky if you're not used to it."

"Do you have a Z97 filter or HDzoom pack?"

Yarden's fingers stopped in midflight and he looked at her with obvious admiration. Not only did she understand the three-second system but also the new state-of-the-art technology.

"We don't have anything quite as sophisticated," Yarden said, glancing over to Nick as if he was to blame, being the company's highest authority on the premises.

"The company is considering updates," Nick said almost too quickly.

Maggie heard a bit of defensiveness in Nick's tone. She ignored it and focused instead on Yarden who was cueing up segments for her to view on monitor after monitor.

"This is one of them." He pointed at the first screen.

Maggie leaned forward. Nick didn't. Had he already seen these? Of course, he had. She wondered how long Morrelli and Yarden had been at it.

From the grainy quality of the video all Maggie could decipher was that the man was average height, clean-cut. He was wearing jeans, a jacket with maybe a logo on the shoulder, and tennis shoes. There was nothing extraordinary about him.

She felt the two men watching her, gauging her reaction, waiting.

Yarden added more views, cueing monitor after monitor until there was a line of grainy freeze-framed images of two different young men with the same backpack walking separately through the crowded mall. Only one instance showed the two of them together.

"I thought there were three?"

"Oh yeah, there were three all right." Yarden's fingers started poking the keys again. "The third one came in with a young woman and another man." He brought up the segment. "We followed him to the food court. Then we…we sort of lost him. We don't have many camera angles on that area and no cameras actually in the food court."

"What about the woman and the other man? Were they involved?"

When Yarden didn't answer Maggie sat back and glanced over at him. He and Nick were exchanging another look. Yarden's ruddy complexion had gone pale. Nick started searching the monitors.

"What is it?" Maggie asked.

"We think one of the bombs went off in the women's restroom," Nick told her as his eyes darted from screen to screen. "You may have just answered our question as to how that could have happened."

CHAPTER
27

For a few minutes Rebecca was back in the bedroom she grew up in, light filtering through yellow gauze curtains, the sound of windchimes outside her second floor window. She could smell fried bacon and imagined her parents down in the kitchen, her mom setting the Sunday breakfast table with bright-colored placemats and long-stem glasses for their orange juice. Her dad would be playing short-order cook, waiting for Rebecca before he started his performance of flipping the pancakes. Those Sunday mornings weren't for show. Her parents really had been happy, the banter out of love not jealousy. She wanted to sink down and soothe herself in that moment, that feeling of calm and security. If only she could ignore the prick at her skin, the ache in her arm, that deep burning sensation.

Her eyes fluttered open. She willed them to stay closed. They wouldn't listen. The blur around her swirled images and noise together. Before her eyes could focus she started to remember: holiday music, Dixon laughing, Patrick smiling. And then…backpacks exploding.

Rebecca didn't realize that she had tried to sit up until she felt hands on her shoulders pushing her back down.

"It's okay."

She recognized the voice and searched for it. Patrick's face bobbed in front of her, slowly coming into focus. There was no smile, only concern. And she tried to remember—how badly had she been hurt? The image of a severed arm lying next to her made her twist around to check both her own. One was wrapped. The other had a needle and tubes in it. But both were there, attached.

"You're all right, sugar," a woman's voice said from someplace over Rebecca's head. "Just relax and lie still a bit."

"Do you remember what happened?" Patrick asked.

She nodded. Her throat felt like sandpaper. She tried to wet her lips. Patrick noticed, fumbled around then brought a bottle of water to her mouth. He was gentle, giving her sips when she wanted to gulp. She knew he saw her frustration but still he insisted on sips.

"Where are we?"

"The hotel across the street," he said.

"Where?"

"Across the street from the mall. They set up a triage area here."

"But the hospital...I thought we were going to the hospital."

"It's okay." He took her hand. "They were able to take care of you here. You don't need to go to the hospital."

She sat up again. This time Patrick helped her instead of holding her back down. Her eyes scanned the room, searching through the chaos for the man with the syringe.

"He's not here," Patrick told her. "I've been watching."

She avoided his eyes and continued her own search. The man with the syringe knew she was still alive. She wiped at her forehead despite the poke of the needle. Her skin was clammy with sweat and she still felt light-headed. Dixon's message rattled in her mind. He said she wasn't safe. That she couldn't trust anyone. Not even Patrick.

Did the man with the syringe give up because he knew she was with Patrick and he couldn't get to her? Or did he no longer *need* to get to her because she was with Patrick?

Rebecca glanced at her friend. His hair was tousled, his jaw bristled with dark stubble. His eyes watched her with an intensity she wasn't used to seeing. What was it? Concern, panic, fatigue? Or something else?

How well did she really know Patrick Murphy?

"You okay?" he asked as he reached for her hand again.

She pulled back, grabbing her bandaged arm as if in pain.

"Did they give me anything? Like for the pain?"

"I think she just localized it." Patrick was already looking around for a nurse or paramedic. "Does it hurt pretty bad?"

Now there was no doubt—concern filled his eyes when he looked back at her.

"Could you see if they have some Advil or something?"

"Yeah, sure. I'll be right back."

Rebecca watched him zigzag through the triage groups and head for a nearby exit. She patted down her pockets carefully and stopped when she saw him glance back. He disappeared from sight and she twisted around to find her coat. Quickly she found Dixon's iPhone. It was turned off. She decided to keep it off.

She scooted to the edge of the covered table, almost forgetting the needle and IV tube in her arm. Another glance over her shoulder. No Patrick. She bit down on her lower lip and pulled the needle out, bending her elbow to stop any bleeding. Then she eased off the table, awkwardly, without use of her hands and trying not to notice the ache in her bandaged arm.

Still no sign of Patrick. She saw an EXIT sign in the other direction and that's where she headed. Within minutes she made her way through the crowded lobby and found an ATM. No one noticed her. There was too much commotion. She kept her head down but her eyes darted around everywhere. She slipped her debit card into the machine, keyed in her PIN and waited. She'd get enough cash for a cab ride, something to eat. Maybe she'd better get enough for a hotel room, but someplace near the hospital.

The card spit out of the machine and the display screen blinked: CARD REFUSED.

There had to be a mistake.

She'd used this debit card a couple of times on their trip and in various locations. She knew she still had about $425 in the account. She slid the card back in and before she could key in the PIN the machine spit it out again, repeating the message.

Rebecca glanced around. Still, no one paid attention to her. There was too much chaos in and out to notice her sudden panic.

She pulled out her one and only credit card. She'd taken a cash advance from the card last month. She had a substantial cash allowance available but had disciplined herself to use it only as a last resort. This definitely qualified. She slid the credit card into the machine, waited and typed in the PIN. Maybe she'd better take out extra, especially if her debit card wasn't working. Just to be safe. All she had in her pockets was the change left from a twenty.

The machine spit this card out, too. CARD REFUSED.

Don't panic, she told herself. There's just something wrong with this machine. She'd find another ATM. No big deal.

She found the exit with confident strides through the midst of rescue personnel and bloodied shoppers. She was in good shape compared to them. That's what she kept telling herself. Then she pushed through the side door and she was outside. When had it gotten dark?

The cold hit her in the face. She had to catch her breath. It had started snowing again. The wind whipped around her. On this side of the hotel there were only lights in the corners of the parking lot. And suddenly the confidence seemed to slide right out of her. She was all alone. Nothing new there. She was used to being on her own. So why did this time feel like she was sliding off a cliff?

CHAPTER
28

There wasn't much to go on, yet Maggie made note of everything. Small details that appeared insignificant at first glance, could end up breaking a case. Despite the grainy black-and-white video she might find something. Except A.D. Kunze expected more than something. He expected her to supply a conclusive profile, one irrefutable enough he could use for a search warrant. He made it sound like she should have names, addresses and social security numbers just by examining the black-and-white, three-second delayed movements of these young homicide bombers.

Unfortunately he wasn't the only one. Television and movies had turned profiling into a sort of magic act that had people believing with a few clues and a wave of the hand, you could pull the rabbit out of the hat, so to speak. Even Kunze insisted there was a scientific formula—which was almost as bad as magic—that if a suspect showed certain characteristics or traits—characteristic number one, two and five from a theoretical psychological profiling chart—then, of course, the suspect fit a specific category. Organized, disorganized. Anger, vengeance. Ritualistic,

chaotic. Two out of three and voilà, just look for the nearest sociopathic narcissist with a speech impediment dressed
in a double-breasted navy blue suit. If only it were that
easy.

Maggie had a premed background, a bachelor's degree
in criminal psychology and a master's in behavioral psychology. Early in her career she had earned a forensic fellowship at Quantico. Yet, even she believed profiling was
more about observation than anything else. The trick—if
there was one—was seeing what others missed, taking account of what may appear obvious to others. And just as
important as paying attention to what was left behind, you
needed to pay attention to what was absent.

Notably absent in this case so far? Hours had passed
and no one had taken credit for the attack. Not even a
suicide note or video…yet. Already it didn't quite fit into
a mass killing category like Virginia Tech or Columbine
High School. Also absent was that none of these young
men looked nervous or anxious. None of them seemed to
fit the profile of a homicide bomber or a mass murderer.

"Is this the one?" Yarden asked.

He had been waiting on her almost to the point of
being annoying. Ordinarily she'd rather be left alone to
run through each tape, over and over as many times as
necessary until she was sure no detail had gone unnoticed.
But this was Yarden's territory. Actually his mastery of the
control panel and ability to follow instructions were saving
them valuable time.

"Yes. If you could rewind it from when we first see
him."

It was the track on the corner monitor from the third-
floor camera in what Yarden had marked as NW1. This
would be the third time Maggie had asked to see this particular track.

There had to be something here that she was missing. What was she not seeing?

Yarden began the tape, fingers ready to freeze-frame or zoom in. But Maggie let it play. She wanted to examine Bomber #1, focusing only on him, picking him out of the distant crowd then watching as he got closer and closer.

His head didn't swivel or dart around. His hands stayed by his side in a comfortable, easy stride. There was nothing to indicate he was nervous or anxious. He didn't glance around, worried about being followed. He didn't look around for cameras, didn't even seem to care whether or not one caught him on film.

He wore a jacket, jeans, tennis shoes, a baseball cap. Nothing sagged, bulged or flapped over to hide any weapons or to disguise his appearance. Nor was there anything to indicate he belonged to a gang. No backward cap, no special hand signals, no T-shirt with a message. He appeared to be dressed in regular street clothes.

Maggie guessed his age at somewhere between eighteen and twenty-six. Like the others he was undeniably Caucasian. Light-colored hair curled over the collar of his jacket but not over his ears. Sideburns were long but trimmed, and on the morning after Thanksgiving, Maggie couldn't help but notice he had taken time to shave. Was that something a twenty-year-old took time out to do, especially if he knew he was going to the mall to blow himself up?

Maybe it meant nothing. She knew homicide bombers often followed their daily routine even on the day of their deaths. They didn't want to alarm or tip off family members or friends. Still, she wrote it down in her small notebook.

She wasn't used to jotting things down. Never had a problem keeping it all in her head. Writing stuff down, that was her partner, R.J. Tully. He scratched out notes about everything and on anything that was available: a napkin, a dry cleaning receipt, a ticket stub. Maggie had been content to commit details to memory until A.D. Raymond Kunze came along. Now it seemed important to keep a record of her thought process. He couldn't sideswipe her if there was documentation. Suddenly she was becoming one of those bureaucrats she hated, concerned about covering her ass. Was it that, or did she simply not want Kunze to win, to break her spirit?

On the video Bomber #1 crossed right below the camera. Not even a glance in its direction. Did he even know it was there? A clean-cut, good-looking, college-aged guy with his entire future ahead of him. Nice clothes, athletic physique, an air of confidence. She wanted him to look up, just for a second so she could see his eyes. So that she might be able to get a glimpse of why he did this? But she already knew. She had already seen this series three times before and each time she had willed his eyes to glance up. Come on, just one glance. And each time Bomber #1 simply walked on by.

CHAPTER 29

Rebecca was gone.

Patrick's first reaction was that she'd been taken against her will. Could that paramedic psycho have followed them?

Damn! He knew he should never have left her alone. He had been so sure the guy wouldn't dare try anything here in the crowded hotel ballroom where triage sites with cots, IVs and real medics lined up one after another. Narrow paths would make it difficult to drag anyone from the room without notice. Or so Patrick thought. What if the guy managed to get to Rebecca and drug her?

Stupid! How could he be so stupid?

"You looking for your girlfriend?"

Patrick spun around. It was the old man who had been on the triage cot next to Rebecca. His silver hair sprouted up out of the gauze that now wrapped his head.

"Have you seen her?"

"Yep. She left."

"By herself?"

Was it possible the guy was confused?

"As far as I could tell." He scratched at the gauze. "She just got up and left."

"Just like that?"

"Just like that. Pulled the needle from her arm." He pointed at the IV left on the cot.

"Did you see where she went?"

The man pointed a crooked finger. Patrick had to turn and look over his shoulder. There was an exit clear across the ballroom. That didn't make sense. The closest exit was right behind her where Patrick had gone. She watched him leave. If she was looking for him why would she head in the opposite direction?

"Are you sure?"

"Hey, I may have gotten knocked in the head but there's nothing wrong with my eyesight."

"Sorry. It's just…"

"I know, I know," he nodded. "You're worried about her. She didn't look so good. A little glassy-eyed, if you ask me."

Patrick pulled out his cell phone. No text messages. No voice messages. No missed calls. He didn't know Dixon's iPhone number and Rebecca didn't have a cell phone of her own. What was she thinking? Was she still in shock? Maybe she didn't know what she was doing.

He thanked the old man and headed for the exit. If she was disoriented, she couldn't have gotten far.

The exit opened to a common area. A table and folding chairs had been set up. Two blue uniformed paramedics controlled the flow of the chaos. Patrick could barely see the lobby through the crowd. To his right he saw a bank of elevators and down the hall to the left, another exit. This one probably to the outside.

Patrick stood looking from one area to the other. Which way did Rebecca go? He couldn't imagine her fighting her way through the crowd. She hated crowds and after what she'd just been through? But she wasn't herself. Maybe still in shock. He'd learned how physically debilitating shock could be from his Fire Science classes. If she wandered outside she might not realize how cold it was.

He headed for the exit. Just as he pushed out the door he saw a man in a uniform coming from the parking lot, headed for Patrick.

"You. Wait a minute. Whatya think you're doing?"

CHAPTER
30

Nick leaned back in his chair and rubbed his hands over his face, his fingertips digging at the blur of fatigue. He didn't need to look at his watch. The bristle on his jaw told him it was late. His stomach reminded him he hadn't eaten since earlier in the day. He had a headache. The room was too warm and too dark. The glare from the computer monitors had sucked the liquid from his eyes. And of course it didn't help matters that Maggie O'Dell sat next to him, so close he could smell the scent of her, causing his mind to reel slightly off track—was it shampoo? Lotion? Perfume?

They must have already looked at several miles' worth of tape, trying to find the three young men and track their paths. They followed them through the mall as best they could, accessing the appropriate camera view and going backward. To get to the third floor, each of the young men had to come up one of the escalators. To come into the mall, they had to enter through one of the entrances. And so the reasoning took them, step by step, camera by camera, seg-

ment by segment. It was tedious and now Maggie wanted
to go back through certain segments over and over again.

Yarden was much more patient than Nick. He caught
himself sighing a couple of times but didn't even garner a
glance from Maggie. She was in another zone. And Yarden
was busy proving himself a master of the control panel,
his long fingers never tiring, his mind sharp, his patience
admirable. Never once did he grumble or question or hesitate. He was the quintessential follower, eager to please,
jumping at the next request. And although Nick was tech-
nically Yarden's superior the little man beamed at Maggie,
looking to her first for each instruction no matter whether
Nick had given the last. Truthfully, Nick couldn't blame
him. There was an easy calm about Maggie, a presence
that entered every room with her. One that said, "I know
this is tough but we'll handle it together."

Nick remembered feeling that way four years ago when
she stepped into the chaos a serial killer had left behind
in Platte City, Nebraska. As sheriff Nick was supposed to
have jurisdiction over the case. He was supposed to have
control. He could still conjure up that sense of being overwhelmed, the panic he tried to keep at a low boil somewhere deep inside himself. Even then, Maggie's presence
had reassured him, settled the boil to simmer, made him
believe everything would be okay. So he understood Yarden
being attentive to Maggie's every word, her every command, her every move. Nick was too, but for a slightly different reason. When was it that his true feelings for her had
come to the surface? When had it finally hit him? Really
hit him? Before he canceled his wedding to Jill? Or had
that simply been the excuse that led him to the real conclusion?

As he watched Maggie, now he wondered why it had
taken him so long.

"Stop it right here." Maggie interrupted Nick's thoughts, pointing to a monitor in the upper corner that had caught her attention. "Can you zoom in on his baseball cap?"

Yarden obeyed instantly.

"What is that?" She pushed her chair back and stood for a better view, tapping the screen with her index finger. "We've been focused on finding a front shot but what's that on the side of his cap? It's a logo, isn't it?"

Yarden moved forward, careful to keep from leaning too close.

She'd been taking notes, pages of them in her miniature notebook. As Nick swiveled and stood to take a closer look at the monitor, he glanced down at the notebook before he glanced up. In a brief glimpse, all he caught was the word PROFILE at the top of the page.

"Oh, I know what that is. It's the Golden Gophers," Yarden said, beaming like a school kid answering the tough question for his favorite teacher.

"College team," Nick explained to Maggie.

"Right. University of Minnesota," she said without missing a beat. Nick was impressed. Yarden even more enamored. "Looks like he's wearing a letterman jacket, too," she added. "Jerry, doesn't that look like the university's insignia? It's an *M,* isn't it?"

Yarden was already punching keys and zooming in on the guy's upper left chest where Maggie had been pointing.

"Minnesota fan," Nick said.

"Or he's a student," Maggie countered.

The phone on the wall rang.

It startled all three of them. Yarden looked at it as though he'd never seen it before. He glanced at Maggie, then Nick.

"Must be the guys upstairs," he said, but still didn't move

to answer the phone like he didn't want to be reminded of what was upstairs.

At first Nick thought Yarden was waiting for someone to instruct him once again or to give him permission to answer it. However, one good look at Yarden's face and Nick could tell the apprehension was dread, not uncertainty.

The phone must have rung a dozen times before Yarden pushed himself out of the chair and reached for it.

"Security." A pause and then he added, "This is Jerry. Jerry Yarden."

Nick tried not to watch, but it was impossible to look away. Yarden's entire face crunched together like a man waiting for something or someone to hit him. He nodded and swallowed hard a couple of times, his Adam's apple bobbing above his collar.

By the time he returned the phone's receiver to the wall Yarden had lost all color in his face.

"Security thinks they have another bomber," he said in almost a whisper.

"You're kidding?" Nick asked. "Where?"

"In the southwest parking lot." The Adam's apple bobbed again. "They wanna see you and me upstairs."

Maggie's cell phone started ringing. A couple seconds later, Nick's started ringing, too.

CHAPTER
31

"He may have gotten left behind," Charlie Wurth told Maggie as he helped her into a bulletproof vest.

It didn't make sense this many hours later.

"Maybe he was hiding somewhere inside the mall," Wurth added as if he could sense Maggie's question. "Waiting. You know, thinking he could leave after everything settled down a bit."

Maggie could tell the new Deputy Director of Homeland Security had never worn a Kevlar vest before just by looking at the way he had cinched up the straps of his own vest. His fingers were shaking slightly, just enough that she noticed. He was nervous. Of course, he was nervous. It shouldn't matter, but it managed to ratchet up her anxiety. The adrenaline was already causing her heart to race.

"What makes them think he's one of the bombers?"

"They said he was sneaking around the back."

She raised an eyebrow.

"And a backpack," he quickly added. "A red backpack."

Maggie glanced at the three other men in the small exit

way. They were gearing up, too. In silence. No conversation. Only the snaps and clicks of their equipment. SWAT team. Cool and calm. Or so they appeared. It was chilly here, a draft coming from somewhere and yet she could smell their sweat.

Maggie glanced beyond the exit way. A.D. Kunze was nowhere to be seen.

"He sets that thing off out there," Wurth continued and now Maggie could see beads of sweat on his upper lip, "we're in a heap of trouble."

"I'm a profiler, not a negotiator. What exactly do you want me to do?"

On the phone, Kunze had told Maggie it was "showtime." He followed up with, "Security says they've got a live one. And you need to be able to tell them whether they do or not."

It had sounded like a joke, a dare. But he was serious.

She had had stranger requests but not from her assistant director. Cunningham would have never sent her out like this.

"What exactly is it you want me to do, Deputy Director?" she asked again.

"They've got him cornered. Now, maybe he's just some kid with a red backpack. Scared out of his wits because of all the excitement. But if he's one of the bombers...we can't take that chance. These guys—" Wurth's hand waved at the SWAT team as if he were only now introducing them to Maggie. "They can't take him out if there's a chance that pack's gonna blow. Cops can't approach him either. Same reason."

That was it. End of explanation.

Wurth pulled a ball cap on and started struggling into a blue jacket that had SWAT on the back. He made it look like the Kevlar vest was a straitjacket. It took a couple attempts of poking his arm behind him into the jacket before he found the armhole.

One of the team members handed a blue jacket to Maggie.

"And me?" she had to ask Wurth.

Evidently he thought he had explained everything he needed to explain. He looked up at her as he struggled with the zipper, his fingers still giving him a problem.

"You can tell us if he fits the profile of the other bombers."

He said it as if it were a matter of fact. Maggie wanted to laugh. This was crazy.

"And if I can't?"

He stopped. So did the SWAT team. The look on Wurth's face told her immediately that hadn't been considered.

"I know you're probably a little nervous, Agent O'Dell," Wurth said, quiet and slow, sounding like a child's father. Suddenly she was "Agent O'Dell," when all during the flight she had been Maggie.

"I'm not nervous." Her stomach told her differently but she had learned long ago to set aside the nerves. That wasn't the problem. She knew how to focus. She trusted her gut instinct. She could respond and perform under stress. But this was ridiculous and she wanted to tell Wurth exactly that. Had he ever examined crappy, black-and-white surveillance video? "This isn't the way profiling works."

"Look, Agent O'Dell." This time he took her arm and bent toward her, close enough she could smell the peppermint on his breath, almost as if he thought what he was going to confide wouldn't be heard by the SWAT team despite the crowded exit way. "This may be our only shot to prevent another tragedy. A.D. Kunze is willing to take a risk on your talent. So am I. Now we just need you to be willing to take that risk, too."

He was a smoother politician than she had given him credit for.

"Let me borrow your tie," she told him as she pulled on the blue SWAT jacket.

Wurth looked surprised but didn't question her or hesitate and he tugged at his necktie.

"Anybody have gloves?" she asked and was immediately handed a pair.

She pulled on the gloves, the fingertips too big but they were warm and she wouldn't be handling anything that required perfect dexterity. Then she took Wurth's bright red necktie and wound it around her left wrist, making a knot and letting the ends dangle about six inches.

"When I raise my left hand above my head," she told the SWAT team, and demonstrated, "that means 'take him out.'" They all nodded. She turned to Wurth, waited for his eyes. "Make sure whatever law enforcement is out there now knows the signal."

She had no intention of raising her hand but she knew they would look for a signal. More importantly, they'd wait for a signal. With several law enforcement agencies taking part, it was better they wait for some signal rather than misjudge and react to any sudden movements.

One of the SWAT members was already relaying the message over the radio strapped to his shoulder, but Maggie waited for Wurth's assurance, his commitment, his accountability.

"Absolutely."

She watched his fingers rezip his jacket and this time she noticed they weren't shaking.

"Okay," Maggie said. "Let's do this."

CHAPTER
32

This time Nick led the way while Yarden hung back, always a couple of steps behind. He showed his ID to the guard at the bottom of the second escalator. National Guard, sniper unit. By this time no one made it upstairs without scrutiny and security clearance.

As Nick climbed the stairs—all the escalators had been stopped—he felt his breathing change. He wasn't sure he was prepared to see what was at the top of the third floor. His father used to tell him there wasn't anything worse than seeing a body ripped apart in a car accident, flesh peeled back, burned or mangled. As county sheriff, Nick had a couple of opportunities to judge for himself. But Nick had seen worse—the small blue bodies of two little boys, carved and left by a serial killer in the prairie grass along the Platte River. Could anything top that? He hoped not.

He knew how this worked only because two weeks ago as part of his training for the new job position he had attended a seminar on terrorist attacks and what to look for at any one of the facilities where they provided security. It had been intended to be a guide on how to convince their clients to upgrade their systems. Two weeks ago Nick thought the seminar preached scare tactics. The "what if" scenarios seemed a bit over the top. Now he realized how wrong he had been.

Thanks to that seminar the information was all still fresh to him. So he knew the protocol. In his mind, he tried to prepare himself for what he was about to experience. Rescue mission always came first: treat the injured, put out fires, make the building safe. Those who were wounded and injured were now on the first floor, across the street at the hotel triage area or on their way to a hospital.

Next came the recovery while preserving evidence. At this point, those who were left wouldn't be going anywhere in a hurry. For several hours they would become a part of the crime scene, helping answer questions that they should never have been expected to be asked. Maggie had once told him that even after death, victims were an investigator's best hope for telling them who the killer was.

Almost at the top of the escalator and Nick felt like he was holding his breath. His heart pounded against his rib cage. The entire air smelled scorched up here. Someone had finally turned off the Christmas music. The eerie silence that replaced it was almost worse.

The scene before Nick struck him as surreal. A black crater had been cordoned off. A half dozen crime techs in Tyvek suits silently walked a grid, measuring, mapping, scooping, sifting and photographing all of it, grid by grid. He knew they would eventually do this with each site.

"Dig out the crater," was what they called it. All of the debris within an area fifty percent bigger than the crater itself would need to be examined. The techs were using sterilized equipment to sweep up and sieve. Seemed odd to Nick at first that they'd need sterilized stuff to handle what had already been burned, but what you brought to a crime scene could be just as detrimental as what you took away.

Later those same techs would be on hands and knees doing a fingertip search of the same areas. They'd make sure even the tiniest fragments of evidence didn't go unnoticed. But it wasn't just about collecting debris. They were measuring and examining dents and dished metals, looking for embedded scraps, swabbing for undestroyed explosives, testing for solid residue.

The task appeared insurmountable. And they would have to repeat it two more times at two more blast sites.

"Mr. Morrelli?"

Nick almost forgot why he was here. For a minute he felt invisible, looking in from the outside, tiptoeing on the edges of his dream or someone's nightmare. He turned so suddenly he bumped Yarden, almost knocking him over.

"Sorry."

"No problem." Jerry Yarden looked like he might be sick at any minute, his face ashen, eyes wide.

"Nick Morrelli."

The man approached, watching his step as he made his way over. He wasn't part of the collection team and wore a navy blue suit instead of the Tyvek overalls. Still, he had on paper shoe covers—what looked like a size fifteen. Goggles dangled from his neck alongside a paper face mask. Purple latex gloves stuck out of his jacket pocket.

"You don't recognize me." The man seemed disappointed.

Nick took a better look. He didn't expect to find anyone he knew up here.

"David. David Ceimo. What the hell are you doing here?"

"Good to see you again, Nick." He put out a hand.

"Almost didn't recognize you without your helmet in my gut."

That garnered a wide-mouth grin. Had he smiled first off, Nick would have immediately known the man even without a Mizzou gold and black mouth guard. The safety had sacked Nick twice in one game, a string of quarterback blitzes contributing to the Huskers' embarrassing and rare loss at home to the Univerisity of Missouri. Not a fond memory even now as Ceimo's hand devoured Nick's.

The two men had gone on to make the NCAA All-American team, but if Nick remembered correctly, Ceimo had made it all the way to the big house. Minnesota Vikings, first-round draft. Unfortunately he also remembered the tall, lean Ceimo had been injured his second year, final game of conference play, a huge hit that left him on the turf. To look at him now it hadn't affected him a bit, and though he had trimmed down a bit he still looked like he could tackle anyone who got in his way.

"I'm here for Governor Williams," Ceimo told him. "Chief of staff."

"Congratulations." Nick kept the, "you've got to be kidding," to himself. Why should he be surprised? Ceimo was probably wondering the same thing about him. A one-season quarterback now representing the largest security company in the country? "Have you met Jerry Yarden?"

"No, I don't think so," Ceimo said, extending his hand to Yarden.

"David and I played football against each other."

"That right?" Yarden stood between the men, craning his neck, looking from one to the other. "Seems you know a lot of people here."

Nick ignored the comment and told Ceimo, "Jerry's the head of security here."

"Actually assistant to the director."

Both Nick and Ceimo cocked their heads at almost the same insinuating angle.

"The director's still in New Jersey. There for Thanksgiving," Yarden rattled off in defense.

"Yeah, state fire inspector is stuck in Chicago," Ceimo told Nick and Yarden, crossing his arms and obviously finished with the small talk. Nick didn't mind. "There for the holiday, too. O'Hare's backed up. This snow's canceling flights left and right."

"Governor stuck somewhere, too?" Nick asked. It was an innocent question but Ceimo's glare didn't take it as innocent.

"We've got a problem," he said instead of accounting for the governor's absence. "The governor wanted me to keep you guys informed, as a favor to your boss. Wanted you to have a heads-up. Be one of the first to know in case there's something more we should be looking for."

Yarden was nodding, bobble-head style.

"It's looking like these guys didn't do this on their own."

Nick was just about to tell Ceimo they already knew about the potential fourth bomber in the parking lot.

"They may not have even known they'd volunteered to be shrapnel."

"What do you mean?" Yarden asked.

"You've located the detonators," Nick said. That would be the first step.

"Need the fire inspector to verify, but my bomb expert seems convinced."

Nick couldn't help noticing Ceimo said, "my" bomb expert and wondered why the hell he was telling them any of this? They were simply security. On the totem pole of jurisdiction they came pretty close to the bottom of the stack.

"What exactly is your bomb expert convinced about?" Nick asked, only because it looked like Ceimo was waiting to be asked. He seemed to be enjoying doling out the information slowly.

"Understand only a handful of us know about this, okay?"

"We got that loud and clear." Nick was tired. They all were. Patience wearing thin.

"Bombs were detonated from off-site."

"Off-site?" Yarden didn't understand.

Nick thought he might have heard wrong.

"The bombers didn't detonate their own packs?"

Ceimo nodded. "Someone else did it from outside the immediate perimeter."

"Somebody else? How could they do that?" Yarden still seemed confused.

But Nick wasn't. He knew exactly what Ceimo was suggesting. They'd spent hours viewing miles of tape and the whole time, all three of them—Maggie, Nick and Yarden—kept saying the same thing, "These kids don't look like homicide bombers."

There was a good reason they didn't look the part. They weren't bombers. Poor bastards, probably didn't even know what was in store for them.

CHAPTER
33

The wind stung Maggie's face with tiny ice pellets. It was bitter cold and yet she could feel sweat trickle down the middle of her back. Wurth and one of the SWAT members led her along a breaker wall that separated the parking lot from the hum of interstate traffic.

Deputy Director Wurth walked hunched over, probably from the cold. He had joked earlier that, at least, he didn't have to worry about freezing his ass off in New Orleans, but Maggie couldn't help thinking his trained, hunched-over stride may have been a precaution against getting his ass shot off. Maybe she had been wrong about him being a novice to a Kevlar vest.

An area in the back corner of the parking lot had been cordoned off. Despite what had happened, people still had to be pushed back. Looked like mainly media—cameras and microphones, trails of breath from reporters doing live feeds.

Maggie could see slivers of the scene over the hoods and roofs of cars and SUVs. They had the suspect pinned down between the lanes of parked vehicles though she couldn't see him. Back here, yellowed light streaked with glittering snow pellets was all they had to break up the darkness.

It looked like two different groups of law enforcement. A guess from the different colors of jackets and hats. Most likely county and state. Rifles leveled on bumpers or hoods. Every officer would have his or her service piece drawn. She wasn't sure who had jurisdiction. It didn't matter to her as long as they played by her rules.

She glanced back at Wurth. He wasn't even armed. How could she trust him to keep these guys from firing? They didn't even know him. Most of them were locals and it would be tough to keep the emotion out of this. On the day after Thanksgiving, every single one of them probably knew someone in that mall today: a mother or wife, sister, brother, best friend, neighbor. They thought they had a live one. Adrenaline would be pumping. And the cold would only add to the rush.

"Ready when you are." A voice startled her, crackling over static and coming from her shoulder. She'd forgotten about the two-way radio the SWAT team had strapped to her upper arm. At first it had felt too tight; now she couldn't feel anything.

"No one fires unless they see red," she shouted into her shoulder, the stream of breath tracking to the radio like visible sound waves.

"Roger that."

"Any weapons?" she asked, this time keeping her voice lower.

"Haven't seen any. Only the backpack."

"I'm gonna let him see me, hands out to my sides."

"Roger."

Maggie stood up straight as she came around a set of officers crouched behind an SUV. They acknowledged her presence with only a nod. One of them pointed, indicating the young man was just on the other side.

She saw a piece of camouflage move and realized it was the suspect, right there. He was only five feet away. He glanced at her, did a double take and scooted back but was trapped between two vehicles. He had the backpack clutched to his chest like he knew it was the only thing keeping them from firing.

"It's okay," she yelled to him, holding her hands out from her side to show him she wasn't armed.

His eyes darted around. He was tall and rail-thin. She could see him shivering. God, he was young. And scared.

"I just want to talk to you," she told him. It was hard to keep her voice soothing with the cold air sucking her breath away. His eyes met hers and she recognized something in them.

"Hold your fire," she shouted. "He's not one of them," she yelled to the officers just as the boy pounced at her.

He shoved her back and bolted past her. She hit hard into a car grill. "Don't shoot," she managed to scream, scrambling to regain her balance.

She took off after him, expecting to hear gunfire at her back.

CHAPTER
34

Patrick didn't think the man in uniform was a cop. There had been plenty of cops in the mall. From what he remembered, all of them had their guns drawn and their badges displayed prominently, strapped to a thigh, tacked to a vest. One even had his fastened to the side of his knit stocking cap. This guy didn't have a badge. Just a uniform and an embroidered name tag that read FRANK. Patrick guessed security. Was he with the fake paramedic guy? How hard was it to get a uniform? He wondered if his name was really even Frank.

One thing for certain, the guy was big, burly, solid. One side of his jaw looked crooked. He looked like the type of guy you could hit and he'd never even feel it. He reminded Patrick of a bully who picked on him in junior high. He'd gotten plenty of blackened eyes and bloodied lips. This guy towered over Patrick, too. But maybe he wasn't so fast. And if he didn't have a gun...

"Just think it's odd," Frank said. He had an accent, but not a Minnesota accent. More like Brooklyn which only increased Patrick's paranoia. "Why you coming out the side door like you're sneaking off?"

"It was the first door I came to."

"You get hurt?" He pointed to the blood on Patrick's sleeve. He hadn't realized it was there.

He glanced up at Frank, gauging what direction to go with this guy.

"Yeah, but they patched me up."

"You look a little bit woozy, yet. Might not wanna be slipping out the back until you have all your wits about you."

Okay, maybe Frank was a good guy. That was the downside of not trusting people. Sometimes good guys slipped through the cracks and you didn't recognize them.

"Actually, I was looking for my girlfriend," Patrick confessed. "She got hurt, too. I'm hoping she didn't go wandering out into the cold. Did you see anybody else come out this door?"

Frank stared at him hard. Had Patrick been wrong about him? He glanced around the parking lot and shook his head.

"Some commotion going on around front. Nobody back here." Then he grinned at Patrick, coffee-stained teeth, a gap between the front two. "Just you." Despite the grin he was still examining Patrick. "They found another bomber." His eyes stayed firmly planted on Patrick, watching for his reaction.

"Another—?" Patrick asked.

"Out in the parking lot," he continued, warming his gloved hands together in front of him, as if to show Patrick how huge his hands were. "Asked us to keep a lookout for any others."

"Oh man, I can't believe there're more." Patrick grabbed at his arm as if it suddenly hurt. "Haven't they done enough damage?" Then he rubbed at his eyes as if they were starting to blur. "You know, you're right. I probably should go back in. I don't feel so good."

"What about your girlfriend?" Frank wasn't convinced.

Patrick shrugged and continued to hold his arm right over the stain of Rebecca's blood. "Maybe she didn't come this way. You said you didn't see anybody else. She's probably still inside looking for me."

He turned to go back into the hotel.

"Hey, kid," Frank said and Patrick winced.

He stopped. The door was so close, about five steps away. Maybe he should just make a run for it. But what if the door was locked from the outside?

When he glanced back, Frank had a long nightstick in his huge gloved hand, slapping it against his other hand. Where the hell did that come from?

"Don't go sneaking out any back doors anymore, okay?" Frank told him. "Everyone's a little on edge right now. You know what I mean?"

He flipped a switch. The nightstick was actually a long-handled flashlight. And then Frank turned, shined a tunnel of light in front of him and left into the dark.

Patrick took a couple of gulps of cold air. Paranoid. He was too damned paranoid. He went back into the hotel. Rebecca had to be inside somewhere.

CHAPTER
35

Maggie ignored the ache in her back. Something pinched where she had slammed against the front of the car. At first she had tried to unzip her jacket to get at her Smith & Wesson. It slowed her down too much. The kid wasn't armed. She'd do without it. Besides, she was the only one who could catch him now. They'd all listened to her. Stood down.

Behind her she could hear footsteps crunching but they were too far back. Her radio crackled from her shoulder, "Subject headed south, southeast."

The kid had slipped a couple of times, little traction in his sneakers. Each time she closed the distance between them, two paces, three. Only a car length between them now, but he was wiry, flexible, spinning around bumpers and twisting to avoid rearview mirrors. He was scared. Didn't matter that he wasn't one of the bombers. He didn't understand what had caused all the attention. Maggie wondered if he even understood much English.

As soon as she had gotten a good look at him she knew immediately he wasn't a part of the group of young men she had spent the afternoon watching. He was too young. And he was black. Tall, skinny—almost anorexic thin. But it was that look in his eyes that gave him away, that terrified panic of someone who's been accused and hunted before. She'd seen that look. It wasn't fear from guilt. It was fear of persecution. She was guessing about his lack of English.

There were drifts between the cars and one of them had swallowed Maggie's boot, sucking it right off her foot. Cheap slip-ons. She didn't let it slow her down. Her daily exercise regimen included a three, sometimes four-mile run.

From the radio, more static then, "Don't let him leave the lot."

She heard the clicks of metal behind her. Closer.

Damn it! Was that the sound of rifles getting set? Is that what she was hearing? Someone bracing a weapon against the metal of a vehicle? Taking aim?

"Hold your fire," she yelled into her shoulder, only it came out in gasps, hardly coherent.

"Suspect fleeing. Considered dangerous."

"Hold all fire," she tried again. He's scared, not dangerous. Could they shoot him with her trailing this close?

She heard more movement coming fast behind her. Heavy boots crunching snow, the slap of leather, the clack of metal, shouts garbled by the wind.

The boy slipped again, wiping out and thumping his knee against a bumper. Another two paces lost. Then he glanced over his shoulder. Big mistake. Slowed you down every time. He thought he'd regain momentum by taking a sharp left, and running parallel back in her direction, only with a lane of cars between them. Maggie spun around.

He was right there. Right alongside her. She could see slices of him between the parked vehicles. The cars were all that separated them. She pushed herself. A little faster. Her lungs were already burning from the cold air she'd sucked in. But the wind was at their backs now. Just a little more. She needed to get a step or two in front of him. She'd still lose him if she had to twist between the vehicles. She decided on a shortcut.

Maggie glanced ahead at the long uninterrupted row of vehicles. She chose wisely. Then she jumped on the hood of a compact and let the slide of snow-caked rubber soles on metal propel her right on top of the boy. It knocked him completely off his feet. His elbow jabbed into Maggie's side, catching her right under her vest. It knocked the air out of her. She squeezed her eyes shut against the pain, but still held on.

He was shoving and kicking until she grabbed his arm. One twist and his body went rigid. She pulled his arm back behind him and almost automatically he went down, face down. Her knee was in his back, his legs sprawled.

"You may not feel like it now," she told the boy in machine-gun bursts of breath. Each intake of cold air stabbed her lungs. "But you'll thank me for this later."

Better a knee in the back than a bullet.

When she finally looked up she was surrounded by men in helmets and scoped rifles. One of them held the red backpack that had gotten discarded somewhere along the chase. Another held the boot she had lost.

Charlie Wurth squeezed through the group, a head shorter than the rest of them, looking small and out of place. But he had a huge smile on his face as he offered a gloved hand to help Maggie up.

"Son of a bitch, O'Dell. You are something else."

CHAPTER
36

"It's bigger than we thought," David Ceimo was telling Nick and Jerry Yarden. "Not just three kids getting together and thinking it'd be cool to blow up a shopping mall."

Nick pulled the paper shoe covers on but kept his face mask dangling at his neck. Jerry had geared up completely, reminding Nick of an orange bug. The elastic band that held up the mask made his ears stick out further. And he'd mussed his hair, leaving tuffs sticking straight up. Nick resisted the urge to nudge him, and do a swipe at his own hair like he'd do with his nephew, Timmy, to tell him his hair was all tousled. Instead Nick pulled on a pair of purple latex gloves and followed behind Ceimo and Yarden, staring at Jerry's tufts of orange hair rather than looking down at the trails of blood. Bodies were covered where they lay but he swore he saw what looked like a leg—gnarled fabric and flesh with a loafer—underneath what may have once been a food court table, now twisted metal.

Ceimo was leading them to the first and closest crater. No one paid any attention to them. They continued their slow, painstaking tasks. The buzz and hum and swish of equipment took the place of conversation. Walking amongst the techs in their Tyvek overalls, masks and goggles reminded Nick of walking through a scene of *Star Wars*, a different planet covered in soot and ash with a distinctive smell of burnt dinner. That's how he tried to think about it. Especially the burnt dinner part. Anything to keep his mind from focusing on it really being burnt flesh and singed hair.

A tech noticed their approach. She shoved her goggles up on top of her short blond hair then picked up the tray of debris she was sifting through.

"Jamie's lead on the crater dig. She's our bomb expert," Ceimo told them.

Nick thought she looked like a college kid. On closer inspection he could see small crinkle lines at the corners of her eyes that revealed she was older.

"Go ahead and tell them what you told me," Ceimo told Jamie.

She pointed with a gloved finger to a pile of debris in the center of her tray.

"When you think of an explosion most people automatically think everything is incinerated. But fire is only one portion of an explosion. The other, of course, is blowing things apart. We end up with fragments. Some actually are decipherable." She poked around the debris and now Nick could see what looked like fibers, obviously scorched but some of the ends were still red.

"The backpack," Yarden said.

"Yes, and this metal piece was part of the detonating mechanism."

"Doesn't look like much of anything," Nick couldn't help saying.

"There're several other smaller fragments here." She gently pushed them out of the ash. "I'll piece them together back at the lab, but I recognize it already. You guys remember the Pan Am flight that went down over Lockerbie, Scotland?"

Everyone nodded. It was a long time ago. Nick figured twenty years at least, but anyone in law enforcement recognized the case. A huge passenger jet blowing up in the air.

"That was a mess," Jamie said like she'd been there. The crinkles weren't that deep. "The debris was scattered over miles and yet investigators were able to determine the exact cause. They found a tiny piece of circuit board from an electronic digital timer. It'd been placed inside a radio-cassette player along with Semtex then placed inside a brown Samsonite suitcase." She paused, noting Yarden's dropped jaw. "Yeah, amazing, huh?"

"Are you saying this piece of metal might be some sort of circuit board?" Nick asked.

"No, it's not. It's a bit different. But what I am saying is that we can determine a lot from fragments. Sometimes they're very definable. The devices used to detonate a bomb are sort of like a black box in an airplane. It can tell us a great deal of things. That circuit board found in the Lockerbie bombing was identified as a particular digital timer manufactured by a company in Zurich. Only twenty of the devices had been made. Special ordered and custom made for the Libyan government."

"Wow!"

Nick glanced at Jerry Yarden. Maggie might have some competition. Looked like Yarden had transferred his awestruck attention and affection to Jamie. Nick thought he saw the beginning of a smile at the corner of her mouth but otherwise she seemed unfazed. Instead, she continued.

"This detonating device is something I've only seen once before."

"So you might be able to track it to its manufacturer?"

She hesitated at Nick's question. "There's a good possibility."

"Wait a minute," Ceimo said for the first time. "You didn't tell me that before."

"I'm just saying it's a possibility. Remember I still have to piece the fragments together. But from what I'm seeing so far, this device looks like it may be specialized enough that we might be able to track its manufacturer. It's certainly different. Not digital. Not a preset. For lack of a better definition, it's wireless. It allows the bomb to be detonated with a remote control."

"Could they have each had a remote control on them at the same time?"

Jamie shook her head. "I'm not finding anything to indicate that, but truthfully," she said, shrugging, "the only reason for a remote control device like this is if you don't want to be anywhere near the bomb when you detonate it."

"Why not just use a digital one?" Nick insisted. "Set all of them for the same time? You wouldn't have to be nearby then, either, would you?"

"That's true. But things can go wrong with the digitals. If you get delayed you can't reset them, at least, not so easily or quickly."

"And if he used a remote control, why not just leave the backpacks where he wanted them to go off?"

"We would have noticed them," Yarden said. "We watch for anything left behind."

"Exactly," Jamie agreed. "Too much of a risk that they'd be found before they exploded."

There was a silence. No one wanted to admit what it all meant, that the bombers may have been victims, too.

"There's something else," Jamie finally said. With an

index finger she pulled out another piece of metal. "Not conclusive," she warned, "but the backpacks may have had some kind of padlock on them."

Nick rubbed at his jaw. He remembered how much those guys reminded him of his nephew, Timmy. Older versions but ordinary, clean-cut guys. Enjoyed football. Maybe played. The one had on a letterman jacket. He remembered their confident strides on the video. No nervous jitters. No swiveling heads or darting eyes. Just walking up and down the mall.

What the hell did they think they had locked away in those backpacks? And who convinced them to carry them around a crowded mall?

"You said you've seen this type of detonator before," Nick reminded the bomb expert.

Jamie hesitated, looked to Ceimo.

"It's okay," he told her. "The governor wants Al Banoff's guys up to speed on this."

"I've seen it only in the plans for another bomb. We caught the guy before he completed it. He had the entire blueprint drawn and claimed it was simply a class project. But he'd already begun constructing it. The detonating device was very similar to this one, an advanced wireless system that could be triggered via a remote control. It stood out because it was pretty different from what we're used to seeing. So was the bomb he was planning. That's why he needed to be able to detonate it from as far away as possible."

"What was so different about it?"

"It was supposed to be a dirty bomb."

CHAPTER
37

Asante had cleared airport security with no problems. He presented a boarding pass and driver's license and received only a cursory glance with a wave of a busy hand. Even his duffel bag made it through with a brief pause on the conveyer. No one spoke to him. No one gave him a second look. It was perfect.

Except that here he still sat at his gate. His flight was delayed. No new departure time even hinted at.

He avoided drawing attention to himself but stayed close enough to listen. He'd heard the desk clerk tell another passenger that their plane was on the ground in Chicago and the snowstorm kept it there. As soon as it was cleared for takeoff and on its way, she would alert everyone. Until then, they could only wait.

"No," she told several impatient passengers. "There were no other flights tonight to Las Vegas."

On his handheld computer, Asante had done his own search of other flights on other airlines. Unfortunately the clerk was correct. There were no other flights from Minneapolis to Las Vegas until morning and all of those were booked or overbooked.

"It is after all, Thanksgiving weekend," he overheard the clerk defend herself when one of the passengers complained.

Asante kept calm. Just another glitch.

He had already checked rental cars, too. None available. Even those due back were delayed because of the storm. What Asante had earlier called a godsend was quickly turning into a…a glitch, he reminded himself. Only a glitch.

Sitting so close to the information desk, he'd shut off his phone's ringer and ignored all calls. Now he checked messages. They knew better than to leave text messages. Too easy to trace. There was, however, one voice message. He pushed the button to listen.

"Hi, it's me," the woman's voice said in a cheerful, familiar tone, a wife leaving a quick message for a husband. "Just wanted to let you know Becky hasn't been picked up yet. She's out of cash. On our way to get her now."

Asante smiled. He should have been upset that Rebecca Cory was still wandering around. "She's out of cash," meant that the girl must have tried an ATM machine. Their system would be able to tell them exactly where the ATM machine was located. They'd know exactly where to "get her."

He checked his wristwatch. If the plane was still in Chicago there was no way it would get here within an hour. He had ignored his hunger for too long, and he believed taking care of the basics kept the mind sharp. Food was one of those basics. He set the alarm on his watch for thirty minutes. On his handheld computer, that he continued to keep strapped to his other wrist, he set the alarm for any weather alerts concerning Chicago and Minneapolis. Then he swung his duffel up over his shoulder and headed off to find something to eat.

Despite the delay he was safe here. If the authorities began searching for another person—another John Doe #2—they'd never identify him now. Even if they captured his image on any of the mall's cameras and started canvassing the airport to prevent his escape, they'd never find him. Most airports didn't have cameras in their ticketing or receiving areas. Those were virtually securityless or what Asante liked to call, "security-lite." And the John Doe #2 who had facilitated the mall bombing was no longer anywhere to be found. He had been left down in one of those camera-less areas, stuffed away in the restroom trash and flushed down the toilet.

CHAPTER
38

Maggie shouldn't have been surprised that A.D. Kunze didn't share Deputy Director Wurth's excitement for the way she had handled the parking lot suspect. Turned out the kid was a sixteen-year-old Sudanese refugee, separated from his newly adoptive mother during the bombing. He spoke pretty good English except the panic had dismantled the pretty good. Raw fear and instinct had brought back too many fresh memories of government police in his country. He did the only thing he knew— he ran. Fortunately he hadn't been hurt.

Maggie, on the other hand, knew she might have a bruised rib or two. Not a good idea to go flinging yourself over car hoods or getting shoved into chrome grills of SUVs.

She was still holding her aching side, allowing Wurth and a paramedic to help her take off her vest. Wurth insisted she get checked out and had taken her to the hotel across the street where a triage area had been set up in one of the ballrooms. To avoid the media, he convinced a paramedic to use a small room off the ballroom. They were able to keep the media out. No such luck in keeping Kunze out. He came marching in and immediately began lecturing her.

"What the fuck did you think you were doing out there, O'Dell? You were just supposed to let them know whether or not the kid was one of the bombers." He stood over her, hands on his hips, veins bulging in his thick neck. "We didn't need you running off and playing hero. You could have gotten a bunch of bystanders killed. Not to mention law enforcement officers. We have enough trigger-happy assholes out there without you giving them a good excuse to let loose."

"That's enough." Wurth surprised Maggie as much as he did Kunze.

"What'd you just say to me?"

"Shut the fuck up." Wurth was about five inches shorter and fifty pounds lighter than Kunze but he didn't back down. He stared up at the FBI director and didn't flinch. "Your agent did a courageous thing out there."

"Courageous? You think that little game of catch-me-if-you-can was courageous?"

"She prevented an innocent kid from getting killed. And yeah, on a day when we're all looking to shoot up somebody for what happened here, I'd say what she did was pretty courageous."

"Well, it's too bad you're not her supervisor. Maybe she wouldn't get reprimanded."

"Reprimanded?" That stopped Wurth.

As for Maggie, again, she shouldn't have been surprised. She said nothing. Just closed her eyes briefly from the sharp pain in her side and finished pulling off the protective gear. Kunze had managed to scare off the paramedic, too.

"Forty-five minutes," Kunze said. "That's how much time you two get to clean up before you go live in front of the media and explain what just happened. I'll see you then."

They watched him leave. He disappeared out the door.

Wurth turned to look at her. "What the hell did you ever do to that guy?"

CHAPTER
39

Rebecca started to panic again. The ATM at the gas station/minimart next to the hotel had spit out both her debit card and her credit card. She wasn't sure she had enough money for a cab ride to the hospital. Mall of America was clear out here in the suburbs and she knew the hospital was downtown.

She stood inside the station's shop looking out at the swirling snow. God, it was cold and dark. After the explosion, she'd ripped out the lining of her coat to stop the bleeding in her arm. Each time the shop door opened it made her shiver to think about going out walking in that cold again.

She bought a Snickers bar just so they wouldn't kick her out of the shop, although there was a steady stream of people coming and going. She stared out the window, headlights flickering on and off as cars pulled up to the gas pumps or parked at the shop. She could see her reflection in the glass, only glimpses but enough to feel like she didn't recognize herself. Her arm throbbed. She contemplated buying the travel pack of Tylenol for four-ninety-eight, but that would leave her with even less money, less security.

She took small bites of the candy bar, trying to remember when she had eaten last. All she'd had was the coffee earlier at the food court. Leftover turkey and dressing last night at Dixon's grandparents' house. A heavenly feast. God! That felt like days ago. A lifetime ago.

"Becky?"

Rebecca turned to find a woman smiling at her. None of her family or friends called her Becky. Either Rebecca or Becca. But the woman looked like she knew her.

"I thought that was you," the woman said.

She had paid for her gas and was obviously headed back out the door. Now she moved aside to let someone else out and let go of the door. She was Rebecca's age, maybe a little older, dressed in worn-out jeans and an expensive leather jacket. In one hand, car keys dangled from her fingers, in the other she held a couple bags of chips and her spare change.

"I'm sorry, do I know you?"

"No, not really," the woman admitted and shrugged as if she was sort of embarrassed. "I'm Chad's girlfriend. He pointed you out at the mall. I'm on my way to pick him up. Can I give you lift somewhere?"

Rebecca blinked and tried not to gasp. Chad was dead. She'd seen him explode. Did his girlfriend really not know?

"No, thanks," she managed. "I'm actually waiting for someone."

"Really?" The woman didn't look convinced. "Looks like you got hurt." She pointed at the bloodied sleeve of Rebecca's coat. "Crazy what's happened, huh. Chad got bruised up, too. You sure I can't give you a lift?"

"No really. I don't want to miss my friend."

People were walking in around the woman. She was starting to be in the way of the foot traffic.

"Okay then. See ya."

Rebecca watched the woman walk back to her vehicle. She looked over her shoulder and waved. Rebecca slid over so she could still see out the window but now over a display of ice scrapers. The woman's van was back at one of the corner pumps, the windshield draped in shadows so Rebecca couldn't tell if there was anyone else in the van.

Was it possible that Chad had survived? Could Rebecca be mistaken? In her panic and shock could she have only thought she saw Chad explode? All of it seemed like a nightmare. A bad movie. Maybe she had imagined it.

She squeezed out of sight while keeping her eye on the van. A quick glance around the shop. The guy behind the cash register was watching. She pretended to look at the ice scrapers, picking one up and checking the price. Another wave of customers came in and the guy was too busy to keep track of her. She replaced the ice scraper and moved to the other side of the shop, close to the restrooms, a spot where her view was only a slice of the gas pumps. But she could see the parking lot's exit and the back lot. She watched the van leave. Slowly it pulled out the exit and onto the street. Rebecca felt her shoulders slump from relief.

She pulled Dixon's iPhone out of her pocket and powered it on. Dixon was her only hope. She found his last text message. She didn't need to know the number if she simply pushed Reply.

She tapped out her message:

U STILL THERE?

Within seconds came the response:

WHERE R U?

A GAS 'N SHOP ACROSS FROM MALL. CAN U COME GET ME?

She waited.

ON MY WAY.

Rebecca leaned against the wall, weak with relief. She quickly caught herself. Glanced around. Cash register guy was still busy. She'd be okay. She'd wait here for Dixon.

Then she saw it. The dark-colored van eased its way slowly to the opposite side of the parking lot, creeping to a stop alongside the back Dumpster.

CHAPTER
40

Maggie found a Pepsi machine and ice maker off the crowded lobby. Wurth had managed to get them hotel rooms. Even had her bag delivered from the back of the SUV. She got the impression that once you earned Charlie Wurth's respect he took good care of you. Not something she was used to, especially lately with A.D. Kunze.

As the last of the injured were cared for, the hotel's ballroom, reception area and lobby slowly transformed into an information center for families to reconnect and to find out about loved ones. Screams and cries—some out of sadness, some out of relief—mixed with greetings and a litany of instructions. The front revolving doors swirled continuously, bringing in a constant stream of cold air and a new wave of victims, their families or responders.

Maggie gently eased her way through the crowded lobby, nudging and excusing herself. The constant press of bodies and steady hum of voices made it feel like forever to get across to the bank of elevators.

The hotel was large, an eight-story convention center, but the holidays and its proximity to Mall of America ensured it was packed with regular customers. This overflow of injured and worried families created an additional energy and caused a commotion of its own. In the midst of all of it, Maggie had noticed the disjointed line of guests dragging their suitcases and waiting to check out. A good deal of frightened guests—concerned about the bombings not being over or confined to the mall—wanted to be gone, leaving rooms available for law enforcement and medical personnel. Maggie didn't realize how grateful she was that Wurth had snatched up several of those rooms until she closed the door to her own. Now as she tried to make her way back there with her Diet Pepsi and bucket of ice, she realized how dead tired she was.

Once inside the elevator the noise disappeared, like turning off the volume of a loudspeaker. The cries and shouts and mumblings were replaced by Christmas music. At first, Maggie only noticed the change because of the drastic difference. As she left the elevator and started for her room, the music followed her down the hallway. Then she recognized it as a nice change. A soothing change.

She usually survived the Christmas season by ignoring it as best as possible but there were certain elements that reminded her of a pleasant time in her childhood, what she called the prefire days. Music of the season was one of those things that she took heart in.

Maggie was twelve when her father was killed, a firefighter running back into a flaming house to save the occupants. People told her she should be proud her father died a hero. As a child Maggie thought that was a ridiculous thing to tell her because, of course, she would rather have a live father than a dead hero.

Christmases after his death were usually as unpredictable as they were untenable. It depended on how early in the day—or the evening before—her mother decided to start the festivities and who the guests would be—Jim Beam, José Cuervo or Jack Daniel. If the year had been especially successful, Johnnie Walker might replace all the others.

As an adult, Maggie had tried—in the beginning, at least—to start some new holiday traditions with her now ex-husband, Greg. But as a young and rising star in a prestigious law firm, Greg had always been more concerned with being seen at the right holiday parties and leaving lasting impressions with expensive gifts that he'd later grumble about not being able to afford. There were no quiet moments putting up a tree, no midnight masses with inspiring messages of hope, no family feasts around a crowded table. After a while the Christmas season became something Maggie just got through.

But every once in a while something would remind her of Christmases before the fire—happy, wonderful times that now after twenty years seemed almost a figment of her imagination. Earlier she thought she had seen someone who looked like her father—down in the crowded lobby—so he was already on her mind.

As she placed her key card into her hotel room's door the next song began: "Have Yourself a Merry Little Christmas." Without warning she remembered her father singing the same words and that Christmas came back to her in a flood of memories so vivid they couldn't possibly be made up by her imagination.

The three of them—her mother and father and Maggie—had spent the afternoon trudging through the snow at a Wisconsin tree farm. Their mission to find and cut down "the most magical Christmas tree in the field."

"How will we know it's magical?" She wanted to know but her father just kept shaking his head and saying, "We'll recognize it when we see it."

Maggie had been eleven that Christmas. She was too old to believe in Santa or magic. When her father finally stopped and pointed to the tree he wanted, she thought it looked suspiciously like all the others they had declined. But her father loved to make a special event out of their outings and she and her mother played along. That night they decorated the tree, sipping hot chocolate and singing Christmas carols. At the time they had no idea it was to be their last Christmas together. Perhaps that alone was what ended up being magical about it.

Inside the room, Maggie checked the time. She set aside the ice bucket. The ice was for her bruises, not the soda. She guzzled half the Diet Pepsi while she started pulling off her dirty clothes. Her suitcase lay open on one of the double beds. She wished she had time for a shower before their press conference, but she'd settle for a change of clothes. She turned on the TV only to fill the quiet, glancing briefly. Then she stopped completely.

The scene being played out looked like an episode of the reality show, *Cops*. It was, in fact, the local news. The camera had captured her chase of the young Sudanese boy. It wasn't the first time the channel was playing it. The anchors were commenting as though they had seen it over and over and were now doing an instant replay analysis.

"Here it is," the woman said just as Maggie watched herself jump up onto the hood of the compact car.

"Whoa," the two anchors joined together.

"That had to hurt," the woman added but she said it like she was a proud mother. "We've just learned that agent, Special Agent Margaret O'Dell, is a profiler from Quantico who is here at the request of Governor Williams."

A professional photo of Maggie appeared in the corner of the television screen.

The anchor continued, "Special Agent O'Dell was able to assist and tell local law enforcement that this teenaged boy was not one of the bombers simply by the profile she has already come up with for the homicide bombers. The boy—"

Maggie's cell phone started ringing.

On the television screen a photo of the boy was added alongside Maggie's.

"This is Maggie O'Dell."

"Some good news and some bad news," Charlie Wurth announced without a greeting.

"What's the good news?"

"You don't have to do the press conference. I'll join Chief Merrick and his home team for this one."

"Let me guess. A.D. Kunze doesn't want to exploit my escapade."

"Aw, so you're watching."

"Just turned on the TV. Looks like the local station caught it."

"Au contraire, cheri," he said giving his voice a pretty good New Orleans Cajun spin, "Networks just picked it up. CNN and FOX have it, too. You're a star."

"So I'm guessing that's the bad news."

"No, no. That's not it. Remember how disappointed your supervisor was about a half hour ago? Well, now he's fit to be tied. He did want me to tell you that we're all meeting down in the command center, ground level, room 119. Your presence is greatly appreciated. Why don't you wait and come down in about thirty minutes. I should be finished with the media by then and I'll do my best to play interference."

He was gone before she could thank him. She found the remote and clicked through the channels. Sure enough, there was the chase in various stages on different channels.

Her phone started ringing again. What had Wurth forgotten to tell her?

"This is Maggie O'Dell."

."Hey, it's Nick. What are you doing right now?" He sounded as casual as if he were asking her on a date. Obviously he hadn't seen a television yet.

"Having my nails done, followed by a spa treatment."

He laughed long and hard. Like someone who hadn't laughed in quite some time and didn't expect to right this moment. So long, in fact, that she had to wait for him. It made her smile.

Then he was serious, again. "We heard the fourth bomber was a false alarm. Are you okay?"

"A few bruises. I'm fine."

"Listen, Jerry and I just learned a few interesting things. I know we're all meeting over at the command center in a little bit, but I thought you might like a heads-up."

"So what did you learn?"

He told her about the bomb expert's findings. It only confirmed her suspicions, that the young men carrying the backpacks had no clue what was to happen today.

He told her that Jerry was downloading the best shots they had found of the five suspects and ended by asking if there was anything else she wanted them to bring.

"How 'bout a burger and fries," she said.

"I'll see what I can do."

He hung up before she could tell if he knew she was joking. With Morrelli it was hard to decipher. There had always been chemistry between them but otherwise they seemed out of sync with no common ground to rely on. Maybe she'd simply given up trying to figure it out.

She finished peeling off the rest of her clothes. Ironically the chase had been good for her, mentally as well as physically. A month ago she wasn't sure her body would hold up to those sorts of challenges ever again. She had felt weak and nauseated. A fever and nosebleeds sent her into a tailspin of panic, constantly wondering if the virus she had been exposed to might be replicating itself inside her body. At times she believed she could feel it exploding her blood cells. But she'd been lucky. She'd gone past the incubation stage and still showed no signs of the virus. Yes, she'd dodged yet another bullet, unlike Cunningham.

Now as she examined her injured right side she could see it had already started to turn blue and purple. Next to the scars on her torso, the bruises looked mild. No big deal. She'd accepted the fact that her body was becoming a road map of past cases. Told herself it came with the territory. When you tracked killers for a living, sometimes it got rough. Most of those memories had been safely compartmentalized. Eventually the fear and panic of the exposure would find its own compartment. Now if only she could do the same with her personal life.

Her friend Gwen Patterson, the professional psychologist whose past client list included killers as well as five-star generals, didn't believe in compartments. She oftentimes reminded Maggie that stuffing everything behind doors and into convenient little compartments of the mind sometimes had a way of backfiring.

"One of these days a few walls may crumble. Then what?"

She suggested Maggie find a way to sift through the good and bad. Learn how to hang onto the good stuff. But what if the good—those memories of her father—only reminded her of what's missing in her life? Maybe that's what Nick Morrelli was reminding her of, again. Too many things missing.

Maggie checked the time. A five-minute shower would

definitely do her wonders. And then she needed to learn some things on her own. She pulled out her laptop and plugged it in on her way to the shower.

CHAPTER
41

Henry Lee sat next to his wife's bed, staring at the tubes connecting her to a half a dozen machines. The biggest tube that came out from under the covers at the foot of the bed held his attention. Yellow and red fluids pumped through it, mixing into a spiral of pink. It nauseated him whenever he let himself think that fluid was actually being pumped out of Hannah.

He watched the tubes because he couldn't quite look directly at her. She was bloated beyond recognition, thin lips shoved apart by more tubes down her throat. Her eyelids fluttered and sometimes he caught her looking for him. Did she know he was here? He grabbed her hand and squeezed.

"That's good." The nurse noticed as she came into the intensive care room. "She's going to be a little uncomfortable as she starts to notice the tube down her throat. We're easing back on the morphine so she'll wake up."

"Uncomfortable?" He didn't like the sound of that. He didn't want her to be in pain. He stood and wrapped Hannah's hand in both of his.

"It's okay." The nurse recognized his angst. "We need her to be a little more awake and alert so when we pull the tube out she'll breathe on her own. Otherwise heart patients want to sleep and let the machine continue to do all the work for them."

"But she'll be in pain?" He wasn't satisfied.

"Uncomfortable." The nurse corrected him. "As soon as we get it out, we'll be able to increase the dose again. It won't take long."

Hannah was staring up at him now, eyes blurred but she looked like she was trying to tell him that she hurt. Though her arms were poked with needles and tubes she was attempting to reach up to her throat, glassy eyes imploring him to help her. It killed him to see her like this.

"She'll be okay," the nurse said. "I'm going to need you to step out of the room while we take the tube out."

He didn't move. He didn't want to leave her. Her eyes kept pleading with him. How could he leave?

The nurse put a hand on his shoulder.

"It'll only be a few minutes. I'll come get you just as soon as we're finished."

He tried to keep his face from wincing or showing his concern. No, it wasn't just concern. Who was he fooling? It was fear...pure and simple. He could not lose this woman. Losing a daughter was one thing, like cutting off one of his arms. But Hannah? That would be like ripping out his own heart. You can survive without an arm. It's tough as hell but you find a way. Without Hannah? No, he'd never be strong enough to survive without her.

"I'll be right here, Hannah. The nurse is going to take good care of you." Then he added as if he needed to hear it out loud, "You're going to be just fine."

He walked out of the room, his knees so weak he had to put his hand up against the wall to steady himself. He made it through the double-wide doors that took him out of the Intensive Coronary Care unit, and he felt like he couldn't breathe. The waiting room was still empty. He dropped into one of the unyielding vinyl chairs.

He glanced around. Still no Dixon. Henry hadn't seen the boy since he left with Henry's cell phone to call his friends. He still couldn't believe that they had found a way to use Dixon, to suck his own grandson into this. My God, they went so far as to seek out and target the boy's friends. And why? Because of Henry's apprehension? Because they wanted to ensure his silence?

He closed his eyes and shook his head. He still couldn't believe it. He wanted to call Allan again. Ask him if he knew. Find out what the hell was going on? How could something that had begun with such honorable intentions turn into a greedy and disgusting grab for power and money?

The boy's absence only made Henry more anxious. He was relieved to have Dixon safe and with him, but now he grew impatient with the boy. Of course, he was concerned about his friends but his grandmother had just come out of major heart surgery. He should be here at her side...at Henry's side.

He absolutely hated to admit that he needed someone to be at his side. For forty years he had worked his way up to establish a successful business, a national success. A Fortune 500 success. Even in retirement he had refused to hand it over, insisting on remaining chairman, casting the deciding vote, always in control and on top of things. Or so he believed until now.

Hannah's emergency surgery had certainly caught him off guard. Just like his daughter's death. He had believed there could be no worse day than that dreadful one in April back in 1995. The difference—Hannah was there with him, by his side.

Right now he didn't care about anything else. Didn't care that their strategy had gone so terribly wrong. Or had it? Is this exactly what they wanted to happen?

Henry was beginning to understand that what he considered patriotism and honor, his so-called business associates appeared to see as only methods to raise profit margins and leverage political power. Henry had made a mistake. He realized that now. Family was what mattered most. Family was the most important thing. Everything else— country, business, even honor, were secondary. The tragic irony was that it was his sense of family that had sent him down this path in the first place. Only he had strayed too far. He'd forgotten what his original mission was, letting his pride and pigheaded stubborn ideals jeopardize everything else. Everything including what family he had left. How the hell could he ever make this right again?

On TV the local channels were still live at Mall of America. A press conference was going on but in the corner of the screen a chase scene from earlier played out. Still no confirmation on how many were dead though the estimate had been put at anywhere from twenty-five to fifty. Hundreds more had been injured.

Henry rubbed at his eyes then rubbed his hands together. His fingers were trembling. He glanced down the hallway. Where the hell was Dixon? They had told him earlier that he could use the phone in the waiting room for local calls. He just needed to dial a 9 first. He grabbed the receiver and punched in the number for his cell phone.

Sometimes a boy needed to be reminded of his obligations. Family needed to stick together. And damn it! He needed Dixon here with him, not off checking on his friends.

The phone rang four, five times before a voice answered that Henry didn't recognize.

"It took you long enough to call."

"Who is this?"

"Never mind that. I'm sure you'll want to talk to your grandson."

There was a muffled sound and then, "Granddad? What's going on?"

Only Dixon sounded muffled, too, as though he were being kept a distance from the phone. Then he heard the boy yell out in pain and this time Henry Lee felt his knees give out completely.

CHAPTER
42

Patrick had wandered around the hotel for long enough. He'd been up and down every hallway on every floor, checking stairwells, riding freight elevators and popping through doors to laundry rooms, ready to apologize each time. Rebecca wasn't here.

It was freezing cold outside. He kept alongside the busy highway though there were no sidewalks and little room for pedestrians. On this night he wasn't alone. There was a lot of chaos in and out of the parking lots of businesses that bordered Mall of America.

Would Rebecca have risked going to one of the restaurants? He didn't think so. There were absolutely no taxi cabs. Rescue vehicles and police cruisers still lined the edges, red and blue lights flashing but the sirens off now. News vans with satellites on their roofs and reporters and camera crews took up any other available space. Uniformed cops directed traffic in and out of the hotel parking lot. All of the mall's entrances looked like they were barricaded. A Red Cross RV was stationed near the front of the mall with shuttle vans.

No, there was enough chaos that no one noticed Patrick walking in and out of traffic. And no one would have noticed Rebecca either.

He stopped at a busy intersection, this one still using the traffic lights instead of a uniformed cop. Vehicles headed for the interstate could speed off to the ramp with no wait, unlike those stalled in the other direction. They had to wait in stop-and-go traffic inching their way toward the mall and the hotel.

Earlier he'd tried directory assistance to get a phone number for Dixon Lee. Nothing. There were no directories for cell phones. He got a number for Henry Lee. Practiced what he'd say to the man if he answered.

He dialed. Waited. Only an answering machine.

Of course, Mr. Lee was probably still at the hospital. Patrick didn't have a message rehearsed for the answering machine so he hung up. He was running out of ideas. He was cold. He was hungry and he was worried about Rebecca.

That's when he saw her.

Across the street he recognized her. She had just come out of the Gas 'N Shop. Tentative at first, holding onto the door of the shop as if she might need to run back in.

"Rebecca," he yelled. His voice got lost in the hum of four lanes of traffic between them. He tried to cross against the light and the blast of a car's horn stopped him. One lane of traffic moved slowly. The other didn't need to wait for him and let him know. Evidently the Good Samaritan patience was wearing thin.

He found himself shifting, pacing, while waiting to run across as soon as the light changed. In the meantime, he watched helplessly as Rebecca hesitated then relinquished her hold on the shop's door. Slowly she approached a white sedan, bending to a rolled-down passenger window before getting into the car.

A sigh of relief. Patrick recognized the car. He'd spent two days in that vehicle, riding and driving from Connecticut to Minnesota. Yes, now he could see the *Batman: The Dark Knight* decal on the back window. It was Dixon's car.

Thank goodness.

Patrick started crossing the street as the car left the shop. He ran against the wind and ice. Twice he slipped, almost falling. He waved his arms though the car was driving away from him, leaving the parking lot. He raced around the gas pumps, zigzagging between vehicles, taking a short cut. Dixon's car pulled onto the highway just as a van honked, almost hitting Patrick, so close he could feel the heat of its engine at his side. He jumped onto a curb, out of the woman's way. Now all he could do was watch as Dixon's car gunned its engine and sped toward the interstate ramp without even noticing him.

He was out of breath. His high-tops were caked with snow, his fingertips numb, his hair wet and plastered to his head. He stood there watching the red taillights disappear as pellets of ice pricked at his face.

It was okay, he told himself. He could relax. At least Rebecca was safe.

CHAPTER
43

Maggie shouldered her way through the crowded hallway. The entire floor of conference rooms at the hotel had become a makeshift command center. She passed one door she recognized as the triage room and another where victims reunited with families. Room 119 was at the end of the hall.

She had changed into blue jeans, a turtleneck sweater and leather flats. Her Smith & Wesson stayed back inside her room's safe, along with her badge. All she carried was her smartphone, her ID, a credit card, room key card and a twenty-dollar bill she'd slid into her jeans pocket.

Nick and Jerry Yarden waited outside the door, both smiling at her. She could tell they'd seen the chase scene by now. So had the others. It was obvious as soon as she walked into the room. Heads turned and nodded. Eyes glanced then stayed and stared.

It was a small group. Maybe a dozen. Police chief Daryl Merrick's group was in another room. Merrick had won jurisdiction and ended up lead on the case. He had his hands full recovering bodies and rescuing injured, setting up information centers for victims and families, not to mention juggling a media nightmare. However, it'd be up to the federal agencies—Homeland Security and the FBI—to conduct the investigation, issue warrants and track down the killers. That was this group, gathered in Room 119. Most of its members were still at the scene, sifting through debris and interviewing witnesses. They would still be cataloguing evidence and piecing together theories in the days, even weeks after tonight.

Charlie Wurth was back from the press conference and at the front of the room, setting up a huge dry-erase board. Alongside him a CSI tech plugged in a computer and arranged a projection screen. Nick introduced Maggie to David Ceimo and a bomb expert, named Jamie, while Yarden made his way to the front of the room to hand off a jump drive containing the grainy, blurred images—the best shots they'd found—of the five suspects. Maggie listened to Nick and David Ceimo explain their connection while she watched Yarden with Charlie Wurth. There appeared to be some discussion, then Wurth was pointing to the computer. It looked like he wanted Yarden to stay and help run the show.

"Okay, people," A.D. Kunze said as he made his entrance into the room, pulling the door closed and letting it slam shut behind him. "I know everybody's tired. Let's get to this."

Wurth nodded at Yarden and handed him a wireless remote.

"Go ahead," Wurth told him.

Yarden was a bit hesitant. Maggie could tell he was nervous. The tips of his ears had begun to turn crimson. He was a master at the computer panel but it was different in a dark room with only monitors. Here in front of a group of law enforcement officers it would be a bit out of Yarden's realm.

Yarden glanced down before cueing up the photos on the projection screen. On the computer monitor Maggie could see there were rows of photos, about five photos in each row. The images, now jpegs, would have been downloaded from digital cameras used to record the scene. They were joined by the images Yarden had brought from the surveillance videos.

Yarden pushed a few buttons on the computer keyboard then pointed the wireless remote and clicked. A crime scene photo of one of the craters came onto the projection screen. He clicked again and another image came up alongside. On closer inspection, Maggie could see the smaller image was one of the shots of the same area from a surveillance camera before the explosion.

"We initially believed there were three bombers," Yarden started to explain. "Then we discovered the site of one of the bombs was the women's restroom." He clicked the remote and the "before" shot was replaced by one with a zoomed-in image of the sign.

Yarden waited a few minutes then he cued up three more shots: the grainy images of four men and one young woman. Even on the projection screen Maggie was struck by how indecipherable the images were. They would never be able to identify them.

"What's your assessment, Agent O'Dell?" A.D. Kunze boomed from his perch against the back wall. "You must have a profile established. After all, you were able to determine that young man in the parking lot was not one of the five."

There was silence. These were trained investigators. They knew this was an unfair call-out even if Kunze hadn't used a condescending tone.

"At least one of them may have been a college student," Maggie said. "We were able to make out logos on a ball cap and letterman jacket." She saw Yarden cueing up those close-ups even as she spoke. "All five are Caucasian, between the ages of eighteen and twenty-six. None are wearing anything controversial. Other than the ball cap and letterman jacket there's nothing to indicate by the way that they're dressed that they belong to a specific organization or gang. There's no visible piercings or tattoos. I know there was some expectation to connect these individuals to a group like CAP, but I see no evidence of that from the videos."

"That's Citizens for American Pride," Wurth added. "There were some warnings about an event called into Senator Foster's office." Then he pointed to the photos and he said, "We had three bombs, you have five suspects."

"Right," Maggie continued. "It appears that two of the people came into the mall with one of the bombers. Because one of those backpacks ended up in the women's restroom, we suspect the young woman was involved. And possibly the other young man. I might add that none of the five suspects appear to be overly anxious or nervous. And certainly didn't act like homicide bombers."

"Which follows my theory," Jamie, the bomb expert joined in. "There's preliminary evidence that all three bombs were detonated by remote control. I'm speculating that none of these individuals knew they were carrying explosives. Or if they did, they didn't believe they would be detonated while they were carrying them, otherwise, there's no reason for an off-site remote. Also just from the fragments I can already determine the devices were constructed by someone who knew what he was doing. A professional. Definitely someone who was trained in the use and handling of explosives."

"But in the case you told us about earlier," Nick said, "you mentioned this detonator had some similarities to a guy who drew up a blueprint for a dirty bomb. If I'm re-membering correctly, didn't you say he claimed he did it for a class project? Wasn't he a student?"

"I remember the detonator," Jamie told him. "I'm sorry, I don't remember other details." She glanced around and noticed that wasn't good enough. "I can get details."

Wurth nodded, satisfied.

Kunze didn't look satisfied. "What about groups like CAP?" he asked, looking to Maggie again. "We certainly can't dismiss their involvement simply because none of these kids were wearing AMERICAN PRIDE T-shirts."

"Agreed," Maggie told him. "I did some checking. The ball cap and letterman jacket are from the University of Minnesota here in the twin cities. Citizens for American Pride held two rallies on campus within the last year, the most recent, last month. However, the university hosts a variety of similar events and forums."

"So it's possible these kids were members?" Kunze wanted to know.

"As I said earlier, there's no evidence that points to that, but yes," Maggie conceded, "it's possible."

Kunze seemed satisfied. He left before the meeting was adjourned. Maggie couldn't help but wonder why he was so determined to pin the bombings on this particular group. From her brief research before coming down to the meet-ing, she couldn't find a single incident of violence or crimi-nal behavior attributed to the group. Sure, they had made some outrageous statements but even the so-called warn-ings or threats that Senator Foster's office had received were mild. They also hadn't taken credit for the attack which was odd.

Wurth and Yarden went over more crime scene photos. They created a list of information, evidence and leads. When they were finished David Ceimo offered to take them out for burgers and beer. Maggie realized, as she often did, that only law enforcement officials would think of food after a meeting like this.

CHAPTER
44

Nick scooted into the tall leather-backed booth behind David Ceimo. He wanted to kick himself. He'd hesitated. Overcompensated. He didn't want to look obvious about wanting to sit next to Maggie and now Yarden beat him to it. Not only that but Yarden had managed to fit himself right in between Maggie and Jamie while David Ceimo and Nick took up the other side of the huge corner booth. Deputy Director Charlie Wurth was supposed to join them later. Nick figured he should have invited A.D. Kunze, too, but he couldn't find the FBI guy. He'd left the briefing early and no one seemed to know where he had gone.

Nick was relieved to be away from the scene, even if it would be for an hour or two. As a county sheriff and then a prosecutor, he'd been to plenty of crime scenes. But nothing this massive and never this many fatalities. He had gained a new respect for those left behind still sifting and walking the grids around the craters.

On a busy Friday evening, The Rose and Crown was packed. The English-style pub had a lobby full of guests waiting, but Ceimo's older brother Chris owned the place. He had escorted the five of them personally to the quieter of two rooms. Now he came back with place settings, handing them oversized menus and taking their drink orders himself.

"On the house," Chris told them.

"No," David insisted. "I can't let you do that."

"I'm not letting any first responders pay tonight." The older Ceimo was shorter than his brother, handsome with a quick smile but serious dark eyes. "We all make our livings, in part, because of the mall and the airport. Something like this happens, we have to pitch in somehow. It's the least I can do."

They watched him leave then David said, "His partner brought over a bunch of food to the scene. I had to get him cleared through security. They almost wouldn't allow it till Chief Merrick noticed a pastrami on rye." He smiled, obviously proud of his older brother. "Must have brought four or five dozen sandwiches."

"Yeah, that was nice," Jamie said. "People don't usually think about us needing to eat. My boyfriend always thinks it's gross that we'd even want to, but after six or seven hours you get hungry."

"You want, I can have Chris shut off this television." David pointed to one of the many screens suspended throughout the pub. This one was off to their side about ten feet away, just over Nick's right shoulder. The volume had been muted and closed captions ran along the bottom of the screen.

Nick found himself looking to Maggie. David did, too. Even as they waited for an answer the video footage of the now infamous chase was being played.

"It's okay," she said after it took a second or two for her to realize they were allowing her to make the decision. "If there's an update or a break in the case, where better to find out?"

They all laughed. Nick realized every one of them probably had a story to tell of the news media preempting one of the cases they'd worked on. However, he doubted that any of them had been preempted by a journalist in their own family. His sister, Christine, had done it to him twice in the past. Once even compromising her son, Timmy's safety. He thought she'd learned her lesson, but he didn't trust her. It was almost as if she couldn't help it. Like a drug addict. Even now he avoided returning her calls. Was she concerned or looking for a scoop?

Briefly he realized her calls might concern their dad, but Christine would say so, wouldn't she? His dad's health had been deteriorating the past several months, bad to worse with no hope of recovery. The stroke he'd suffered four years ago had reduced him to a shadow of the man Antonio Morrelli had once been. But some things never changed and Nick thought the old man was stubborn enough to stick around just out of spite and to ruin Christmas for all the rest of them. Maybe deep down that's what Nick hoped. Whether he wanted to admit it or not, he wasn't quite ready for his father's departure, for him to be gone completely and forever from his life.

He scratched at the stubble on his jaw and rubbed at his eyes. When he looked up he found Maggie watching him from across the table. The others were talking about food, their attention buried in the large menu placards. But not Maggie. She had one elbow on the ridge that separated the booth from the wall. Her cheek rested against her hand. David Ceimo sat directly across from her, Yarden right next to her and yet, she was watching Nick from clear across the diagonal of the table.

At first he glanced away. But her eyes were still there

when he looked up again and this time he met them despite
the flutter they stirred in his gut. She looked tired, but she
smiled, just a little. Her eyes were still serious with an intensity he recognized. From the first time he met Maggie
O'Dell he felt like those eyes could examine anyone deeply,
and he knew they missed nothing.

Their drinks came at that moment. Before Chris finished
setting them down, Yarden was pointing at the television
screen, waving his arms to get their attention.

"Holy crap," Yarden blurted as he tried to stand up for
a better look. "They have the bombers."

Nick had to look over his shoulder. Three photos of three
young men were displayed in the middle of the screen.
Names appeared beneath them and on the CC crawl at the
bottom of the screen.

Chris reached up and turned the volume on:

"*...were last seen. Two unnamed sources have verified
the identity of three men allegedly involved in the bombing
at Mall of America. All three are college students, two at
the University of Minnesota and one at the University of
New Haven in Connecticut. Again, the three young men
are, Chad Hendricks of St. Paul, Minnesota; Tyler Bennett
also of St. Paul, Minnesota and Patrick Murphy of Green
Bay, Wisconsin.*"

"Son of a bitch." Ceimo was the first to speak. "What
sources? Where the hell did they get photos and names?"
He was pulling his smartphone from his jacket pocket, as
he slid across the booth's bench. Nick barely got out of the
bench and out of his way.

Nick glanced around the table as he sat back down. Both
Yarden and Jamie's eyes were still glued to the television
screen. Maggie's face had gone white and she was digging
for her own cell phone.

"What is it?" Nick asked her. She looked like she had seen a ghost.

"Patrick Murphy."

He noticed her fingers had a slight tremble as she punched at her cell phone's menu. He could see she was searching for a number.

She glanced back up at him. He thought he saw a glimpse of panic before she looked back down. Without giving him her eyes again, she said, "Patrick Murphy is my stepbrother."

CHAPTER
45

Maggie excused herself, suddenly feeling claustrophobic up against the wall. Yarden and the bomb expert named Jamie couldn't move quick enough to release her from the corner of the booth. She needed to get out of the noise and the crowd and the prying concern of Nick Morrelli's eyes. She escaped to the restroom, only to find a long line waiting for the stalls. But it was quiet here if you didn't count the cell phone conversations.

On her own phone she searched the queue for Patrick's number. She had called him a week ago—ten days at most—to invite him to Thanksgiving. He already had plans. He was going out of town with friends to spend the long holiday with them. She pretended like it was no big deal.

Maggie blamed herself. She was the adult, twelve years older and yet, she had no idea how to take on the role of the decision-maker, the family planner. No idea how to be or act like a big sister. Hell, she had no idea how to act like a family.

Now as she searched her phone's menu she wondered

why she hadn't memorized his phone number. She was good with numbers and details. Even as she jotted things down while viewing the videotapes she knew she didn't need the notes. The discovery of Patrick two years ago had brought with it a whole storm, not just about having a brother but all her preconceptions about her father. The parent she loved and missed and remembered with adoration had actually led a secret life. And for two decades her mother continued to keep his secret. Patrick reminded Maggie of that every single time she saw him or talked to him. It was crazy and she needed to find a way around it if she ever intended to have a relationship with him. But not having his phone number was another reminder that she evidently wasn't ready. Now here she was hoping Patrick's number was in her phone's call history.

Her fingers kept hitting more than the arrow buttons. She had to focus, to concentrate despite the flushing toilets and the nagging little girl who wanted to go into the stall by herself. Even from behind the stalls there were conversations. People on their phones. Couldn't they go to the restroom without talking about their day? Though tonight's conversations were sprinkled with excitement and concern about the bombing and the newly released suspects.

Finally, Maggie found the number. She started to hit "return call" then glanced around again and stopped. How exactly was she going to do this? She moved away from the line, back into another corner by a sink that had an Out of Order sign posted on the mirror in front of it.

She hit the button, closed her eyes and waited. It didn't need to ring twice.

"Becca?" It was Patrick, anxious and out of breath.

She had no idea who Becca was. Of course not. She had no idea who any of her brother's friends were.

"It's Maggie, Patrick."

The silence lasted so long she was afraid he had hung up.

"Patrick, are you involved in this?"

She wished he'd ask what? Maybe even pretend he had no idea what she was talking about.

"I wasn't with Chad and Tyler, if that's what you're asking."

Maggie leaned against the tiled wall. God! He knew who they were. If he hadn't known them, he wouldn't call them by name. They'd only be the other two suspects.

"You know them?"

"They were friends of one of the friends I was with." He let out a long sigh. "That sounds lame, doesn't it?"

He sounded so young. Had she ever been that young, that naïve? She noted that he said "were." Past tense. Did he know the two young men were dead?

"You're wanted for questioning," she told him and hated that she sounded entirely like an FBI agent and not at all like a sister. Why could she not get a hang of this?

"Yeah, I just saw."

"Where are you?"

Silence.

"Patrick, you're going to have to trust me or I can't help you."

"Let me think about it."

She was pacing as much as the corner allowed, getting frustrated. What was there to think about? Letting her help him or trusting her?

"I'll let you know," he said in what sounded like a rush. And then he was gone. Silence.

"Damn it!"

Her anger surprised her and drew looks. Even a couple of stall conversations came to a halt. Maggie pretended to ignore it all and she stomped toward the door. This time the line parted for her long before she had to ask or squeeze through.

CHAPTER
46

Asante finished the cheeseburger and fries, leaving a reasonable tip. An ordinary meal that wouldn't stand out and an ordinary tip that wouldn't leave a negative or overly positive impression. Ordinary, he had learned long ago, was the key to being invisible.

As he headed back to his gate he noticed groups of people at all the other gates amassed under the television monitors. He stopped, as did the others walking in front and behind him even though he already knew what the commotion was. The local television station had finally decided to release the photos his crew had anonymously submitted. He watched for a while then continued through the terminal, turning his head as he passed other televisions. He had to, at least, pretend to be interested and surprised and appropriately disgusted.

The waiting area for his gate was full, not a single seat available. The regulars who raced to board first were already standing near the door, their oversized carry-ons left in the way, making it impossible for anyone to overtake their position or even pass by.

Asante had always hated airport travel. In recent years it had become only worse. There were no longer manners or etiquette. People treated the waiting areas like their living rooms, tossing coats and bags on seats that should be left for other passengers. They gobbled down fast food while talking on their cell phones, carrying on conversations that others shouldn't have to listen to. They let their kids scream and crawl and run around. It was almost as bad as a mall. And yes, though he treated each of his projects as professional assignments, it had brought him a slight pleasure to blow up the largest shopping mall in America. Likewise it would give him considerable pleasure to blow up one of the busiest airports during the busiest travel day of the year.

As he drew near the information desk he was pleased to see he wouldn't have to ask any questions or depend on eavesdropping on others as they questioned the airline clerk. Posted below their flight number and destination was now a departure time. He still had an hour wait, but the posted time meant the plane had left—or at least been cleared to leave—Chicago.

He settled close to one of the television monitors. It was only an hour. He could pretend to be interested in the calamity for an hour.

CHAPTER
47

Patrick shoved his hands deep into his jacket pockets. His cell phone stayed buried in his fist. How could he trust Maggie? He barely knew her. It hadn't been that long ago that he discovered she existed. That they shared a father. She got the legal version. He got the illegitimate one. Both their mothers kept them from knowing about each other, some twisted pact Patrick's mother said was "a profound mistake." Of course she called it that only after the secret had been found out.

Now Patrick stood under the awning of a restaurant adjacent to the mall. He had walked into the place hoping to finally get out of the cold, sit down and have something to eat. The restaurant was packed, but he had found an empty bar stool in the lounge and ordered a Sam Adams. He was taking the first sips while he looked over a menu. That's when the news alert came on.

The television monitors were back behind the bar, high up, and everyone was watching or pointing.

Patrick almost choked. He still couldn't believe it was his picture, his name. He had just taken a drink of the beer.

Could barely swallow. Why did the police think he had something to do with the bombing? And now Maggie did, too. He didn't even know Chad and Tyler. Had never met them. Dixon pointed them out at the mall this morning. That was it.

Now here Patrick was out in the cold, again, shivering, teeth chattering. Soaking wet from his head to his toes. He made his way back to the hotel, avoided making eye contact with anyone, keeping his head down. Though he honestly wondered if anyone could recognize him in his present condition.

By now he figured he knew the hotel better than anywhere else. If he needed to hide, it seemed the best place. He took the stairwell to the fourth floor, knowing from his previous search that this was one of the quieter floors. He waited to make sure no one was in the laundry room before he went in. Helped himself to enough towels to dry himself off. He even found a pair of work coveralls.

He peeled out of his wet clothes, rolled them up in some towels and threw them into one of the dryers. The coveralls were a size too big. He had to turn up the cuffs. But they were dry and warm. He decided to take off his wet high-tops and his socks and threw them into the dryer, too. If any of the maids caught him he knew enough Spanish to make up a good story. At this time of night he didn't expect to see much housekeeping staff.

From the laundry room, he heard the freight elevator. It was stopping at the fourth floor. He recognized the screech of the doors sliding open. He looked into the hallway but ducked back into the laundry room just as he caught a glimpse of the man stepping out. A huge man in a blue uniform. Patrick's stomach did a flip as he pressed himself against the inside wall, hidden partially by the racks of folded towels, and held his breath.

He didn't think he could fool the security guard named Frank a second time tonight.

CHAPTER
48

Maggie hadn't gotten far and her phone started to ring. She didn't recognize the number. The area code was local. Could Patrick be calling from a pay phone? Or perhaps a friend's?

"This is Maggie O'Dell."

Silence.

Then a man's gravelly voice said, "Special Agent Margaret O'Dell?"

That was what the television reports had called her. She shifted her weight, crossed her arms, exhaustion giving way to alarm. It was someone who had seen her infamous chase. Someone who could access her unlisted cell phone number.

"Who is this?" she asked, none too politely.

"I have some information about the incident…at the mall. What happened there."

The caller sounded out of breath, fatigued, hesitant. Maggie guessed from his voice that he was older than the college-aged young men the news media said were responsible for the "incident."

"Are you saying you saw what happened?"

"No."

"But you were at the mall."

"No...no, I wasn't there." He was getting frustrated. She needed to wait. People revealed more during silences than after questions. "I know things."

Silence again.

"I'm listening," she finally said when she thought she might lose him.

"I have information. That's all that you need to know right now." He was almost angry and definitely frustrated, physically exhausted. "Look, my wife just had surgery. I'm a little tired," he said, not an apology, Maggie thought, so much as a way to calm himself down. "I'll tell you everything I know. Only you. Nobody else. You're the agent that saved that boy, right?"

Before she answered, he continued, "But you have to come to me. You have to come to where I say, so I know they won't be listening."

"Okay," Maggie told him. Did he really have information? Or was he a conspiracy theory nut, trying to hone in on some attention for himself? And how did he get her cell phone number?

"They have my grandson," he burst out without prompting. "That's where the bastards crossed the line."

She knew asking him who "they" were would get her nowhere. He wouldn't even give his name. He told her exactly where he wanted them to meet. She had no problems with the locale or his laundry list of instructions, though she wasn't sure how she would pull it off. Definitely not with A.D. Kunze's help. But by the time the man had hung up Maggie realized she knew the one person who could make this happen. She started searching for the governor's right-hand man.

She found David Ceimo in the restaurant's kitchen, his cell phone pressed so hard against his face there was a red indentation on his cheek.

"I want to know where they got this information. Anonymous doesn't cut it," he yelled over the clanging of pots and pans. "I don't care. Find out."

Ceimo shrugged and attempted a smile when he saw her. She leaned against a steel rack to let the chef squeeze between them.

"Any luck?"

"The photos were e-mailed anonymously to someone at the TV station." He raked a flap of his thick brown hair off his forehead only to have it fall back. His fingers made a second unsuccessful swipe. "They claim two sources confirmed."

"Sources close to the investigation?"

"Not from what I'm hearing. Just 'two independent sources.'" And he air-marked the quotes. "How did we get to this place where our news media only sensationalizes the news instead of reports it?"

They had to move out of the way again while a waiter tried to remove a tray from the refrigerator. The kitchen, though spotless, had little room for any extra personnel. Maggie moved to the other side of a narrow, long table, what looked like the kitchen's more extensive version of that evening's dessert tray.

"I just received an interesting phone call," she told him, glancing down at the tiramisu and cheesecake that came between them. "With an interesting request."

Ceimo's eyes narrowed on her. He was better at blocking out the kitchen activity. Maggie's training kept her eyes darting around, looking for anything and trying to catch everything. Her stomach, however, kept reminding her that they hadn't had a chance to eat, drawing her eyes down to the desserts.

"And this request?" Ceimo was impatient.

"The caller claims he has information."

"What kind of information?"

"He'll only share it in person. And only with me."

"He saw you on TV," Ceimo said, surprising her. There was more to the governor's aide than she expected. Nick Morrelli had introduced David Ceimo as an old football rival. His good looks and charm—not unlike Nick's—had made her misjudge his intellect, just as she caught herself doing with Nick.

"What if he's just some wacko?"

"Wackos are my specialty," she said and started giving him the details.

CHAPTER
49

Nick wished he could find an excuse to stay in Ceimo's SUV and tag along with him and Maggie. The two were obviously on some secret mission. He found himself a little jealous. That was ridiculous. Of course, he knew it was. Maggie asked Ceimo only because of his connections. Nick wondered if it had something to do with her stepbrother. He wanted to ask. Would have asked, but once again, he ended up in the wrong place, sandwiched between Yarden and Jamie in the back of the SUV.

"Let me know if there's anything I can do," he managed to say just as Ceimo dumped them out in front of the hotel.

Nick followed Yarden and Jamie down a hallway back to the command center. It hadn't been that long ago that they had left. Charlie Wurth was still here and Kunze had returned.

Nick poured himself a cup of coffee and was dumping cream into it when Kunze said to him, "Wurth said O'Dell was with you."

"She was."

Kunze glanced at the door again.

"She went somewhere with Mr. Ceimo," Yarden offered.

"Where exactly did they go?"

"They didn't say." Nick shrugged, sipped his coffee.

Kunze grumbled under his breath, digging his cell phone out of his jacket pocket. He stomped across the room, punching in numbers just as Deputy Director Charlie Wurth asked everyone to take a seat.

Wurth started writing on a huge white dry-erase board at the front of the room.

"Here's what we know so far about these guys. We haven't had much time to dig. Everything's still coming in. Feel free to chime in if you've got questions or information to add. No need for formalities."

On the dry-erase board under POI (persons of interest) he listed the names of the three young men the news media had released:

CHAD HENDRICKS, age 19, St. Paul, Minnesota

TYLER BENNETT, age 19, St. Paul, Minnesota

PATRICK MURPHY, age 23, Green Bay, Wisconsin.

He drew a bracket that connected Chad and Tyler, then jotted, "roommates at UnivM."

"We have two agents with a search warrant on their way to the dorm room these two men shared on campus. It looks like they also went to the same elementary school and high school."

A.D. Kunze passed out copies with all three of the young men's photos. He stopped at Nick and Yarden's table.

"Can the surveillance video verify these three were the ones with the red backpacks?"

Both Nick and Yarden took a closer look. Nick didn't like being put on the spot. Neither did Yarden.

"You saw the quality of the shots we had. It's tough to

tell," Nick said. "Hendricks for sure." He pointed at Chad's photo. It was a head shot. Probably from a sports roster. He was definitely the kid in the Golden Gopher ball cap. They had looked at that video enough times to safely identify him. Yarden was doing his bobble-headed nod.

"This one could be Bennett." He tapped Tyler's photo. "But Patrick Murphy...I don't think we have good enough video to identify him." He wanted to get back to the surveillance room, back to the video. If he looked a bit harder he wondered if he would recognize the man Maggie said was her stepbrother.

"Definitely Hendricks and Bennett," Yarden said, sounding confident. He wasn't just backing Nick up. Yarden may be timid but he was good at his job. "We couldn't get a good look at the third bomber or the two people he had with him. They all disappeared into the food court."

"What do you mean disappeared?" A.D. Kunze asked.

"The food court doesn't have any cameras."

"None?"

"No, sir."

Nick stopped himself from defending the antiquated security system that originally had been designed to track shoplifters, not terrorists.

"Mall security doesn't extend to that area," Yarden started to explain but Charlie Wurth stopped him.

"We never expected our shopping centers to be targets for terrorist attacks," Wurth said. "Same reason mall security officers are not armed. There are changes that are long overdue."

"Interesting that the TV station didn't have the girl's photo," Nick said.

He had everyone's attention now. Even A.D. Kunze stood quietly.

"So what does that mean?" Charlie Wurth asked.

"Could mean that whoever leaked those photos to the media didn't know the girl ended up with one of the bombs." A.D. Kunze crossed his arms over his chest. "At least it wasn't anyone from our group. Let's make sure it stays that way."

"Is there any evidence that the bombers died with the backpacks?" Wurth asked Jamie.

"Preliminary says yes to two of the three. The restroom bomb didn't appear to have human remains mixed with it."

"You can tell that?" Nick couldn't imagine what it must be like to sift through and determine that conclusion.

"Without getting into the gory details—" Jamie must have read his mind "—yes, we can."

"So there's a chance that three of the five escaped?" A.D. Kunze said it like it was an outrage.

"Don't forget the asshole with the remote," Wurth reminded them. "He got away, too. I'd place all my bets on him being the one who leaked the photos to the media."

A knock at the door stopped Wurth. Everyone twisted around to the door at the back of the room. Kunze was closest. Instead of just opening it and letting the intruder in, he stepped out. In seconds he was back. No one had moved, taking their cue from Wurth who waited.

"Morrelli, Yarden." Kunze waved them over.

He didn't give them any hints. He escorted them out the door without another word. On his way out to join them, he waved a hand at Wurth to continue.

Kunze led them to a couple waiting off to the side. The man wore a long cashmere overcoat. The woman's was leather, no less expensive.

Jerry Yarden seemed to recognize them before Kunze

began the introductions. His ears were red again, his eyes wide. Neither a good sign.

"The Chapmans arrived while you both were out. I asked them to stop back. Mr. and Mrs. Chapman, this is Nick Morrelli and Jerry Yarden from UAS, United Allied Security. The Chapmans are the majority owners of Mall of America."

Nick relaxed. The well-dressed couple probably just wanted to give them commendations. He didn't realize how wrong he was until Mrs. Chapman furrowed her brow and said, "What in the world went wrong?"

CHAPTER 50

Rebecca should have trusted her gut instinct.

Even before she got into Dixon's car she knew something wasn't quite right. He didn't turn to look at her directly, and instead, kept the left side of his face out of her sight. Yet if she had seen his black eye she still would have gotten into the car. She would have been concerned and would've wanted to hear what had happened.

No, it wasn't that he wouldn't look her in the eyes. It was something else. A tension, a fear so palpable she had felt it.

However, her gut instinct could never have predicted a gunman crouched in the backseat. Nor would she have predicted that the woman from the van, the one who had called her Becky and offered her a ride, would be slamming her face down into the snow and binding her wrists with plastic ties.

Now all alone in what felt like a dark, cold hole with the smell of gasoline all around her, Rebecca's mind raced. Who were these people? Why were they doing this? Had Dixon been involved in the mall bombing? Was Patrick?

What did they want with her? She didn't know anything. She hadn't seen anything.

Her eyes started to adjust to the darkness. It was a cellar or a crawl space. Wood rafters for a ceiling that wasn't even four feet from the floor. Not really a floor, just cold, hard concrete. The walls were concrete blocks. No windows. One small three-foot-by-three-foot door above. A trapdoor with no stairs. It didn't fit tight or in the rush, was left askew. Light from above seeped in around the left side. They had flung her down and with her wrists tied together she landed hard on her wounded arm. She felt a trickle of blood and knew some of the sutures had ripped. The pain was secondary. Nothing could override her fear.

Up until now she had been with Dixon. They left his car in the long-term parking lot at the airport. It had still been snowing. Rebecca searched for signs of life, security vehicles, a shuttle bus, other motorists, passengers returning to their vehicles. There was no one. Even if she dared to scream no one would hear her.

The woman in the van had followed close behind. It was there, in between the vehicles of the parking lot, that the woman pulled Rebecca from the car and pushed her down into the snow, binding her wrists so tight Rebecca felt the plastic bite into her skin. They shoved Dixon and Rebecca into the back of the van. The gunman crawled up beside them.

Dixon wouldn't meet her eyes. He looked awful. His lip was split on the same side as the black eye. His hair stuck up in places where it had been yanked. In the headlights of passing traffic she saw that his coat had been ripped and his jeans stained at the knees.

She wanted to ask him what was going on. She wanted to make him look at her and tell her whether he had anything to do with the bombing. But the panic had closed off her throat. It took all her effort to breathe, to keep from hyperventilating. Her arm throbbed.

They had parked in a long narrow alley, some place downtown. Again, there was no one to see them hustled from the van through the back entrance of a building, a brick building four—maybe five—stories high with long, dark corridors, institutional linoleum, blank sterile white walls. Rebecca tried to notice everything. Isn't that what they did in the movies? Even blindfolded and gagged they'd remember how many railroad tracks the car had bumped over or the sound of water under a bridge. Noting and recording her surroundings made her concentrate on something other than the pounding of her heart.

Now she tried to do the same thing here, alone in the dark. It simmered her panic.

She could hear muffled voices. Thumping footsteps overhead. Not just footsteps. It sounded like they were moving furniture. In the room above, she remembered metal desks and rolling chairs, file cabinets and a shelf with electronic boxes. There were several computers left on, their screen savers the only illumination in the room when they first entered. Everything had looked new, the walls a freshly painted white, plain and sterile like the corridors. Oddly there had been nothing personal in the room. No coffee mugs, no jacket over a chair, no container with pens, no plaques or pictures. It looked almost as if someone had quickly put together a makeshift office that was meant to be temporary.

Her eyes stared at the trapdoor, first waiting for someone to reappear. As time passed she still watched, wondering if the door wasn't closed properly and was out of line to cause that sliver of light, then maybe it wasn't locked. Could she shove it open? A bit of hope fluttered until she realized that with her hands tied behind her back she'd never be able to push it open or climb out.

She started looking around the musty area for something sharp to rub the plastic tie against. There had to be something here. That's when she noticed why the smell of gasoline was so strong. There were pools of it on the hard, cold concrete floor. She must have fallen in it because now she could smell the damp spots on her jeans and coat. Two cans marked gasoline sat on a shelf with their caps off. But they were set upright, not tipped over.

Rebecca realized this crawl space hadn't been splattered with gasoline by accident. Someone intentionally poured it out all over the floor.

CHAPTER
51

Saint Mary's Hospital
Minneapolis, Minnesota

Henry Lee wanted to continue pacing. He had been able to pace all he wanted downstairs in the cafeteria, watching for the FBI agent while pretending to sip coffee and burn off nervous energy. Not much of a ruse—he had been nervous, anxious and angry. Pacing helped.

Though disappointed, he felt a slight bit calmer back here, sitting at Hannah's side, holding her hand and listening to the machines wheeze and hum. There were still too many machines attached to her. But she was sleeping, resting, breathing on her own, now that the tube had been removed from her throat.

Henry glanced at his wristwatch. He had waited in the cafeteria ten minutes longer than his own self-imposed deadline, though the whole time he had been anxious to get back to Intensive Coronary Care. He shouldn't have been surprised that the FBI agent didn't meet his request. She must have thought he was some psycho and had passed on the message as a hoax.

Probably just as well. The hospital cafeteria had been a bad idea. He hadn't been thinking clearly. It was risky. They might be watching him. He couldn't see them, couldn't pick them out, but he wondered if they were here. After all, they must have taken Dixon from the hospital. If they had recognized the FBI agent from the TV news clips and saw him talking to her, they would most certainly kill Dixon.

Henry wasn't sure what he'd do now. He had five hours before they would allow him to talk to Dixon again. He had called his cell phone number anyway. It rang five times before it clicked over and he heard his own voice ask if he wanted to leave a message. He called it three more times. Each time it was the same. That meant they had left the phone on, left it somewhere to ring, probably just out of Dixon's reach, taunting him, reminding him who was in control.

Henry was worried sick about the boy. He tried to keep from conjuring up images of what they were doing to him. These were ruthless people who didn't mind blowing up innocent women and children in a shopping mall. People who had an agenda beyond what they were hired to do. He feared they would kill Dixon whether Henry "behaved" or not.

Maybe it was the fatigue, maybe it was sheer madness, maybe it was the realization that he had nothing to lose. They could take the project and twist it into their own selfish scheme, but by God, he would not allow them to take his grandson down with them. They had crossed a line and for that, he'd send them all to hell even if it meant he had to go along with them.

A nurse had left when Henry returned to the room. He'd

lost track of the in-and-out traffic. Now a white-coated doctor came in, still gowned up from surgery. Henry ignored them all unless they spoke to him first. He didn't want them interrupting his thoughts.

This doctor checked the machines, like all the others. Then she stood on the other side of Hannah and did something that surprised Henry. The doctor took a tissue from the side table and gently wiped a small line of drool that had escaped down Hannah's chin.

Henry raised his eyes to meet the doctor's.

"Hello, Mr. Lee."

Henry simply nodded. At first he thought she was just another doctor, a polite one taking time to introduce herself. But she held his eyes and little by little he recognized her beyond the black square-framed eyeglasses and the hair that was slicked back to accommodate the surgical cap. She looked smaller in the scrubs, white coat and blue paper shoe covers, but she had donned the role of doctor or surgeon with an air of grace and confidence that had fooled him.

It was too late to hide his surprise or the sigh of relief. She'd come, after all.

CHAPTER 52

"How did you find out my name?" Henry Lee wanted to know, but Maggie could see he was pleased rather than upset about it. "And how did you find me?"

"There's a consult room next door. Security key card entry only," she told him in the same calm voice she might use had she really been one of his wife's doctors, updating him, comforting him. "It's already been swept for bugs. We have it for the next twenty minutes."

He stared at her as if she were speaking a foreign language and he needed an interpreter. Finally he nodded. She waited while he tucked his wife's hand under the covers. He had been holding it all this time and looked reluctant to let go. Then he followed Maggie without further hesitation.

"I'm sorry about your wife," Maggie told him as they settled into comfortable chairs in the next room. "It sounds like she made it through surgery quite well."

"That's what they keep telling me." He sounded like he didn't believe them.

She reminded herself that his wife's condition wasn't

her concern, though she admired his obvious devotion to her.

In the short amount of time since his phone call, Maggie had learned quite a bit about Henry Lee. With David Ceimo's connections as the governor's chief of staff, he had been able to track the anonymous phone call to Maggie's cell phone. The call had come from a waiting room in Saint Mary's Hospital's ICC.

In their brief conversation the caller had let it slip that his wife had just had surgery. On the day after Thanksgiving, there were no planned surgeries. Maggie had been able to find out that there were, in fact, only two emergency surgeries. One, an appendectomy. The other, a triple bypass. Another quick phone call to ICC—this one a bit of a finagle—and Maggie was able to get the patient's name. From there she discovered her anonymous caller's name. While David Ceimo took care of getting her hospital credentials and security clearance, Maggie searched everything she could find about Henry Lee by using her smartphone's Internet connection.

Turned out the man had an outstanding reputation as a business mogul, taking several companies and building them into national Fortune 500 successes. Now retired and remaining chairman of his empire, he used his clout to lobby for homeland security measures. He was far from the wacko she had expected.

"I'll only tell you what I know if I'm promised immunity from prosecution." He said it like it was something he had memorized, perhaps rehearsed. There was none of his earlier passion in this request.

"I don't have the authority to make that promise."

In the past A.D. Cunningham had backed her up with any deals she believed necessary. She was pretty sure A.D. Kunze would not.

"I can assure you that I'll talk to the authorities about your cooperation," she told him, "but that's as much as I can promise."

He studied her with tired and hooded, watery blue eyes. She could see him evaluating his options. She waited while his eyes left hers, darted down to his wringing hands then back to hers.

"They have my grandson," he said and cleared his throat, an unsuccessful attempt to hide the hitch in his voice. "Will you at least try to get him back?"

"I'll do everything in my power to try to get him back."

Then Maggie sat forward and waited, not wanting to throw out questions that might limit the information he gave.

"I'm a patriot," he chose to open with.

It surprised Maggie, but she kept from showing it. One of the companies Henry Lee owned was a security provider. From the brief background search, she had expected to come here and get information from him that might involve some breach of security or perhaps a failure to report a warning.

What Maggie O'Dell didn't expect was a confession.

CHAPTER
53

Nick stood at Jerry Yarden's side as Yarden gave his long-winded and animated version of what security had done to try and foil the attack. The Chapmans nodded, thin-lipped and unblinking. Nick was relieved when his cell phone started ringing.

"Sorry, I've got to take this call," he told them, excusing himself and escaping down the hall without even looking to see who was calling. "This is Nick Morrelli," he said with just a hint of importance mixed with a dab of irritation for the Chapmans' benefit.

"Finally. I can't believe you answered."

It was his sister, Christine. True enough, he had ignored her previous calls and not returned any of her messages. He hadn't been ready to divulge any details that he suspected the news reporter in her would be wagering for.

"Yeah, sorry. It's been crazy here."

He glanced back down the hall. The Chapmans had forgotten him already and were focused on poor Jerry. Nick took another hallway, searching for somewhere a bit quieter.

"We've been watching," Christine said. "It's hard to imagine. I can't even pretend to know what it must be like to be there in the middle of it."

He found a small, empty room off the elevators and ducked inside. Stacked, dirty coffee cups filled a table. Folding chairs were left in no particular pattern. Nick sat down in one against the wall.

"The director of security and I were just getting our asses chewed by a couple of the owners of the mall."

"You're kidding. What did they think could have been done?"

Nick heard the interest in Christine's voice and immediately hoped he wasn't sorry he had told her that.

"It's kind of late," he said, glancing at his watch and wanting to prevent any follow-up questions. "Is everything okay?"

"I didn't want to add to your stress, but I knew you'd want us to call you." He didn't like the change in her voice. "We had to have Dad taken by ambulance to Lakeside Hospital's emergency room."

Nick shot out of the chair, gripping the phone tight against his ear.

"Is he okay?" He found himself bracing one hand against the wall.

"They've got him stabilized."

"What happened?"

"Mom noticed his breathing was more...I guess raspy. That's how she described it." There was a long pause. "Nick, I don't think she's gonna be able to take care of him from here on out. It's getting harder and harder."

He needed to sit back down. Found the chair again.

"Okay," he offered as his best gesture of agreement. "What are you thinking?"

He'd never been in on these conversations. It had always

been Christine and his mom making the decisions regarding his dad's care. He had been off in Boston, 1300 miles away, up until several months ago when he moved back to Omaha. Now he realized how lucky he had been all those years, and he couldn't help but wonder why Christine decided to foist this on him this time?

That wasn't fair. He knew that wasn't fair. But he was exhausted, overwhelmed and 400 miles from home. What could he do about it?

"You know she won't agree to moving him anywhere outside of home," Christine said. "But she's being stubborn about having some outside help. She keeps saying Dad doesn't want some stranger helping him pee. It's ridiculous."

He glanced around the room. He wanted to ask her why all of this needed to be decided right now? He was safe, stabilized, she had told him. Christine was always worrying about things before they happened.

"How long will they keep him in the hospital?"

"His doctor wants to run some tests. Probably through the weekend."

"Can we talk about it when I get home?"

Silence. Had it been the wrong thing to say?

"Sure, that's fine," she finally said.

Nick recognized that tone. It meant waiting was anything but fine. Passive aggressive. Wasn't that what they called it. Both of them had the symptoms. Number one on the list was "hates confrontation."

"It's just that I'm a little overwhelmed right this minute," he tried to explain and knew it sounded lame as soon as it escaped his mouth.

"I just wanted to talk to you about it, Nick." She was upset but doing her best to keep it from her voice. "I'm fully aware that when it comes time to actually fix it, that I'll be the one doing it by myself."

He didn't know what to say. He felt like she had slugged him in the gut. He felt like an asshole.

"I've gotta go," she said and he heard the click before he could respond.

He closed his eyes and leaned his head back against the wall. He wasn't good at this family stuff. That's why they'd never asked him before. But if Christine knew that, why was she expecting something different from him? Why now?

CHAPTER
54

Maggie tried not to interrupt Henry Lee. She refrained from crossing her arms or any other nonverbal gestures that might stop him. Her psychology background had taught her to listen without giving any indication of prejudice. Sometimes an impassive listener gathered more valuable information than a seasoned interrogator. Human nature dictated certain behaviors, like filling in long silences or attempting to please a receptive listener.

"My daughter, Dixon's mother, was one of the 168 people who were murdered on April 19, 1995. Four thousand eight hundred pounds of ammonium nitrate and jet fuel driven right up to the front of the Alfred P. Murrah Federal Building in Oklahoma City."

There was still enough emotion to cause the blue eyes to go watery, again. He took an irritated swipe at them and continued, "I didn't believe it could happen. Thought we'd never allow it again. But we Americans have short attention spans. We become complacent. Six years later, 9/11."

He sat back, sat forward, couldn't get comfortable. Didn't seem to know what to do with his hands.

Maggie waited out his silence and his fidgeting.

"We've become complacent again," he told her. "This was meant to be a wake-up call. This administration keeps tearing down our policies on terror, weakening our security systems. They're leaving us vulnerable for another attack. And mark my word, there will be another attack." The anger was creeping back into his voice.

"It'll be some major sporting event or in one of our shopping centers or an airport. They've broken down the barriers we worked so hard to build. Closing down Gitmo. It's crazy. Treating those monsters to three square meals while all they want to do is get back out there and slaughter innocent Americans."

"Thirty-two innocent Americans were killed today." She couldn't help it. She didn't want to listen to his diatribe and let him believe her silence might excuse, condone or possibly understand it.

"Dear God, thirty-two?" He covered his face with trembling hands. "That wasn't supposed to happen," he said through his fingers as they rubbed at his disbelief. "I swear to you, that wasn't supposed to happen."

"What exactly was supposed to happen, Mr. Lee?"

"A disruption. That's all." He shook his head and sat forward, hands wringing. "Our group…and it's an influential group of high-level, upstanding individuals…"

"Citizens for American Pride?"

He let out a breath, something that sounded between a snort and a chuckle.

"CAP? It's a smokescreen, a distraction. That organization has nothing to do with this."

"Then I don't understand, what group are you talking about?"

"No one knows about us. We've managed to keep it secret for almost fifteen years. We've influenced business contracts—billions of dollars—making sure that American companies are awarded. We've manipulated government policy. Nothing different than what lobbyists do, only we have members who are…let's just say, a bit closer to actually making government policy."

"Are you saying members of Congress are a part of this secret group?"

He shrugged and she knew he was monitoring what he told her, perhaps deciding as he went along.

"We're not thugs," he said. "That's all I'm saying. Sometimes our methods may have seemed a bit unconventional. We did what we felt was necessary to influence, to persuade, to keep America on track. Yes, we pushed the envelope. But no innocent lives were lost. I promise you that."

Now he glanced around the room as if checking to see if it was, indeed, secure. "This was meant as a wake-up. The devices—electronic jamming devices—were supposed to be in those backpacks. They were designed specifically to disrupt computer and satellite feeds. I helped create them myself. It was supposed to be a virtual electronic blackout, appropriately timed to occur on what the retail world calls 'Black Friday.' A day of substantial profits would be turned upside down to show how easily a terrorist could walk in and do the same, maybe worse."

"You certainly proved the worse part."

Maggie bit down on her lower lip. Calm, steady, impassive—she could do this without injecting emotion. She kept from balling her hands into fists, willed her feet to stay planted when she wanted to pace.

"You're right. Someone certainly proved it. Someone with his own agenda. Those boys didn't have anything to do with this."

"You know the boys involved?"

"They were friends of my grandson. Chad, Tyler and Dixon got hoodwinked into carrying those backpacks. And Patrick—they shouldn't even have his picture. He didn't have anything to do with this. Patrick and Becca just went to the mall to be with Dixon."

"You know Patrick Murphy?"

"Patrick and Becca celebrated Thanksgiving at my home yesterday, spent the last two nights with us. They go to University of New Haven with Dixon. Came from Connecticut all together. Drove two days. Good kids. Good, decent kids."

He was shaking his head and didn't notice Maggie swallowing hard.

Patrick had been telling the truth. He didn't have anything to do with the bombing. She shouldn't have been so hard on him, should have trusted him instead of asking him to trust her. Now she was sitting with the man who Patrick had spent Thanksgiving with and he seemed to know more about her brother's character than she did. Suddenly her stomach did a flip as she realized something.

"Was Patrick with Dixon when he was taken?"

"No, neither was Becca."

The relief was hard to contain but Henry Lee didn't seem to notice as he stared at his hands again.

"Dixon said he left the backpack with them. Are Patrick and Becca alive?"

Maggie saw the realization in his eyes. He hadn't thought of it until now, that Dixon's friends may have been killed in the blast.

"Patrick is alive. I don't know about Becca."

Henry Lee shook his head. "Dixon was here at the hospital with me," he told her. "I was so relieved that he was safe. Then those bastards took him from here. That's how I know they must be watching."

He stopped, took a couple of deep breaths to steer himself away from the anger. "Dixon was worried about his friends. He borrowed my smartphone. He was talking to them." He paused and squinted, looking for the right term. "Texting them, making sure they were okay. That's how those bastards are making me keep in touch, controlling how I keep in touch. With my own goddamn phone."

"Who exactly are *they*, Mr. Lee? Who is it that has your grandson, who switched bombs with jamming devices?"

"The one in charge calls himself the Project Manager." He looked away. Took several more deep breaths as if steeling himself for what came next. "And he's getting ready to make another attack on Sunday."

CHAPTER
55

Just Patrick's luck. Looked like security guard Frank used this laundry room as his break room.

Patrick climbed into and folded himself inside one of the large commercial dryers, barely clicking the door shut before the giant sauntered in. He pressed himself against the metal drum, hoping anything that showed through the round window would only look like a pile of clothes waiting to be sorted. He could see just a sliver of Frank and what looked like a three-day supply of vending machine snacks. The security guard sat down at one of the tables, popped a can of soda, ripped open a bag of chips and propped up a paperback novel.

Great. A nice, long break.

Patrick tried to ignore the cramp in his legs. One leg twisted up under the other. He'd better get used to it. Frank was settling in. The dryer next door rattled and vibrated with the towels and his clothes, thumping his own high-tops against the back of Patrick's head. He might get away with some movement. The sound would get lost in the hum of the other dryer, but he couldn't chance setting his own creaking or whining.

Then he remembered his cell phone. He hadn't shut it off. He hoped Becca wouldn't choose now to call him. Or Maggie.

It reminded him that Becca hadn't called him. He couldn't call her. He didn't have Dixon's phone number. But she had his number. Why hadn't she called? Now that she was safe with Dixon, why wasn't she at least checking to make sure he was okay? When she escaped from the triage area had she intended to escape from him, too?

The thumping already gave him a headache. He chanced another peek. Frank had barely made a dent in his junk food stash.

Patrick's leg cramped, and he gritted his teeth against the pain. He leaned back, tried to stretch. The metal drum groaned and he froze. He braced himself and tried to listen over the vibration of the next-door dryer. No footsteps. He didn't see a chunk of blue uniform. Maybe the groan had sounded louder inside than outside.

This was crazy. All through high school and college he worked hard, kept to himself, tried to do the right thing, stayed out of trouble. Didn't date, didn't do drugs, didn't binge drink, didn't go looking for a fight. Or at least he didn't make a habit out of any one of those things. It'd been hard enough taking care of himself. Paying for college. Making enough extra money to eat, buy gas for his car and pay the rent. How the hell did he end up with his picture plastered all over the network and cable news? How did he end up alone, on the run? In a fucking dryer?

He closed his eyes and clenched his jaw against the thumping. It was exhausting having only yourself to depend on. He thought maybe Becca had felt the same way. He didn't want to admit how disappointed he was that she left without a word to him, that she didn't call or text. If he admitted that he was disappointed then he'd have to admit that she mattered. He had trusted that she was his friend. Didn't friends look out for each other?

Maggie said he needed to trust her.

He remembered when she called and invited him to her home for Thanksgiving. She offered to pay for his flight or train ticket. Said he could spend the weekend if he wanted. She had a big house with a huge backyard. She was anxious to introduce him to her white Lab, Harvey. In the last two years since they'd discovered each other, Patrick could count on one hand the times they had seen or talked to each other. He didn't know this woman who was trying to suddenly be his big sister.

Then it occurred to him that she, at least, was trying. What had he done? Not much of anything.

From what little he knew about Maggie, he realized she had worked hard to get where she was, working her way through college, earning a forensic fellowship at Quantico. And it sounded like her life hadn't been much easier than his after their father died. She had only hinted about her mother's alcoholism, but Patrick had worked in Champs long enough to recognize the difference between someone who chose to stay away from alcohol and someone who had to stay away.

The first time he met Maggie she had come to Champs in the hope of seeing him when he was working. Only she had no idea what he looked like. He remembered watching this lady sitting by the bar as she glanced around like she was searching for someone. It was a college bar. She looked out of place. Not because she was older but because she was too classy for Champs. Then to make matters worse—to prove even further that she didn't belong—she ordered a Diet Pepsi.

The memory brought a smile just as the next-door dryer came to a sudden stop. No more vibration. No more thumping.

Patrick stayed pressed against the drum, not daring to move. The quiet was worse than the thumping. He risked a glance, moving only his head and keeping the drum from groaning again. The table was empty. No snack food, no paperback novel.

He craned his neck. No Frank. Was it possible he was gone?

Patrick dared to eased himself up on his elbows, creaking the drum just enough so he could see the rest of the room. Empty. Finally he could get out. If only he could twist himself out of this pretzel.

He pushed the door of the dryer. It didn't open. He put his shoulder to it and began to shove his weight against it.

The door didn't budge.

CHAPTER 56

Henry could tell the FBI agent didn't like him. Despite the compassion she'd shown earlier with Hannah, it was obvious she was having a difficult time listening to his reason for any of this. He didn't care. If he took into account what others thought of him he'd never have built the business empire he had today.

This agent, this young woman looked half his age. What did she know about making decisions that would change the world? He didn't give a crap whether or not she liked him. She could judge him all she wanted. The only thing he cared about now was that she helped him get Dixon back. Nothing else mattered.

"Where is the next attack supposed to take place?" she asked.

He could tell that her patience was wearing thin. She didn't realize it but he had caught plenty in her eyes, read the brief flickers of emotion she thought she could conceal. Henry had hired and fired more people than this woman had probably met in her young life. He saw that she wasn't just getting impatient, she was anxious, exhausted, cautious, suspicious. Not only did she not like him, she didn't trust him.

"I don't know the exact location," he told her. His hands no longer trembled. A good sign. He didn't like not being in control.

She raised an eyebrow. It was the first facial expression she had allowed.

"Sunday is the second busiest travel day of the year," he explained. "It'll be an airport. But I honestly don't know which one. We provided a list, but the choice was left to the Project Manager."

"Why an airport? I thought the jamming devices were designed to cause a commotion in the retail industry? Stall the computers? Play havoc with their profits."

"No, no you don't understand." He shook his head. He thought he had been clear. "This isn't about money. This is about keeping America safe. Keep terrorists from striking us again. This administration has destroyed all the safeguards we worked so hard to put into effect. What better place and time to remind Americans than a mall on the busiest shopping day of the year. Likewise, an airport on the second busiest travel day, stalling travelers returning home."

"Did you know it would be Mall of America?"

"Yes, of course. It's the largest mall in America."

"Then why don't you know which airport?"

He nodded. She was smart. But she still didn't quite understand.

"The largest mall in America made sense, no question about it. But if we knew which airport, we might give it away or incriminate ourselves."

"You're going to give me the list." It wasn't a question.

He hesitated then reminded himself it didn't matter. It was a small exchange for Dixon's life.

"Of course. I don't have it memorized. I'll need to e-mail it to you."

She pulled out her smartphone.

"You'll e-mail it to me before I leave."

Maybe he had done his own misjudging of her as well. She was sharp, quick…gutsy.

"So tell me about this man who calls himself the Project Manager," she prompted him.

"I wasn't the one who hired him," he told her.

"He was hired?"

Another slip of emotion. He could see it, though subtle, it was there in her eyes. Surprise? No, Henry thought it was more a flicker of disgust.

"None of us met him. He made certain we had no idea who he was, what he looked like, where he'd come from."

"Why did you believe you could trust him?"

Henry shrugged. Good question.

"He came to us highly recommended by someone we trusted."

"Are you telling me this man you hired to upset retail business and stall air travel, has his own agenda?"

"Either he has his own agenda or he's following orders from someone in our group. Someone who believes we need bombs rather than jamming devices to wake up America." Somehow he couldn't bring himself to tell her that the group he defended and vowed to protect had gone a step too far, ignoring his warnings, betraying years of integrity and honor in exchange for what? Power? Greed?

"You realize I could take you in for questioning," she told him. "I could make you tell us who that someone is."

"I know my rights, Agent O'Dell, and I employ some of the best attorneys in the country. I'd clam up and you'd have nothing. You need this information and I want my grandson back alive."

Her earlier sympathy had diminished.

"If you want your grandson back you'll need to tell me something. I don't know if you're aware of this but Chad Hendricks and Tyler Bennett are dead."

He winced, closed his eyes. He had suspected as much.

"Their backpacks blew up while on their backs, detonated from outside the mall." Her voice had gained an edge to it. "They were just walking around the mall, thinking they'd cause some commotion—according to you—by jamming a few computers, holding up some lines of shoppers, irritating those greedy retail owners. They had no idea they'd be blown into pieces."

His eyes met hers and he watched her carefully put away the anger, pretending the emotion was a tool of her interrogation practice.

"It's okay," he said. "It doesn't matter to me if you enjoy taking swipes at me."

That surprised her. He could see she wanted to cross her arms but stopped herself. She flexed the fingers of one hand, no doubt preventing them from balling up into a fist.

"Think whatever you must about me," he continued. "I deserve it. But my grandson doesn't deserve to pay for any of my mistakes."

"Let's get back to the Project Manager, Mr. Lee. There has to be some information you can give me about him."

"There is one thing. Though I don't know if it means much. He referred to himself as John Doe #2. I was told he said it as if it were a resumé enhancer."

"I'm not sure I understand."

"My daughter was killed in the bombing in Oklahoma

City. The Project Manager knew more about all of us than we knew about him. I figured it was some twisted reference to the alleged third terrorist. For my benefit, perhaps. Remember, they referred to him as John Doe #2? Maybe he said it because it was true."

"Are you suggesting the man you hired as the Project Manager *is* John Doe #2 from the Oklahoma City bombing?"

Henry shrugged.

"That he even existed was mere speculation, rumor at best."

Henry noticed that Agent O'Dell looked like she was already considering it, wondering if, indeed, John Doe #2 may have been real after all.

"That's all I know," he said. "Did you want me to download that list for you?" He pointed to the smartphone in her hand.

She stared at him a second or two, the information taking time to sink in. He wondered if she had any idea how much of a risk he was taking by telling her any of this.

"So we have a deal?" he asked, waiting for her eyes to meet his. "You'll get my grandson back from this bastard?"

He knew there wasn't anything else she could say. She simply nodded.

CHAPTER
57

Saturday, November 24
McCarran International Airport
Las Vegas, Nevada

Asante didn't want to waste any more time, but he waited behind three other first-class passengers. He couldn't be the first to deboard the plane. Being first would be noticed by the flight attendants as too anxious. Being first would be out of the ordinary.

Most of the passengers—even those who looked ready to hit the casinos' gambling floors—were exhausted because of the long delay. Asante tried to blend in with them though he had no intention of stepping foot in a casino. Not on this trip.

Las Vegas had been an excellent choice, especially with the unexpected delay. Most airports closed down after midnight. Not Las Vegas. It was just as noisy at this hour as any other time of day. Even before he came up out of the gateway he heard the clicks and pings of slot machines. Asante glanced at them and wanted to shake his head.

They filled the middle area of the terminal. The majority of the machines were in play by passengers waiting for their flights and needing to extend their addiction for as long as possible.

He shouldered his way through the crowds and started following the signs for baggage claim. He adjusted the duffel bag as he turned on his headset, already planted on top of his ear. Then he punched the keypad on his phone. The call connected in seconds.

"Good flight?" the woman's voice asked in place of a greeting.

"A bit delayed but I'm back on track."

"Becky is enjoying her reunion with her college buddy."

Again, they kept the conversation like a husband and wife checking in with each other. He had trained them well, keeping it minimal and never mentioning full names or using a name as traceable as Dixon.

"Good. And what about our friend, Hank? How is he?"

"He's staying put. Seems to be behaving."

"Glad to hear that. So are we ready to clean house tomorrow?"

"Can't wait," she said with a laugh.

A nice added touch, Asante thought.

"In fact," she continued, "we're making the final preparations."

"Call if there are problems. I'll talk to you later."

He found the escalator for baggage claim and got on with a dozen others.

Glitches, he smiled to himself. That was the thing about glitches—they could be fixed, rerouted or simply deleted.

At the bottom of the escalator while everyone else

headed for the luggage carousels, Asante went the other direction to a small room off to the side. There, a row of foot lockers lined each wall. He found #83 and expertly fingered the combination padlock. One twist left, two twists to the right and it slid open.

Inside the locker, taped to the inside door was a sealed, plain manila envelope with more cash than he'd need. Stacked one on top of another was a twenty-six inch Pullman and its twin, both black canvas, their corners sufficiently scuffed to look like they belonged to a seasoned traveler. He took the two Pullmans out and dropped the duffel bag on top of one. Then he plucked off the envelope, tucking it into one of the bag's side pockets. Finished, he hung his coat in the locker, closed the door and replaced the padlock.

Now all that was left was finding a ride.

He headed for the exits. The warm air hit him in the face. What a difference a few hours and a thousand miles made. Despite going from one extreme to another and despite already breaking a sweat, the warmth felt good.

He started looking for the shuttle buses. He'd catch the next one going to long-term parking. At this time of night he was certain he'd be able to pick out the vehicle of his choice.

CHAPTER
58

Still in scrubs, Maggie climbed into Ceimo's SUV. He'd been waiting in the emergency room parking lot, at the emergency room entrance, the only way to enter or leave the hospital after midnight. Thankfully he had the vehicle's heater turned up. She reached over and clicked the button for her seat to heat up, too. It'd take more than this, however, to get rid of the chill that Henry Lee had left her with.

Before she had time to get comfortable Ceimo told her, "Kunze and Wurth have called. I had to tell him we were following up on a lead. But that's all I told them."

She nodded, grateful.

She had confessed to David Ceimo as soon as she asked for his help that she wouldn't be telling anyone else but him, not until after she had talked to Henry Lee. She knew A.D. Kunze wouldn't have allowed her to go. This was one of those times she would have to ask for forgiveness rather than permission.

Yes, she bent the rules every once in a while, but not without caution. At least, she had learned that lesson. Okay, so her version of "caution" didn't always coincide with her superiors'. There was a time or two that even Cunningham had not been pleased with her. When lives are concerned and time is ticking away, following the rules just to be following the rules, didn't make sense. A.D. Kunze wouldn't agree. That's why earlier, as soon as Maggie had entered the hospital, she turned off her phone, clicking it on temporarily only for Henry Lee to download the list.

"So," Ceimo asked. "Were you able to find out anything at all?"

"Sunday," she said. "There's another attack planned on Sunday."

"Sunday as in this Sunday? As in tomorrow?"

She glanced at the vehicle's green-lighted dials and searched for the clock. She'd lost track of time. Of course, he was right. It was already Saturday morning. They had less than twenty-four hours.

"Yes, the Sunday after Thanksgiving, the second busiest day for airline travel."

"Son of a bitch."

"I have a list of possible airports. Seven of them. We don't know which one's been targeted."

"Minneapolis?"

"Not on the list."

She heard him let out a sigh of relief.

"Sorry," he said, catching himself.

"No need to apologize."

She watched out the side window. Snow covered everything: bus stop benches, light poles, newspaper dispensers. The wind swirled it around and made it dance in the headlights. The white lights on trees already decorated for the holidays, twinkled on frosted branches. It looked like a winter wonderland.

"What can I do?" He wanted to know.

She chose carefully what to ask for and even more carefully what to tell David Ceimo, deciding it was best to leave any speculation out. She gave him as many facts and details as she could about Dixon Lee's abduction. That was the promise she would need help in delivering, though at the moment it seemed impossible with the little information they had.

Ceimo assured her that the governor would be willing to do whatever was necessary. Henry Lee and his empire of Fortune 500 businesses were important to the state of Minnesota. They employed over 6,000 people and brought in irreplaceable state tax revenues. Ceimo agreed that they'd need to work quickly and secretly. The fewer people involved the better chances they had to find Dixon Lee still alive.

However, she mentioned nothing to Ceimo about the outrageous supposition that the Project Manager, the man responsible for the mall bombing, could be the infamous John Doe #2, the so-called third terrorist who was rumored to have assisted—or according to some conspiracy theorists, guided—Timothy McVeigh and Terry Nichols in the Oklahoma City bombing. The idea was crazy. Or was it?

By the time Ceimo dropped Maggie off at the hotel, the crowds had dissipated. This time when she took a detour for her ice and Diet Pepsi, there were, thankfully, no lines to elbow and nudge her way through. Several blue-blazered hotel clerks smiled at her. One told her where there were still some refreshments. Another asked if there was anything else they could do for her. It wasn't until she got into the elevators and caught a glance of herself in the mirrored

walls that she realized why they had paid so much attention to her. She was still in hospital scrubs and the white
lab coat.

This time she tried to block out the Christmas music
that followed her from the elevator to her room. There
was nothing soothing about chestnuts roasting on an open
fire. She was exhausted. Her bruised side ached where the
Sudanese boy had shoved her against a car grill. Her
stomach reminded her it was still empty. And her shoulders
felt a tremendous new weight, a burden put there by Henry
Lee's revelation.

As soon as she got inside her room she popped the Diet
Pepsi open and began sipping. Then she pulled out her
phone and started dialing what would be the first of several calls.

She steeled herself. It was time to call A.D. Kunze and
Charlie Wurth. She'd need to tell them everything. Earlier
she'd made a judgment call to not ask for Kunze's permission but now it was time to ask forgiveness.

CHAPTER 59

Patrick struggled to breathe. There were ventilation traps in these things, weren't there? He was sure of it. There had to be. He told himself it wasn't like being underwater or stuffed in an airtight compartment. He couldn't suck up all the air. There'd be enough. He needed to settle down. He needed to just breathe.

He told himself that firefighters oftentimes found themselves in tight squeezes. Didn't they? What had he read? What had they taught him in any of his Fire Science classes? Could he access some information, some advice, some trick? Some "what if" you're caught without your pickax? Pickax? He didn't even have a screwdriver.

Who was he fooling? No professional firefighter would climb inside a commercial dryer and shut the door.

Sweat trickled down his back and down his face. He had to constantly wipe it out of his eyes. The overalls stuck to him. It was crazy hot inside the dryer. How long had it been? It felt like hours, but he knew that it hadn't been long. Twenty minutes? Forty? Maybe an hour.

He'd exhausted himself with the initial panic. His

shoulder ached where he had slammed it over and over against the immovable door. The only thing that stopped him from yelling for help was explaining to Frank's meaty face why he was stuck in a dryer.

He concentrated on peeling and plucking out the rubber seal around the door. The last piece, finally. Only it didn't make a difference. Not even a slight bit looser. The sucker still wouldn't budge. Now his fingertips hurt from squeezing them between the metal, hoping to bend or pry open the door. His injured palm hadn't started bleeding again but it was throbbing. He was running out of ideas. And eventually out of air, despite his theory about the vents.

Okay, so this was bad but at least it wasn't a freezer.

That first time he'd met Maggie she was working a case in Connecticut. The killer ended up making national headlines—a psycho who cut the diseased body parts from his victims, collecting his specimens in Mason jars then stuffing the bodies in fifty-five-gallon drums hidden in an abandoned rock quarry. The guy managed to throw Maggie into a chest freezer and left her there to die. By the time anyone found her, hypothermia had set in. Hypothermia so bad the doctors had to drain all her blood out of her body, warm it up and put it back in. Amazing what they could do. Amazing that she had survived. Actually Maggie was pretty amazing. Why was he only now realizing that?

Back then she had been a total stranger to Patrick. He felt bad for her but not much else. Still, he came to see her, sat at her hospital bed a few times and kept her company. But what else could he do? Besides, that fall he had plenty of other things that required his attention.

After that, he and Maggie had gotten together for lunch or dinner a few times. He liked hearing the stories about their dad, but, like Maggie, Thomas O'Dell was a stranger to Patrick, too. There was nothing tangible to connect to.

No memories. No photos. Nothing handed down. Patrick didn't even get the man's surname.

To make matters worse, his mother told him the subject of his father was "off limits." She wouldn't discuss it and insisted he respect her wishes. She said she knew she could count on him to not make this issue a problem. How could she not see that refusing to talk about "the subject," "this issue," actually prevented Patrick from knowing about *himself?* As a result, he had opted to spend Thanksgiving with friends who thought they knew him so well they could leave him to fend on his own, instead of spending the holiday with family who didn't know him at all.

They all thought he was the mature, independent twenty-three-year-old who could handle anything and everything thrown his way because he'd taken care of himself so well for so long. Maybe he was sick and tired of taking care of himself. Maybe he wanted to lean on someone else for a change.

The heat continued to soar inside the dryer. He laid his head back against the drum. Not exactly the right time to count on someone else. If everyone thought he was so capable then certainly he should be able to get the fuck out of this dryer. Maybe he just needed to sit back and look at things differently.

He couldn't remember where the hinges were. What side? Had there been a handle that he had to pull up on? He'd been in such a panic he just climbed in and swung the door closed behind him. Was it possible he was knocking his shoulder against the hinged side?

Maybe he needed to take a different approach.

Patrick twisted and turned his body, making the metal drum whine. He slid and shoved himself so that his back leaned against the back of the dryer. His knees splayed out to each side of him in order for him to plant his bare feet on the door. He didn't care if he broke the round glass and cut his feet. He needed to breathe. He needed out of here. He pulled back his legs and kicked both heels against the door as hard as he could.

The door popped open.

CHAPTER
60

Nick had been punching buttons back in the video surveillance room, trying to follow the sequence Jerry Yarden had taught him, when he got Maggie's call. Moments earlier he'd finally convinced Yarden to go home, be with his family, get some rest, although Nick imagined home for Yarden was a small studio apartment and his family probably a cat, maybe two cats. He tried to hide his surprise when Yarden—humble but proud—opened his wallet to show Nick his family: a beautiful brunette, three handsome boys and a small white fluff-ball of a dog on his wife's lap. Nick hadn't even been right about the cat.

"You sure you'll be okay?" Yarden's parting words, accompanied by a glance at the panel of keyboards and monitors. Nick wondered if Yarden worried about leaving Nick alone or leaving his surveillance equipment alone with Nick.

"I'll be fine. Go hug your wife and kids, Jerry. You did good, real good. If I need you, I'll call."

Nick had been feeling like there wasn't much more he could do. He was exhausted but he avoided going to his hotel room. Before he arrived in Minnesota he'd reserved a room at the same hotel that was now the command center, but he hadn't had a chance to get back there and even open his suitcase. He kept checking his watch. He had called his boss, Al Banoff, to give him an update. It was too late, or rather too early in the morning, to call Christine and check on his father.

So instead of his hotel room, Nick had gone back to the mall. He went back to the video surveillance room and started cueing up video segment after segment of the third bomber. He had the image of Patrick Murphy stamped into his mind now and he wanted to see if the third bomber, or the bomber's friend, could be Murphy. But in all the segments they had found, as soon as the two young men and woman got off the escalators onto the third floor, they disappeared into the food court and disappeared out of surveillance range.

Then Maggie called.

Okay, it was silly but he felt a new surge of adrenaline just hearing her voice. Having her ask for his help was a bonus. Inviting him to her hotel room… It was a case, he reprimanded himself. They were working a case—a horrendous, sad, scary case. So why did his heart start pounding a little faster? Why did the gusts of wind that bit and pulled at his coattail not chill him? As he entered the hotel lobby, after walking all the way from the mall, he stripped off his leather gloves to find his palms sweating. He actually had sweaty palms. It was ridiculous. He was ridiculous.

He stopped at his own room to pick up his laptop computer, the one request Maggie had made of him. Once in his room, he shed his coat, took one look at himself in the mirror and continued to pull off his shoes and socks, trousers, shirt and tie. He would be a few minutes late, but he needed something to revive him. He needed a shower.

CHAPTER
61

Henry Lee stared at the wall clock in the ICC waiting room. He'd been here for a good fifteen minutes, watching the hands of the clock crawl. The wait strained his already frayed nerves. Just five more minutes and he could make his next call to Dixon.

Someone had left the Saturday *Tribune* on the unmanned and empty registration desk. Headlines and colored photos of the bombing dominated the front page. He didn't want to see any of it. Couldn't even look at it.

He tried to keep still. He'd bitten half his fingernails to the quick—just like his grandson. It had been an old habit he thought he'd replaced with single malt Scotch, but he hadn't been able to have a drink since Thanksgiving. Now here it was Saturday morning.

In twenty-four hours there'd be another attack.

He shook his head. No one could stop the attack. He didn't have much faith that Special Agent Margaret O'Dell would be able to do anything. Maybe warn the airports and Homeland Security. He'd done his part, done what he could.

Henry wanted to believe that the young FBI agent would find a way to save Dixon but deep down he knew he'd forced her to make a promise she had no way of keeping. It'd be up to Henry to take control. If he expected to see Dixon again he'd need to bargain with them this time. Put away his anger and negotiate a deal.

The people who had Dixon were hired mercenaries, minions of the Project Manager. They could be bought. That's what he convinced himself. He didn't care how much money they wanted, he'd get it. In his mind he'd already started accessing accounts and determining which one had liquid assets. The holiday weekend would make it tricky but not impossible.

Finally. It was time. He could call.

His hands resumed their annoying tremble, making it an effort to punch in the correct numbers on the waiting room's desk phone.

He counted the rings…three, four… They had to pick up. He'd waited the allotted five hours they told him to wait. But instead of an answer there was a click and his own voice instructed him to leave a message.

"No." He slammed down the receiver.

His cell phone was still on. It wouldn't ring five times if they'd shut it off or if the battery had run down. Why would they ignore it? Besides, they had to talk to him. How would they get any ransom if they didn't talk to him? Isn't that what they wanted? Yes, they had to talk to him. It was in their best interest to talk to him.

He dialed again, punching in the numbers quickly as if he might trick his fingers from shaking. He took a deep breath, ignored the acid backing up into his throat. The phone rang and rang until yet another click, then, "This is Henry Lee, please leave a message at the tone."

CHAPTER
62

When Maggie opened her hotel room door she had to stop herself from smiling. Nick Morrelli smelled as good as he looked, fresh from a shower, his hair still wet and tousled. He hadn't taken time to shave but the dark stubble only made him look more handsome, made those damn charming dimples even more pronounced. He'd changed into blue jeans and replaced his shirt and tie with a crew-neck sweater, baby blue that matched his eyes and made them sparkle. Leave it to Morrelli, she couldn't help thinking, to capitalize on every opportunity.

Maggie was still dressed in the hospital scrubs. She hadn't taken time to change. There was too much to do. No time to waste. Plus the cotton scrubs were comfortable.

"Room service shut down at one," she said as she led Nick into her room. "But the front desk clerk brought up some leftovers."

She pointed at a tray with an assortment of fruit, cheeses and crackers on the desk.

"Help yourself," she told him as she grabbed a couple of grapes.

"Wow, that was nice of them."

"It's amazing the service a doctor garners," she said, tugging on the hem of the blue scrub top.

"Very smart. I'll have to remember that. Dressing like a lawyer gets you nothing free."

She smiled as she went back to her place in the corner where two wingback chairs sat side by side, a floor lamp between them. She'd moved one of the bedside tables in front of her chair where she could leave her laptop. Almost everything else in the room remained the same. Her suitcase still lay on the otherwise untouched bed.

Nick loaded a paper plate with chunks of melon, grapes, strawberries, cubes of cheese and a line of crackers. Maggie tried not to watch as he performed a balancing act while he crossed the room to the other wingback chair. He glanced at her with a sheepish smile.

"I can't even remember the last time I ate," he said, sliding his laptop case from under his arm to the cushion of the chair.

Maggie made room on the table for him to set the plate down.

"I know. We had to leave The Rose and Crown before we got a chance to order."

"Yeah, where did you leave Ceimo, by the way?"

"He's off doing me a favor."

"Really?"

Maggie checked his eyes. She recognized that look. He was jealous. He noticed that she could tell.

"Any word on your brother?" he asked.

Good change of subject. Mentioning the pub reminded Maggie of Patrick, too.

"No. He's been ignoring my calls. Hopefully he's somewhere warm and safe."

If Nick was expecting a longer explanation he didn't push for it.

"So what's the game plan here?" he asked, pointing to her laptop as he popped a cube of cheese into his mouth.

She had told him very little over the phone except that an informant had given her some information, she needed his help, and she wanted him to be a part of the task force.

"We have two hours before we meet with Kunze and Wurth downstairs. They're already working on some details. In the meantime I'm plowing through some files and court documents and I thought who better to give me a hand than an attorney."

"Especially one you can ply with free food."

"Exactly."

He put his plate aside, moved his laptop and sat down in the chair next to her where he could see what was on the computer screen.

"You think this has something to do with the Oklahoma City bombing?"

"Not my idea. Someone else suggested it. In fact, the informant I met with told me the mastermind of this bombing implied that he was John Doe #2. Absurd, I know. Most likely he said it only for the effect, but I still have to check it out. I'm looking for John Doe #2 suspects to see if anyone accused or suspected could possibly be this bomber. How much do you know about the Oklahoma City bombing?"

"I remember at the time being freaked out. There were rumors that McVeigh had been scoping out the federal building in Omaha before he chose Oklahoma City. Plus, Junction City, Kansas, is only a couple hundred miles from Omaha."

"So you're familiar with some of the details." And she was pleased he still remembered some of those details.

Junction City, Kansas, was where McVeigh and Nichols rented the Ryder truck they used to contain and transport their mobile bomb.

"I started teaching law at UNL the year before McVeigh's execution. The whole thing made a good case study. The guy was a defense attorney's nightmare."

"Because he admitted to planning and carrying out the plot?" Maggie tapped her laptop's keyboard to bring up the document she'd just read.

"His first attorney...Jones, I think. I can't recall his name," Nick started then scratched at his jaw, trying to remember.

"Stephen Jones."

"Jones claimed McVeigh wasn't being honest with him. He changed his story even when they talked privately. Jones believed there were others involved. Not just Terry Nichols."

"And McVeigh was protecting them?"

"Or McVeigh wanted his own role to be elevated. Sort of fit with the notion that he wanted to be a martyr."

"No one's claiming to be a martyr here. In fact, no one's making any claims for this one," Maggie said with a shrug. "I've been sorting through file after file. If it is the same guy he didn't use the same M.O. I can't find anything that's similar about this bombing and Oklahoma City. The bombs alone were dramatically different. Four thousand eight hundred pounds of ammonium nitrate and jet fuel stuffed into a Ryder rental truck is a huge contrast to three backpacks."

She ran her fingers through her hair, resisting the urge to yank. This felt like a waste of time. Henry Lee hadn't given her anything to go on.

"Bomb-making technology's changed in...what is it? Fifteen years since Oklahoma City? Maybe he didn't need a Ryder truck this time."

She looked over at Nick. He was right in a sense. Post 9/11, three backpacks stuffed with explosives in the middle of a crowded mall would possibly be as damaging to the American psyche as 4,800 pounds of ammonium nitrate and jet fuel.

"I have to tell you," Nick started again and paused. "I never thought John Doe #2 was an absurd idea."

"Really?"

"Too many coincidences. I know eye witnesses are notoriously unreliable but there were too many people who swore they saw someone with McVeigh. Someone who didn't come close to fitting the description of Terry Nichols. Just a lot of unanswered questions."

"I never would have pegged Nick Morrelli for a conspiracy theorist."

"If the case was so clear-cut why are you bothering to go through this stuff? Why not dismiss what the guy said?"

She sat back and let out a frustrated sigh. Her eyes felt swollen, her wounded side wouldn't stop aching.

"Because I have nothing else. A.D. Kunze is doing a background check on the informant. Wurth is looking to see if there've been warnings or bomb threats at any of the airports. All the informant gave me was a warning. Another attack. Tomorrow."

She let it sink in, watching Nick rub at his jaw like someone had punched him. Yes, that was what it felt like. Being punched without warning.

"He told me it'll be an airport," she continued, pulling herself back to the front of the chair and clicking up the list Henry Lee had downloaded to her e-mail address. She had gone over it at least a dozen times trying to find some hidden clue as to why these seven were chosen and which one would be the target.

"He gave me a list," she told Nick, "but didn't give me

a clue as to which airport will be hit. Wurth is trying to warn all of them, but where do we send extra reinforcements?"

She hadn't noticed that Nick had edged forward to get a closer look, his brow furrowed, his arm leaning against her arm.

"Where did you get this?"

"Why?"

"I've seen this list before. This exact list."

CHAPTER
63

A thunderstorm of noise raged above. Rebecca had no idea what her captors were doing. It sounded like claps of thunder. She imagined sledgehammers against metal. Glass shattered. Heavy objects banged against the floor, or what was her ceiling. She wouldn't have been surprised to see something crashing through the wood rafters.

She no longer cared what they were doing. As long as they stayed up there, they wouldn't be hurting her. She had searched the entire crawl space, hunched over, arms still twisted and tied behind her back. She tried to keep down the nausea of fear. The overwhelming smell of gasoline burned her lungs and gagged her. It brought on the dry heaves. Nothing in her stomach except acid. All she wanted was something sharp—a left-behind tool, scissors, something jagged, anything—to cut the plastic tie that bound her wrists together.

There was nothing. The empty gas cans. Some shelves. A monstrosity of a furnace rumbled in the corner. Rebecca stared at it. The huge metal box had rusted on the bottom. Pipes going in and out of the contraption had been piecemealed together. She looked closely for bolts or screws that might be protruding. Then she found a bent piece of metal at one of the corners that made up the furnace's storage cabinet. Someone had hammered it back into place but it still stuck out, battered metal, the edges ragged…and sharp.

Excitement dared to shove aside the nausea.

The bent metal was a bit high. She'd need to do some maneuvering to back up to it and raise her arms up. Pain shot through her wounded arm and Rebecca had to stop. Had to sit down. She waited it out. Steadied her breath. Then she tried again, slowly raising her arms up behind her. She'd have to bring her wrists high enough to bring the plastic down onto the sharp metal corner. She could do it but could she keep her arms raised for that long while she rubbed against the jagged edge, using it like a serrated knife?

Just a little higher. She almost had it when all the noise from above came to a sudden stop.

She brought her arms down and waited, listening. Maybe they would start up again. They might be taking a break. Or leaving. Could they be leaving? She heard voices. Raised voices. An argument. Then the trapdoor started to creak open.

Rebecca scooted farther into the corner though she knew there wasn't anywhere to hide. If she had only a few more minutes she could have cut her wrists free and at least been able to defend herself. She'd kick this time, she decided. And scream. She didn't care if no one heard her.

The light from the open trapdoor had a bluish tint, not as glaring as she'd expected but she still found herself squinting after being in the dim-lit crawl space. She tried to slow her breathing so she could listen, but her heart pounded in her ears.

Someone was coming down. She could see shadows hovering over the opening. The voices were louder but she couldn't make out the words. A scuffle, rubber soles squeaking against linoleum, dragging or being dragged. Then without warning a body tumbled down through the hole, thumping hard against the concrete.

The trapdoor slammed shut and tight, this time closing off all light, but not before Rebecca recognized the motionless body. It was Dixon.

CHAPTER 64

Nick realized it was silly—okay, even childish—but despite all the stress and urgency he still felt disappointed. Maggie had called him to help, not because she needed a friend, not because she wanted to lean on him, but only because he was a lawyer and he'd be able to sort through the files and court documents quickly and efficiently. Well, it seemed his help might pay off beyond her expectations.

"You've seen this exact list of airports?" She sounded like she didn't believe him.

"Two weeks ago. UAS—United Allied Security sent me to a seminar on terrorist attacks. It was part of my training for the new job position. Mostly the basics—what to look for, how better to prepare and assist those facilities where UAS provides security systems or equipment."

Nick had learned a lot at the seminar but he didn't like that it sounded like a sales conference, even including a guide on how to convince clients to upgrade their old systems. At the time, he thought some of the scenarios they presented seemed a bit far-fetched and wondered if they were simply using scare tactics to increase revenues and bonuses for UAS.

"And you saw this list at your seminar?"

"It's a list of the airports being pitched upgrades."

"Being pitched what exactly?"

"At shopping malls UAS provides security personnel and equipment. All airport security is now under TSA but our company—at least for those airports under contract with us—maintains and replaces all the security equipment."

"Like the scanners?"

"Scanners, cameras, metal detectors, even the wands. But the pitch wasn't only for upgrading current equipment. The plan called for a whole new security package in the passenger arrival and departure areas."

She looked like she didn't understand.

"Right now most airports don't have much security in the ticketing or baggage claim areas. You don't see a camera until you get to the security checkpoint area."

"We're protecting the passengers in the air but not on the ground," she said, nodding.

"Exactly. UAS has been pushing for airports to have metal detectors and cameras in those outside perimeter areas."

"Why were these seven chosen?"

"That, I don't know."

Maggie was pacing the length of the hotel room, a nervous habit Nick had forgotten.

"Where did *you* get the list?" he asked her, though he realized she probably couldn't and wouldn't tell him.

"Who owns United Allied Security?" she asked instead of answering.

"I believe the holding company is HL Enterprises."

"As in Henry Lee Enterprises?" She stopped pacing to

stare at him, only it wasn't Nick she was seeing. Something had struck a chord.

"Yeah, that's right. HL Enterprises already owns several companies that are security related, one that produces the equipment, another one that designs and builds structures. I think they took over UAS a couple of years ago. You know how that works—Lee infused a truckload of cash in exchange for the majority voting stock."

She started pacing again. This time Nick watched. He tried to piece together where she was going with all this.

"You think UAS is the target of this group?" Even as he asked it he didn't think the idea made sense.

Maggie didn't look like she discounted the idea. Instead, she stopped again. This time she sat down next to him so she could look at the list she'd left open on her computer screen. She turned and reached over to put her hand on his arm. Waited for his eyes.

"I asked for your help because I need someone I can trust to help figure this out."

It took Nick off guard. He knew his face registered his surprise before he could control it.

"I don't trust A.D. Kunze. I had to tell him everything but I don't trust what—if anything—he'll do with the information simply because it's coming from me."

"What is it with that guy?"

"He blames Tully and me for Cunningham's death."

"That's ridiculous."

"Yes, it is, but he's interim director and he has the ability to make us miserable. I think that's the only reason I'm here. He knew this would be an impossible profiling assignment. I think he wanted me to fail. Even the parking lot fiasco, I think he expected me to screw up. You saw those surveillance videos. Very unlikely that we'd ID those young men from the videos or from any profile I'd come up with. And here's the thing," she said, gripping his arm now, "it didn't matter."

"What do you mean it didn't matter?"

"It didn't matter who the young men were that carried the backpacks. They were incidentals. They were cutaways." There was an urgency in her eyes, a frenetic pace to her words as if she was thinking out loud and Nick was simply there to hear it.

"Back in their dorm room they'll find Web sites in their computer caches for how to make bombs," she continued. "They may even find traces of bomb-making material. But no matter how much time and effort we put into finding out who Chad Hendricks and Tyler Bennett were, or if Patrick was even involved, none of it will matter. The cutaways won't lead us to who really did this. They can't lead us, because they didn't know who planned this. They didn't even know what was planned for them. There is no path because the Project Manager didn't leave one. He took care of everything."

"Wait a minute. Who exactly is *the Project Manager?*"

"That's what I need your help in finding out. If I can't connect him to any of the John Doe #2 suspects then I need to try and figure out where he's going to attack next."

CHAPTER
65

Maggie suggested they turn on the TV. She wanted some background noise as long as that noise didn't include news alerts or footage of her chase scene or interviews with neighbors who knew Chad or Tyler. Nick handled the assignment by stopping at a channel that was playing Christmas movies all weekend to celebrate the beginning of the holiday season.

"One of my favorites," he said, causing Maggie look up long enough to identify Ralphie in *A Christmas Story*. Why was she not surprised that a movie about a little boy wanting a Red Rider BB gun was Nick Morrelli's favorite.

They had an hour until they met Kunze and Wurth downstairs. Maggie still hoped to find something, anything that might steer them in the right direction. While she and Nick sifted through court documents and FBI files online she kept trying to put some rhyme or reason to the Project Manager's choice of airport.

Nick had made a good point about the impact of the attack. The number of casualties may not be his priority. Was he more interested in the effect on the American psyche? A crowded shopping center in the middle of the country the day after Thanksgiving. That was something everyone could relate to, making it even more frightening because of that. It wasn't a ritzy resort, a five-star hotel, a nightclub or casino. A shopping center in the heartland struck at the very heart of every single American who would be thinking, *"That could have happened to me."*

Maggie brought up the list of airports on her computer screen, again. Was there something equally telling in which airport the Project Manager had chosen? The list—according to Henry Lee—hadn't been written in any order:

McCarran International Airport, Las Vegas, Nevada

General Mitchell International Airport, Milwaukee, Wisconsin

Salt Lake City International Airport, Salt Lake City, Utah

Sky Harbor International Airport, Phoenix, Arizona

Cleveland-Hopkins International Airport, Cleveland, Ohio

Reagan Washington National Airport, Washington, D.C.

Detroit Metropolitan Wayne County Airport, Detroit, Michigan

"Believe it or not, Las Vegas is the number one busiest airport for the Thanksgiving weekend." Nick interrupted her thoughts, glancing over at her computer screen.

"Why doesn't that surprise me?"

"It'd be a pretty big impact."

She considered it then shook her head.

"I don't think he chose Vegas."

"Gut instinct?" Nick asked.

"Think about how you prefaced it with 'believe it or not.' It might be a reality, but not everyone would relate to choosing a gambling casino over Grandma's house for

Thanksgiving. He's hoping the impact here is the idea that it could happen to anyone."

Nick pointed the remote at the TV and muted Ralphie right before he got a mouthful of Lava soap.

"What about another Midwest hit? Could he be looking for someplace close? Milwaukee's about a five- or six-hour drive. Detroit's a bit farther. Maybe ten hours."

"Too difficult a drive in that snowstorm. My guess, he was at the airport and gone before they were putting the wounded in ambulances."

"There were flight delays because of the snow," Nick said. "Ceimo mentioned the state fire inspector was stuck in Chicago and Yarden's supervisor was trying to get back from New Jersey."

"How much in advance was this storm predicted?"

Nick furrowed his brow, giving it serious thought.

"They were talking about it early in the week," Nick told her. "I only remember because I promised Christine I'd go with her to buy a Christmas tree on Friday. I was hoping the storm would make her cancel." He shrugged. "It's a good day for college football."

She nodded and smiled, remembering her own plans for Friday. Was that only yesterday?

"Anyway, the storm ended up missing Omaha. Do you think he factored in the snowstorm?"

Her turn to shrug.

"I'm looking at a logical process of elimination. How many of these airports are hubs for an airline?"

Nick leaned closer and took a look. Pointing with his index finger, he went over the list, one by one.

"Milwaukee is Midwest Airlines, Salt Lake City and Cleveland are Delta, Sky Harbor is Southwest and US Airways. Detroit was a limited hub for Northwest. Why? Are you thinking it might be a hub?"

"Actually I'm thinking the opposite. You said UAS has been trying to get airports to upgrade the arrival and departure areas, right? At an airport that's a hub aren't the majority of their passengers simply making a connecting flight?"

She caught the glint in his eyes as he followed her logic.

"So most passengers wouldn't be going through the ticketing area or picking up baggage," she continued. "Not a big enough impact. And Reagan National on the Sunday after a holiday will be a good deal of politicians returning to Capitol Hill."

"You just eliminated every airport on the list."

"Both Las Vegas and Phoenix would be destination airports?" she asked, thinking out loud and not really expecting an answer from Nick. "Someplace where families would go for Thanksgiving for a treat to get away. Maybe get out of the winter cold."

"I just remembered something," he said. "Airports depend on state and federal revenues so we usually take that into consideration when we're talking to them about upgrades. Phoenix is being considered for a chunk of federal dollars. Something to do with Homeland Security. The city's number two in the world, second only to Mexico City, for kidnappings."

Maggie remembered what Henry Lee said about his group influencing government policies.

"It has to be Phoenix."

She hugged him, excited, relieved. She kissed his cheek, but his lips found hers. She let herself sink into him, maybe a moment too long. By the time she pulled away she was out of breath.

"Nick, this isn't a good idea. We're both exhausted."

"I'm not that exhausted."

He ran his hand over her shoulder, fingers caressing the back of her neck. His other hand wrapped around her waist, gently nudging her back against him, enough to show her he wasn't too exhausted. His lips brushed her neck, her earlobe…maybe she wasn't too exhausted either.

A knock at the door decided for them.

"Damn. Can't we ignore it?" But he let her pull away.

"Maybe it's housekeeping?"

"Too early," he said. "And room service doesn't begin until 6:00 a.m. I checked."

She crossed the room, instinctively reminding herself where she had left her Smith & Wesson.

When she checked the peephole she had to do a double take. She was exhausted. Was it possible her imagination was playing tricks on her?

She undid the locks and pulled the door wide open.

"Hi," Patrick said, looking embarrassed and shy. His hair was tousled, clothes wrinkled.

"How in the world did you find me?" she asked him.

"I used housekeeping's direct line to the front desk. 'Ms. O'Dell needs more towels. What room is she in?'" He said it with a convincing Spanish accent.

She didn't say another word. Instead she followed her instinct this time and simply hugged him.

CHAPTER
66

Rebecca was sure Dixon was dead.

She couldn't see him in the dark. There was no sliver of light this time from the sealed trapdoor. She listened for moans or breathing but heard only the rumble of the furnace.

She hunched over, paralyzed in the corner. With her hands bound behind her, there was nothing she could do for him if he was alive and hurt.

"Dixon?" she called for the second or third time. Her voice sounded foreign to her, strained and small.

There was no response.

She searched in the dark and found the jagged metal on the corner of the furnace. She stretched, made contact. It hurt to hold her arms at that high of an angle. She hooked the plastic between her wrists onto the metal and started rubbing it back and forth. Her wounded arm throbbed but she kept pulling and sawing the plastic tie against the sharp edge. She had no idea if she was making any progress.

By now her eyes had adjusted to the dark. It wasn't pitch-black. She could make out Dixon's body. Still no movement. She was too far away to see if he was breathing. Her nerves were raw. Every little sound made her catch her breath, stopping to listen. The silence above should have comforted her. Silence meant no one would be coming down to hurt her like they had Dixon. Instead, it set her on edge. Why would they just leave her to be found or to escape?

She kept sawing. God, her arm hurt. Her lungs felt on fire from the gasoline fumes. She wanted to scream and shout. Get angry because it was better than feeling afraid.

"What the hell did you get us into, Dixon Lee?" she yelled.

"Becca?"

She jumped, pulling her wrists down, and heard a pop. Her wrists were free.

"Dixon?"

"Where are you?"

She could see him move, a shadowed bulk still lying on the concrete floor.

"I'm here," she told him as she felt her way over to him. On closer inspection she saw that his arms were bound behind him. He was struggling to sit up, twisting and rocking.

"Are you hurt?" she asked.

"I'm okay. Sore. Maybe a bum ankle. How 'bout you? Are you okay?"

She touched his shoulder, startling him.

"You got your wrists undone."

"We'll do yours, too. Let me just check and make sure nothing's broken," she told him as she ran her fingers over his arms.

"There's no time, Becca. We've got to get out of here."

He struggled to stand up and fell against her. She caught him by the waist as he slid to his knees. Her fingers were wet and sticky.

"Oh my God, Dixon, you're bleeding."

"Becca, we've got to get out. They've got the whole place rigged to blow."

CHAPTER
67

Maggie braced herself for A.D. Kunze's reaction. From Patrick's initial telling she knew he might have information that could be helpful. She just wasn't sure Kunze would see it that way. Charlie Wurth saved her again. He called Chief Merrick and asked him to send a police sketch artist instead of an arresting officer.

"It might not do any good," she told them. "If the man Patrick saw is the Project Manager he'll make sure that he looks different."

"I won't forget those eyes," Patrick said. "Or the way he walked."

"Unfortunately, he can change both."

"He may not even be there if he uses another group of young people," Kunze reminded them.

"I don't think he'll use cutaways this time," Maggie said, cautiously watching for Kunze to disagree. He cocked his head to the side, encouraging her to continue. "He doesn't have to go to the trouble. He's already set the stage. Another bombing this soon. Everyone will be looking for young, white, college-aged males."

It was just the five of them: Maggie, Patrick, Nick, Kunze and Wurth in the room set aside for the investigators. Ceimo was scheduled to join them. The sun was out today, streaming through the window, a welcome sight. Maggie couldn't help but notice how beautiful the glittering snowy landscape was.

"So what are you predicting he will do?" Wurth asked.

When she turned away from the window and back to them, they were all watching her, waiting.

"The bomb expert," Wurth continued. "She said the detonator he used was similar to the plans she saw for a dirty bomb. Should I be telling my people that's what we might have here?"

Maggie crossed her arms over her chest. She had changed into trousers and a knit sweater but left her matching blazer in her room. Now she wished she had it. They were looking to her for instruction, for guidance. What if she was wrong? Even Kunze was waiting for her to give them some direction.

"I don't think it'll be a dirty bomb. He's looking for psychological impact, not total carnage. He had the opportunity here at the mall. There could have easily been hundreds killed." She stopped, expecting comments. There were none. "My best guess is that it will be a suitcase bomb. He'll bring it in himself and leave it somewhere in the crowded ticket area or in baggage claim."

"If he puts it on a baggage carousel there's no way we'll find it in time," Wurth said, shoving his shirtsleeves up. "Christ almighty, this is not good."

"That's why we need to catch him as soon as he enters the airport."

"But you said yourself, he'll look different. Even if we have a sketch," Kunze said.

"I know I'll recognize him." Patrick startled all of them. They had forgotten about him, waiting in the corner for the police sketch artist to arrive. "Just put me someplace where I can watch."

"You're not going to Phoenix with us," Maggie said and immediately regretted that she sounded like an over-protective big sister.

She had already explained her rationale for Sky Harbor being the target. Wurth hadn't disagreed with the logic, but said he was putting federal air marshals in every airport on the list.

"You said yourself," Patrick argued, "that he thinks he doesn't need to use anyone else now because they'll be looking for young, white, college guys. So maybe he won't walk differently. Maybe he won't need to disguise himself. I'm telling you, I'll never forget those eyes."

"It couldn't hurt," Wurth said. "I say we bring the kid along."

CHAPTER
68

The trapdoor wouldn't move. Rebecca tried to find something other than her hands to ram it with while Dixon tried to saw his plastic tie. At least she had found a light switch, although the single, low-wattage bulb set between the rafters lit only the area below it.

Dixon had told her not to worry about his bleeding. "Just a flesh wound," he called it and Rebecca couldn't help thinking he sounded like one of the heroes in the graphic novels he loved to read.

"How do you know they rigged the place?"

"They told me. They laughed about it." He sounded out of breath. "It was right after they let my granddad's phone ring and ring. They told him if he called back at a certain time he'd get to talk to me again. But they wouldn't let me answer. It was still ringing when they threw the phone up on one of the shelves where I couldn't reach it."

He shook his head, then started sawing at the plastic again.

Then Rebecca smelled something besides gasoline. It was seeping down from the air vents.

"Dixon. Do you smell that?"

He sniffed the air.

"Holy crap," he said. "Smoke." He tried to saw faster.

Rebecca banged on the trapdoor, using her battered hands. What if the fire was already in the room above? They didn't have to rig a bomb. With all the spilled gasoline, all they had to do was light a match. It'd explode once the flame reached the fumes down here. It was hopeless.

She heard Dixon's plastic snap. He rushed over to help her. That's when they heard someone yelling above. Boots stomped. Wood cracked. Maybe they had decided to come back and kill them before they left them to burn. Rebecca crouched with Dixon in the corner.

The trapdoor started to split and the metal point of an ax came through. The smell of smoke was stronger. The voices louder. More boots thumping. A bright light shined down as the last of the trapdoor came away.

"Dixon Lee," someone shouted. "Are you down there?"

Rebecca held onto his arm as Dixon started to crawl forward. Above them, surrounding the hole where the trapdoor had been, were three men in SWAT team uniforms.

CHAPTER
69

Nick almost didn't recognize David Ceimo. He came into the hotel conference room wearing a leather bomber jacket and aviator sunglasses pushed up on top of his thick mass of hair. And he was smiling.

Patrick had just finished with the police sketch artist, who didn't really sketch but manipulated the bomber's face on a computer screen, using a special computer program. Wurth had been on the phone nonstop, using one of the hotel's landlines instead of his cell phone. Kunze and Maggie pored over more files. Everyone, however, stopped what they were doing when Ceimo walked into the room.

"Just got the call. We have him," he said directly to Maggie. "He's alive and safe."

"Thank God."

Nick glanced around. Seemed Maggie was the only one who knew what Ceimo was talking about.

"Some of the bomber's cohorts kidnapped Henry Lee's grandson earlier today," Ceimo explained.

"Dixon?" Patrick shot up. "Becca was with Dixon."

"She's still with him. She's safe," Ceimo told him. "They had them locked up in the basement of a vacant office building. They must have been using it as a makeshift command center. Had computers, cables, wireless equipment—the works."

"Was there anything left behind that might tell us where the next attack is planned?" Wurth asked.

"Everything was smashed. The kid—Dixon, said they had portable drives on the computers that they bagged up and took with them. The basement reeked with gasoline. They started a small fire in one of the hallways. Probably expected the whole place to blow up. And it would have had the SWAT team gotten there a few minutes later."

Nick watched Maggie. She wasn't surprised by any of what Ceimo was telling them. This must have been the favor she'd asked of him.

"How did you know where they were?" Nick asked.

He noticed the look Ceimo and Maggie exchanged before Ceimo answered, as if he were getting permission.

"Dixon had his grandfather's cell phone. The kidnappers left it on for Mr. Lee to call. We were able to track their location by using the cell phone's internal GPS signal."

"Son of a bitch," Kunze muttered.

"Outsmarted the assholes," Ceimo said with that same smile that he had on his face when he came into the room. "They thought they had Mr. Lee under their thumb, so they got a bit cocky leaving the cell phone on. The boy said they taunted him with its ringing. They had no intention of returning him to his grandfather. Or the girl. Unfortunately, the kidnappers were gone before we got there." He pointed to the police sketch artist. "The kids are giving us descriptions."

"And Mr. Lee?" Maggie wanted to know.

"I've sent someone over to the hospital to let him know.

He won't be able to see Dixon until after this is over. They're probably still having him watched."

"Wait a minute. Henry Lee? Is that who we're talking about?" Nick asked Maggie. "The head of HL Enterprises, the owner of United Allied Security, he was your informant?"

She glanced around the room, then nodded.

CHAPTER 70

Maggie gave one of her hotel room key cards to Patrick.

"Go get some sleep," she told him. Actually it didn't take much convincing once Ceimo promised to let him talk to Rebecca.

Charlie Wurth recommended they all go get a few hours of sleep. There was nothing more they could do here. As soon as Wurth informed Senator Foster about a second plot, he offered the use of his jet, but it wouldn't be ready to take off for Phoenix until late afternoon. Wurth, himself, didn't leave, continuing to work the phones, a landline and his cell phone, all the while punching keys on his laptop computer.

Before Maggie could pack up her own laptop, Nick was at her side.

"I can't believe you didn't tell me your informant was Henry Lee."

He sounded upset. She checked his eyes. He was hurt.

"I told you I couldn't. At least not until we knew his grandson was safe."

"But Ceimo knew."

She took a deep breath. Is that what this was about? A spark of jealousy between two old football rivals. Just when she thought Nick Morrelli could actually be a grown-up. Back in her hotel room, for a minute or two, she thought perhaps he had changed.

"He was able to help," she explained, "using the governor's influence."

"If you honestly trusted me, you would have told me it was Henry Lee. But because I work for one of his companies...what'd you think, I would run off and tell my boss, Al Banoff?"

"Wait a minute," Maggie said, putting up her hands in surrender. "I didn't even know Mr. Lee was the majority owner of UAS."

"Yeah, that's what you said." He didn't believe her.

"Why would I lie? Is that what you're insinuating? That I lied?"

"I don't know, did you? You could trust Ceimo, but not me. Maybe you thought I was somehow involved in all of this...this ridiculous plot to strong-arm malls and airports to upgrade their security?"

"Of course not." She was getting impatient. "If anything, they sent you to make sure their plot wasn't revealed."

That stopped him. As soon as she saw his jaw clench tight and twitch with tension, she knew she had said the wrong thing.

"I didn't mean it that way," she started to apologize. "I only meant that they may have taken advantage of sending someone new."

"Someone green. Someone who didn't know what the fuck he was doing."

"Nick."

"Forget about it." He waved her off. "There're more important things to worry about right now."

But she could tell he was still upset as he turned to leave, jaw still tight, shoulders squared. He didn't just walk away from her, he left the room.

When she turned back, A.D. Kunze was there.

He pointed with his chin at the exit. "Don't worry about it. He'll get over it." He lifted a file folder he had in his hand. "I have something I want you to see."

"What is it?"

He looked around the room. Ceimo had left. Patrick and Nick were gone. Wurth was the only one and he was busy multitasking in the corner. Still, Kunze motioned for her to sit down at one of the tables in the opposite corner.

"It's a debriefing file." He handed it to her. "From Oklahoma City."

"An agent who worked the scene?"

He nodded.

"How did you get it?" Usually debriefing files weren't easily accessed. Sometimes debriefings, especially in cases with gruesome casualties, were done more for the mental health of the agent than as a source of information.

"Never mind that. I downloaded a copy. Take it back with you. Sift through it."

She opened the file folder. At first glance, the blacked out names, an assortment of inked-in rectangles, were what caught her attention.

"We had 43,000 lead sheets," Kunze told her. "Interviewed 35,000 witnesses. It was overwhelming. You can't even imagine. Some of the witnesses..." He shook his head, remembering. "I did some of the early interviews. I can tell you about them as if the interview was last week. Rodney Johnson. The guy was in a parking lot across from Fifth Street. He saw two men running from the federal building, in step, one behind the other. Couldn't figure out why they were running. A minute later the blast blew out the windows in his pickup.

"He gave a description of both men. One fit Tim McVeigh. The other had an olive complexion, dark hair, muscular build, Carolina Panthers' ball cap. Not even close to being Terry Nichols.

"Same thing in Junction City, Kansas, where McVeigh got the Ryder truck. Joanna Van Buren at the Subway shop said there were three men who came in for lunch. She remembered because she had to break a fifty-dollar bill for McVeigh. She called us almost immediately when the story broke. Another agent and I went to Junction City. Interviewed her and two other clerks. They ID'd McVeigh, gave vague descriptions of the other two. Again, one of them had an olive complexion, dark hair, muscular build. The sandwich shop had a security camera. I thought we lucked out. I confiscated the video."

He must have seen the anticipation in Maggie's eyes as she sat up, because he was shaking his head.

"The video disappeared before I had a chance to even look at it. Don't even ask," he told her. "Over twenty witnesses saw McVeigh with someone other than Terry Nichols. The descriptions were amazingly similar."

"But there was a sketch that was released early on."

"Here's the thing." Kunze hesitated. "Most of the interviews were done before that sketch was even made. Eyewitnesses are often unreliable. That's what we're told, right? But over a dozen people describing what sounds like the exact same guy?"

"So what are you telling me? That John Doe #2 was real? That he may be the Project Manager?"

"I can't tell you whether or not he was real. We were

never given the opportunity to find out. Are you familiar with Occam's razor?"

"A little." The exhaustion made it difficult to concentrate. She rubbed at her eyes as she said, "It has something to do with the simplest explanation being the correct one."

He nodded, looking at his hands before folding them together on top of the table. He intertwined the fingers.

"That's what we were told to follow," he finally said. "Occam's razor is the principle that if you have two or more theories and the conclusion is the same, the simplest of the theories is usually the correct one. All of our theories, no matter how many men McVeigh was seen with or whether he was seen over and over again with this same olive complexion man, the conclusion always included McVeigh. So you razor out all the things you can't explain, all the stuff that requires speculation, any hypothetical conclusions."

"In other words, you were held back from finding out who John Doe #2 really was."

"Certain people weren't interested in a complex plot. As soon as they had McVeigh there was an urgency to tailor our investigation to ensure his prosecution. We had to at least nail him, right? Anything beyond that…razor it down." He paused, watching her eyes as if he needed to know how all this information was registering.

Maggie simply waited.

"Look, I have no idea if this Project Manager could even be the same man," Kunze said. "That doesn't really matter. But the reference to Oklahoma City is unsettling. I think it means that this is something more than a greedy security corporation. It's something more than causing a commotion, a wake-up call by switching jamming devices with bombs."

"You don't think this Project Manager is a rogue terrorist taking advantage of the opportunity?"

He shrugged.

"After Oklahoma City there was a journalist—" Kunze's voice got quieter and he leaned closer "—who suggested McVeigh and Nichols were actually duped by a federal informant acting as a provocateur."

"Are you suggesting the government provoked the Oklahoma City bombing?"

"Not the government as in the administration. God no. But maybe someone within the government. Someone with enough power and political ties. Someone upset that we virtually ignored the warning of the first World Trade Center bombing in '93. Someone who thought there should be a wake-up call. Sound familiar?"

"You believe Henry Lee's secret group exists?"

Another big-shouldered shrug.

"You thought it was CAP," she reminded him.

"He told you it was a smokescreen, a distraction. He didn't deny a connection. Could be how they recruited those college kids. They may have used CAP just like they used those kids."

"And they being…?"

"Is it so far-fetched to believe there might be other businessmen like Henry Lee who started with honorable intentions then got sidetracked? He mentioned business contracts. There were a helluva lot of contracts that came after Oklahoma City to reconstruct federal buildings, add security equipment, personnel."

"I have to tell you," she told Kunze. "I'm not much for conspiracy theories." Perhaps she was simply exhausted but she couldn't connect the dots Kunze was laying out in front of her.

"Just keep in mind, there's some major legislation

coming down concerning Homeland Security. Not just the dollars for Phoenix. There're a couple of huge bills coming up for a vote, maybe before the holidays. I don't know all the details but it reinstates some stiff regulations for security, regulations that need to be in place before the beneficiaries receive any of the federal dollars attached to the bill."

"Let me get this straight." She braced her elbows on the table and laid her chin in her hands. "You think this Project Manager, by making a reference to Oklahoma City, was tipping his hat, so to speak? Perhaps revealing that, just like Oklahoma City, these bombings are being orchestrated as a government conspiracy?"

Kunze started to interrupt but she put up her hand. "Correction, not the government but a group of business-men with political ties, have hired a professional terrorist to carry out two fatal attacks just to move a bill through Congress?"

A.D. Kunze sat back and released a sigh. "You're right. It does sound far-fetched." He stood and stretched his arms above his head, rotating his thick neck back and forth and definitely putting an end to their conversation whether or not he was finished. Then as if it was an afterthought, he pointed to the file folder. "Do me a favor. Just skim through that."

CHAPTER
71

In flight
Leaving Minneapolis

Patrick had never been on a private jet before. The huge leather captain chairs swiveled and reclined. The walls were paneled, the floor carpeted. They were being served beverages in crystal glassware. The pewter coasters were indented into the wooden side table and had the Senator's initials, A.F., engraved. It was pretty amazing and yet all he could think about was his phone conversation with Rebecca.

It was short, way too short.

"I'm so sorry," was one of the first things she said. After all she had been through and she was apologizing to him.

"Dixon made me think you might be involved somehow," she explained. "He was scared. He made a mistake. I was scared. Can you ever forgive me?"

He was simply relieved to hear her voice, to know she was finally safe. He couldn't, however, tell her about

Phoenix. Couldn't explain what was going on, except that he would see her in a couple of days.

He looked around the inside of the plane, wondering what exactly he had gotten himself into. A couple of days ago he would have steered clear, content to be on the sidelines. He still wasn't sure why he wanted to do this, needed to do this.

Deputy Director Wurth and Mr. Morrelli were at the back of the plane. They had a map of Sky Harbor spread out on a table and were going over details. Assistant Director Kunze had taken one of the chairs on the other side of the aisle and was stretched out, fast asleep, or at least it sounded like it from his heavy breathing.

Maggie sat directly across from Patrick, staring out the window into the night. She had been reading what looked like poor photocopies of documents that had black rectangles stamped throughout the pages. Classified stuff, no doubt. He didn't think the documents held all her attention. She looked preoccupied, thinking about something else. But then how would he know? He kept telling himself that Maggie didn't know him at all. Yet how hard had he tried to get to know her?

One thing he did know—she wasn't happy that he was coming along.

"I guess I really just want to help," he said, out of the blue, almost as if he had only now found the answer for himself.

She looked over at him as if she had forgotten he was there.

"I don't want you to get hurt."

He smiled at that. Couldn't help it. He caught himself trying to hide it with a swipe of his fingers to his mouth. If she'd only seen what he had already gone through in the last twenty-four hours.

"What?" she asked, her voice sounding defensive.

"I've never had anyone worry about me."

"Your mom worries about you."

This time he laughed. She obviously didn't know his mom either. "I've worried about my mom for a lot more years than she's worried about me."

Her eyes met his and there was something he recognized before she looked away.

She glanced out the window again.

"We have more in common than either of us realize," she told him.

"Probably why I need to go along."

This time she smiled.

"I really can take care of myself," he told her and only hoped she never found out about the dryer incident.

They sat in silence, a bit awkward, but Patrick knew she was letting him control the silence. Leaving the decision to him and what, if anything, he wanted to share. Maybe it was time he told her some things about himself if he ever wanted her to get to know him.

"I changed my major," he said.

Before he could continue, she surprised him by saying, "I know. Fire Science. How do you like it?"

CHAPTER
72

Something nagged at Maggie ever since they'd left Minneapolis. She couldn't put her finger on it. Even Patrick's charm and boyish naivety couldn't distract her. She was pleased that he wanted to move their relationship beyond the barriers they had imposed, though both of them seemed to tiptoe around each other. He was a good kid, smart, kind and self-reliant. But she knew he had no idea what he was getting himself into. His adventure over the last day may have left him feeling invincible. But tracking professional killers was something that should be left to the professionals.

She'd already talked to Charlie Wurth about how they could utilize Patrick at Sky Harbor, but only at the lowest level of risk. She wanted him in her sights at all times. All of them would be connected with a wireless communication system. Not two-way radios that could be tapped into, but something limited only to their task force. They'd all wear Kevlar vests under their traveling clothes. And GPS tracking systems. She tried to put in place as many precautions as possible, but she knew if Patrick ended up getting hurt she'd never forgive herself.

She glanced at Nick poring over the maps with Wurth in the back of the plane. How could he believe she didn't trust him? That she'd lied to him? Who was she fooling? As soon as she had seen him sitting at the controls in front of the surveillance monitors and knew he was the investigator for the security company, she didn't trust his judgment. Whatever chemistry existed between them didn't seem to run deep enough to include trust and loyalty.

She had almost let herself get lost in their kiss, lost in Nick Morrelli's charm. It felt so right at the time, but there had to be something more, an anchor more solid than chemistry. Or was it simply her? Would she ever be able to trust a man enough to let him into her life? Had she not learned anything in the last two months?

Before boarding she had checked her voice messages. There was an early-morning one from Ben. He joked about her leaping over cars, said he was worried about her and to call when she got the opportunity. He didn't sound like a doctor simply worried about a patient. Outside of Gwen and her partner, R.J. Tully, she wasn't used to having someone worry about her. She wasn't used to having someone want to take care of her. She wasn't sure how she felt about it.

Suddenly she realized what was nagging her. It wasn't Patrick or Nick or even Ben. It was something A.D. Kunze had said earlier. Why couldn't she put her finger on it? She'd read a good deal of the debriefing file before realizing it was a debriefing of Special Agent Raymond Kunze. He'd failed to mention that not only had he conducted some of the early witness interviews, he was also one of the first agents on the scene.

She glanced over at him. He was stretched out and sleeping, a blanket pulled up to his chin. Fourteen years ago

Kunze would have been about her age, an experienced agent who had probably already seen his share of the horrors people could do to each other. But nothing prepares you for mass murder.

During their trip from D.C. yesterday he had mentioned Oklahoma City. He'd come to this scene at the personal request of the Minnesota governor and the state's senior senator and he'd even brought along a profiler to connect the dots. For someone who, after fourteen years, still believed that John Doe #2 assisted Timothy McVeigh and then disappeared into the Oklahoma City landscape, Kunze had been anxious to wrap up the mall bombing in a neat, simple package. Had he purposely tried to sway the investigation in the wrong direction by insisting they consider Citizens for American Pride, a fringe, white supremacist group? A group that had never perpetrated violence in the past. Had Kunze already known about Henry Lee's secret group? Or suspected that it existed?

Maggie pulled her laptop case out from under her seat and started rifling through the contents. She pulled out the file folder she'd received on their flight from D.C. Inside were the warnings or what Kunze and Senator Foster had considered warnings. The copies of memorandums were poor quality. They mentioned phone calls and e-mails, but there were no transcripts of the calls, no copies of the e-mails. The memorandums talked about vague warnings but went into great detail about the group called Citizens for American Pride, CAP for short. What Maggie was most interested in, was where the warnings had been sent. Who received the e-mails and phone calls? Why had Kunze been so convinced the group was responsible?

Finally on the last page, toward the bottom, there was a brief note, almost a footnote: "Approximate times of e-mails and phone calls not recorded by Senator Foster's staff."

So it had been the senator who had received the warnings.

Maggie slumped down in the leather chair, tapping the corner of the file folder against the chair arm. It was exhausting trying to figure out any of this. Henry Lee had told her that Citizens for American Pride was a smokescreen, a distraction. But Kunze still believed the group might be involved. He'd even suggested they may have been used.

There were a lot of things about this case that didn't add up, no matter how hard she tried to look for the obvious. Smokescreens, kidnapping, hired bombers and secret organizations.

Kunze had mentioned Occam's razor and now Maggie remembered another adage: Don't speculate about hypothetical components. The simplest answer was usually the correct one. Was Phoenix the simplest answer or mere speculation? Was it possible that they were headed to the wrong airport? Could the Project Manager have chosen Las Vegas?

She shifted in her captain's chair, sank the back of her head into the soft leather and closed her eyes. One thing A.D. Kunze didn't quite understand and William of Occam would never have considered or included in his principle was exactly what Maggie counted on—gut instinct. She'd bet her life on it any day of the week and hopefully she could count on it one more time.

CHAPTER
73

Everything had gone smoothly. No more glitches. Asante was pleased.

The crew in Minneapolis had disbanded, destroying or taking with them anything that could be incriminating. And if they had gotten sloppy, or even if they were detained, it didn't matter. None of them had met him or seen what he looked like. They knew absolutely nothing about him. He had a new SIM card in his cell phone. He'd even reprogrammed his computer. The numbers they had been using to reach him, no longer existed. There was no way to connect any of them to Asante, which was just another mark of a brilliant project manager. Even members of his crew were cutaways. No one would be able to reach him now. Not the people he'd hired, nor the men who had hired him. Everything was in place.

The white Chevy TrailBlazer he'd chosen from the Las Vegas airport's long-term parking lot had proven to be a comfortable ride. It had also been a plus that the SUV didn't have an OnStar navigation system. The owner had accidentally left a printout of his flight itinerary on the passenger seat. He wouldn't be returning until the following week.

As extra insurance, before Asante left the parking lot he drove around until he found another white Chevy SUV. The second one was an older model Chevy Blazer, but it had served his purpose. He exchanged the two SUVs' license plates easily in the middle of the night with no one around to notice.

Asante had driven straight through, all three hundred and fifty-nine miles with only one interruption. He'd exited his route to stop at a storage facility a few minutes after crossing the Nevada/Arizona border. The entire trip had taken him just over six hours.

Now he ate dinner in his hotel room, a feast by room service standards. He could see the airport from his window, continuous blinking lights as the last of the evening flights came in and went out. That was one thing he liked about Phoenix. You could see forever without buildings getting in the way. He wondered if the blast tomorrow morning could be seen from this very window.

Asante finished the last of his dessert, wiped his mouth with the cloth napkin and shoved the tray aside. Standing, he could see the hotel's parking lot from this window, too. The Pullmans were in the Chevy TrailBlazer, packed and ready. Everything else he needed for tomorrow he had pulled from his duffel bag and laid out on the second double bed.

He fingered the Carolina Panthers baseball cap. It was beginning to show some wear though he'd taken good care of it over the years. He'd never watched a Panthers game in his life. In fact, he'd bought the cap at a convenience store in Junction City, Kansas. It had been an impulse buy at the time. Asante didn't believe in lucky charms but this ordinary ball cap had come close to being one.

He rubbed his hands together and glanced around the room. Everything was in place. No glitches. He'd get a good night's sleep.

CHAPTER 74

Sunday, November 25
Sky Harbor International Airport
Phoenix, Arizona

Nick wished he had Jerry Yarden here to help him. The quirky little man had an eye for details and a knack for electronic security equipment. He would have had everything in place by now. Instead Nick had been at it since midnight, working with two security technicians, installing and preparing equipment he'd only just learned to operate a few weeks ago.

Because Sky Harbor had been one of the airports on UAS's list for equipment upgrades they had also been sent samples of the new system. Last night when they arrived at the airport, Nick had contacted UAS's manager on-site. The man had been taken off guard by the surprise visit but impressed with Nick's credentials. That he had the Deputy Director of Homeland Security along with him had probably helped. Nick obtained the sample equipment and the two technicians with only the explanation that they would be conducting a test. Then he set out to install the wireless cameras in the areas he and Charlie Wurth had selected. Areas that up until now didn't have cameras.

These new models were small but if the Project Manager was the professional they all expected him to be, Nick didn't want to take any chances that he'd notice them. His technicians took on the challenge with enthusiasm, looking for ways to hide or obscure the cameras while allowing them to have full functionality. Nick was pleased with the results, though none of the cameras would matter if he wasn't able to identify the Project Manager from the police artist's sketch. Just the thought made his heart pound and his palms sweat.

Wurth was being selective as to who he alerted and he'd convinced Nick that no one else under the employment of UAS should be included. Other than Henry Lee, they had no evidence that anyone at UAS was involved in the attack, but Wurth insisted they take the extra precaution. He didn't want to risk word trickling through the ranks and getting to the Project Manager. Nick agreed.

Wurth did, however, warn TSA. He had air marshals on-site. He had arranged for a bomb squad and sniper unit from Quantico to arrive last night. In the early morning hours while Nick and Wurth roamed around the airport, Wurth pointed out team coordinators for the bomb squad. They were dressed as housekeeping, busy securing their stations. Their carts were identical to the airport housekeeping staff, only—according to Wurth—these carts contained what Wurth called "safe containers" instead of bathroom cleaner.

Wurth had also pointed out a hallway that now was blocked off with UNDER CONSTRUCTION signs and sawhorses.

"There's an exit and armored vehicle stationed and ready to take the bomb to a vacant airstrip."

Nick liked how Charlie Wurth made it all sound so organized and simple. Like maybe it could really work, they could actually prevent this attack.

"We'll have all three terminals covered," Nick told Wurth as they finished their final pass-through. "We'll have limited views of the ticketing areas. Once he leaves those areas I won't be able to follow him."

"Understood."

"Here in Terminal 4 there are ticket kiosks on the second level." Nick pointed up the escalators. "The one to the right of the escalator is sort of hidden out of view. It'd be easy to leave a bag there and not have anyone notice for a short while."

"I'll get someone stationed to watch."

The two stood in front of the long line of US Airways counters. Both of them had their arms crossed over their chests, feet spread apart, standing tall and straight as they took one last look around. Staff had started to come in, opening doors, turning on computers. But it was still quiet compared to what it would be like an hour from now.

"We're ready," Wurth said without moving from his stance and sounding confident.

Nick simply nodded. He wondered if Charlie Wurth had problems with his heart banging against his rib cage.

CHAPTER 75

Terminal 4a
Sky Harbor International Airport

Maggie watched Patrick from above the ticket area. She stayed on the second floor, close to the rail, but away from the escalators. Looking down on him in his blue jeans and gray hooded sweatshirt, she couldn't shake the feeling of how much he looked like those college boys at Mall of America.

Wurth had equipped all of them with wireless headsets that slipped on over the ear and allowed them to communicate with each other while looking like ordinary passengers, talking on their cell phones. They agreed to keep conversation to a minimum but Maggie insisted Patrick do check-ins at fifteen-minute intervals.

"If I can't see you, I want to hear you," she told him earlier as she helped him into his Kevlar vest.

They had been wandering around for a couple of hours now, disguised as passengers, carry-on cases over their shoulders. Patrick had a worn duffel bag and a smartphone.

He stopped periodically to look like he was reading or sending text messages. An ordinary kid going back home or back to college after a Thanksgiving holiday. Maggie was impressed. He looked convincing despite his eyes wandering around the entire area, not stopping on any one face long enough to be suspicious. He was better at this than she expected.

Somewhere Nick was watching monitors that corresponded with the new wireless cameras he had installed, several in each terminal's ticket areas. He'd studied the sketch of the Project Manager. They'd all studied the sketch, but only Patrick seemed totally convinced that he'd recognize the man.

New passengers came up the escalators. The first flights of the morning had already left. Maggie felt certain it was to be another morning attack but it could end up being a long day.

She opened a paperback novel and leaned on the rail. It looked like she was reading but her eyes were still looking down below, watching the entrances, scanning the figures in the check-in lines and examining any of the men lingering off to the sides. She also kept checking the faces coming up on the escalator.

"At the newspaper stand," she said, suddenly noticing a man stopped there, wearing a navy blue jacket, trousers, sunglasses and dragging a large, black Pullman.

She glanced down at Patrick and saw him casually wander closer, pretending to be interested in the headlines of the newspaper through the glass on the machine.

"Nope, I don't think so," he said, this time holding up the phone to his ear so anyone who might not see the wireless headset would know he was on the cell phone. "I'm gonna stop off at the restroom. Talk to you later."

The ticket area quickly got crowded again. Bodies and

luggage pressed tight, waiting to check in, lined up at self-serve kiosks. She noticed A.D. Kunze down below talking to a woman in a housekeeping uniform. She certainly didn't look like a sniper or a member of the bomb squad, but then that was the whole idea, wasn't it.

When Maggie glanced back she didn't see Patrick. Her breath caught as she searched, straining to keep from looking like she was searching. Where had he gone?

"Patrick?"

In answer, she heard a toilet flush. She saw Kunze look up at her but he didn't smile until he turned away.

Okay, so she was being an overprotective big sister. A few minutes later she noticed Patrick come out of the restroom but he disappeared out of her sight again, just behind the down escalator.

Relax, she told herself. She needed to relax.

CHAPTER
76

Patrick followed the guy from the restroom. He tried to maintain his laid-back, casual pace despite wanting to hurry. He didn't want to lose him in the crowd.

From the back he thought he recognized the Project Manager's walk. Something about the shoulders, thrown back, chest out, almost like a soldier. Yeah, that was it. He kinda walked like a soldier, at attention, alert to everything and everyone around him. Even his head went from side to side, observing without stopping.

He wanted to be sure. He knew there were snipers, air marshals and agents, waiting. One word from him and they'd be swarming the place. He couldn't say anything until he was absolutely sure. He didn't want to screw up. Maggie was counting on him.

The guy went around the corner like he was getting on the escalator. Patrick waited a step or two, pretending to check his phone. He didn't want to follow so close especially if they both got on the escalator. He'd backtrack around the other way. Maybe he could get a better look from the other side.

He turned to do just that and almost bumped into the guy.

"You forgot that I could recognize you, too," he told Patrick, flashing him a smile as he pressed him against the wall of the escalator, pinning him in with a heavy, black Pullman.

CHAPTER
77

Maggie leaned against the railing and glanced at her watch. It hadn't been five minutes. He had been out of her sight for only five minutes. She restrained herself from calling him again.

If Nick had seen the Project Manager come through any of the front doors he would have alerted them. Unless he disguised himself.

No, don't do that, she told herself. Don't speculate. She didn't need to second-guess herself.

Was it possible the Project Manager had someone else drop off the bag? Had he already been here and left it somewhere?

She looked out over the floor below now packed with passengers and their luggage, little kids dragging behind parents, senior citizens shuffling through the tight passes. She tried to watch for bags that didn't move along with any passengers in the long, slow check-in lines. Wurth walked past her, keeping to the railing. He was doing the same thing, watching for bags left behind. A.D. Kunze did the same down below.

Maggie glanced back looking for Patrick. She was just about to call him when she saw him come out from behind the barrier. Only now he was dragging a black Pullman behind him. Her stomach fell to her knees even before she saw the glint of the handcuffs.

"He's got Patrick," she whispered into her headset.

"Yes, he does," came a voice she didn't recognize.

CHAPTER 78

Patrick couldn't see Maggie's face from where he stood. He tried not to look directly at her. He knew that's what the Project Manager was waiting for. He could talk to them with Patrick's headset but he didn't know exactly who they were or where they were. He was standing off to the side now, about thirty feet away, watching and waiting for Patrick to give away their locations.

Damn it! He really screwed this up.

It happened so quickly. One minute the guy was in front of him, disappearing around the corner and the next minute he was behind Patrick, slipping the cuffs on him and chaining him to the handle of the Pullman.

The guy looked different enough that Patrick hadn't been sure. Back at the mall he had worn a ball cap but his hair had also been much longer and dark. Now it was bristle-short and almost blond. He'd had facial hair, too, a clipped goatee. Now he was clean-shaven. He wore a golf shirt, navy canvas jacket, khaki trousers and leather loafers. No ball cap. But it was the walk that drew Patrick's attention.

By the time he was able to look the guy in the eyes, it was too late.

Off to the side Patrick could see A.D. Kunze. He stopped himself from looking over. Out of the corner of his eyes he could see that Kunze wasn't looking at him, either. He was talking to a cleaning woman, standing by her cart.

He glanced up to Maggie. Son of a bitch! The Project Manager caught him and followed his line of vision. But Maggie was gone.

He saw the guy's lips moving. He was talking to them, using Patrick's headset. What the hell was he telling them? He'd moved away from Patrick quickly. So quickly Patrick wasn't sure if anyone had seen him. Would they know which one he was? Could they tell?

Patrick glanced around again while the Project Manager still searched the upper level, scanning the railing where Maggie had been earlier. Then Patrick saw her. She was coming down the escalator, smiling and chatting with a woman next to her. The Project Manager turned his back to Patrick, just for a second or two and Patrick used the opportunity to point him out. He swung his free hand up, jerked his index finger at the man's back then brought his hand to his head and raked his fingers through his hair just as the Project Manager turned around.

Did Maggie see it? Did any of the others? It might have been too late, because now the guy was leaving. After all, he didn't need to be near the bomb to detonate it by remote control.

CHAPTER
79

Maggie tried to keep the panic from showing. It felt like something had her by the throat. She had to concentrate on breathing. She had to remind herself to slow down. Look by moving her eyes, not her head. Stay calm. Move nonchalantly. No nervous twitches. No jerks or twists around.

She tried to figure out who Patrick was looking at. None of the men around him looked like the sketch. The only olive complexion belonged to a guy with short, spiky sunbleached hair, dressed in khakis and a navy blue jacket.

She eased her way toward the escalator.

"I have a remote," the voice came again over her headset. "You don't have any choice but to let me walk out of here."

No one answered him. There was silence. They could no longer talk to each other now. Their communication system was useless.

She started down the escalator and asked the woman next to her if she'd had a good holiday. The woman started telling her about her trip while Maggie smiled at her and looked over her shoulder. Patrick looked miserable. He glanced in her direction. She wasn't sure if he'd seen her. Then suddenly she saw him raise his hand. He jerked a finger in one direction and ended up pushing back his hair. He had pointed to someone. He was giving them a signal, telling them who the Project Manager was.

Maggie came off the escalator, turning in Patrick's direction. She was close enough now to catch his eyes. He flicked his away, looking over in the same direction he had pointed.

The Project Manager had to be the man in the navy blue jacket and khakis. He was walking away, headed toward an exit but able to keep an eye on Patrick.

"You'll let me leave," he said and this time she could see his lips move. He still hadn't noticed her, and he no longer looked from side to side.

Kunze was closest to Patrick. He and the cleaning woman were edging their way forward. It didn't look like he had identified the Project Manager yet. Maggie examined the railing above, but she couldn't see Wurth. Was she the only one?

She looked back at Patrick and this time their eyes met. He pointed again and mouthed something to her. He was telling her to go after him. Don't let him get away. But how could she leave Patrick chained to a suitcase bomb?

The Project Manager was at the front doors, walking out. What would stop him from detonating the bomb once he was out of impact range? She had to stop him.

Maggie waved at Kunze to help Patrick. He moved in with the cleaning woman and her cart. Maggie took off running, dodging her way around passengers. She dug her right hand under her jacket, gripped the butt of her Smith & Wesson but kept it in its shoulder holster.

She slammed out the door onto the sidewalk and stopped.

She'd seen him turn to his right but she couldn't see him now through the line of curb-side check-ins. She pushed her way through, stumbling over luggage and feet. He was there, up ahead, five car lengths, getting into the passenger side of a black sedan. Maggie shoved herself between startled passengers but the car was already pulling away. She saw the license plate and watched helplessly as it sped away.

Out of breath, she leaned against a concrete bench. And that's when it happened. The explosion sent vibrations under her feet almost knocking her over.

It was too late. She was too late.

CHAPTER 80

Maggie waited though her patience was wearing thin. She didn't want to talk about it anymore. Nothing she said would change things. No amount of debriefing could remove the guilt and regret.

A.D. Raymond Kunze came in alone this time. He sat down across from her. He didn't say anything. Instead he folded his hands on top of the table, intertwining the fingers, a gesture Maggie recognized. What was it, again? She tried to access her memory to psychology of body language. Cupped hands, at the beginning of a conversation, often meant holding a fragile idea. It made her tense up even more.

"There was no way any of us could have known about a second bomb," he finally said.

She nodded. Shifted in the hardback chair, stiff from

sitting too long. She wanted to stand, pace, burn off her nervous energy.

"It damaged a parking garage. Almost a hundred vehicles. Dozens of injuries but only two fatalities."

He said it like it was a scrape, a minor mistake. She agreed that next to Oklahoma City, next to Mall of America, this one was minor, indeed.

"It could have been so much worse," he said when she didn't respond.

"Any leads to catching him?"

"He's like a ghost. Gone. Vanished. We think he blew up the parking garage to destroy the vehicle he may have used."

"What about the black sedan?"

Kunze looked away. Stared at his hands. Glanced at her but wouldn't meet her eyes.

"I got the license plate number," she insisted. She had tried to look up the number herself, using her security clearance and still she came up short. Each time she was denied access. A reference code was given instead.

"You were upset," he said, but the tone was way too gentle for Kunze. "You must have remembered the number wrong. It happens. Nerves. The adrenaline. Makes us transpose a number or two."

She stared at him. She knew even he didn't believe what he had just said. And she couldn't help wondering if that's how it had happened in the Oklahoma City case. Is that how they explained away evidence that didn't fit their theory? Someone must have gotten it wrong?

"I looked up the number myself."

He didn't seem surprised.

"It gave me a reference code. I don't have the clearance to track it, but I think it may have been a federal government vehicle."

This time he met her eyes and held them. "Leave it alone, O'Dell. Just leave it alone."

"Did you know?" she asked him.

"I still don't know," he told her frankly without hesitation. "And I don't want to know. Neither do you. Go home. Take some time off. Be glad we saved an airport full of people from being blown to pieces."

"But the case is far from finished."

"It is for you," and again, he said it much too gently for Kunze. "You're officially off the case. Too personal, considering what happened with your brother."

She wanted to challenge him. Was it because it had become personal or had she gotten too close to the truth? A truth Kunze seemed willing to ignore.

He pushed his chair away from the table, scraping and screeching across the floor and closing the subject. He stood and opened the door, dismissing her before she could argue.

She followed him into the hallway. Charlie Wurth and Nick Morrelli were three doors down. They had just come out of their debriefing rooms. A door clicked behind her. She turned around to see another agent bringing Patrick out of his room. He looked exhausted and she caught him unconsciously rubbing his wrist where the handcuff had bit into his skin and left a mark.

The gesture brought back that feeling again, the one that took her knees out from under her like a roller-coaster ride with the bottom falling out and the walls spinning out of control. She thought the suitcase bomb attached to Patrick's wrist had exploded. But instead, it had been the parking garage, a second bomb.

Within seconds after Maggie raced for the exit, the bomb squad had already cut the handcuffs off of Patrick. Several more seconds and they had the suitcase contained and transported it to a deserted airstrip. The lead safe container prevented the wireless remote from detonating the bomb.

"Congratulations," Charlie Wurth said to Kunze, offering his hand. "I just heard the news."

Everyone's eyes were on Kunze and he suddenly looked a bit embarrassed by the attention. Maggie figured he had received some commendation; she didn't expect what came next.

"A.D. Kunze is officially your new boss," Wurth said to Maggie with a genuine smile.

She looked to Kunze. It was true. He was nodding, trying to smile as he accepted the other men's congratulations. And all the while Maggie couldn't help thinking that he had sold out again.

"We're finished here," Kunze said to them, ready to change the subject. "I'll get someone to drive us back to the hotel or the airport."

"Thanks, but Patrick and I have a ride." She was glad that she had an excuse.

Charlie Wurth shook Patrick's hand, then Maggie's, holding Maggie's a bit longer as he said, "You come work for me anytime, Agent O'Dell. Homeland Security would be honored to have you." He held her eyes and she could see he meant the offer.

"Thanks. I'll think about that."

She didn't look back at A.D. Kunze.

Nick insisted he walk them out. Maggie led the way, stopping in the lobby.

"I guess this is goodbye again," Nick said as he gave Patrick a one-armed hug, that guy-thing that looked awkward but friendly. When he hugged Maggie he held her close and she felt his lips brush against her cheek before he released her.

She checked his eyes and shouldn't have been surprised to see the sparkle had dimmed. He hadn't gotten over the hurt, the disappointment. She wondered if he meant this was goodbye for good.

"When do you head back to Omaha?"

"I've got a flight later today. My dad's been in the hospital."

"Is he okay?"

"It's all part of the process since the stroke. Looks like he'll be home for Christmas."

"Can we give you a ride?" she offered. "I rented a car this morning."

"Thanks, but no. I actually have someone picking me up."

"Take care," she told him, feeling like the short phrase was inadequate.

As Maggie and Patrick made their way down the steps she thought she saw Jamie, the blond bomb expert, parking in one of the visitor's slots out front.

CHAPTER
81

Maggie dropped Patrick off at the hotel after they had lunch at The Rose and Crown. She had a couple of errands to run before their evening flight to Washington, D.C.

She had typed the addresses into the rental car's navigation system and let it guide her while her mind raced off in other directions. A.D. Kunze was satisfied to leave some unanswered questions in exchange for the official title he was only supposed to hold as interim. He'd done it before after Oklahoma City. His conscience had stumbled when he confided as much to her, handing off his own debriefing file. So what happened? Maggie wondered if maybe it simply got easier each time you sold a chunk of your soul.

Was he setting up CAP to take the fall from the very beginning? Would Chad Hendricks and Tyler Bennett get blamed for blowing up Mall of America and killing what now amounted to forty-three innocent people? And although there were no cutaways, no scapegoats to blame for Phoenix, Kunze hadn't stopped local law enforcement from conducting a search for two young white males, possibly college students, who were suspected in stealing the now incinerated Chevy TrailBlazer.

And what could Maggie do? She was officially off the case.

Late last night when sleep wouldn't come, she had pored over more documents, more files and news articles, Congressional amendments and proposals. She had hoped A.D. Kunze would be willing to hear her out. She hadn't realized he had already made up his own mind.

After leaving the FBI building, she'd made several phone calls going only on hunches, calling in a favor and counting on a promise. Not much, certainly not enough to bet an entire career on.

She found herself back downtown, back on Washington Avenue, less than four blocks away from the FBI building.

Charlie Wurth was waiting for her in the lobby.

"You sure you want to do this?" he asked her as they went through the security checkpoint.

"Absolutely. But I'll understand if you've changed your mind."

"*Au contraire, cheri.* I figure I owe you one. Besides, I got my job by being a rabble-rouser. But do you suppose our friend may have changed his mind?"

"He said he'd meet us here." Even as she said it Maggie wasn't sure it was a promise that would be kept.

They took the elevator and rode in silence. Now with their coats over their arms, Maggie noticed that Wurth had changed from this morning into a steel-blue suit with a lemon-yellow shirt and orange necktie. It made her navy blue suit look bland and official. Shoulder to shoulder, they marched down the hallway to the set of office suites at the end.

"Hello. Do you have an appointment today?" a young woman asked as they walked around the huge reception desk, ignoring her and going directly to the open doorway behind the desk.

"Excuse me," she said, trying to stop them.

"It's okay," Senator Foster said from inside the office. "Come on in, Deputy Director Wurth, Agent O'Dell." He stood up behind his marble-topped desk and waved them in. "So glad to see you're back safe and sound."

"Actually we have some questions to ask you." Wurth was cool and calm. "About the bill you're cosponsoring among other things."

During Maggie's frenetic search through Internet documents she discovered that Senator Foster was one of the cosponsors of a Homeland Security bill with a hefty price tag, due to Congress before the holidays. The same bill Kunze had mentioned that would elevate security requirements in airports, shopping complexes and sports stadiums. The one Nick had said would send federal funds to Phoenix.

"Certainly," Senator Foster said. His fingers smoothed his silver hair while Maggie looked for any sign of him being nervous or anxious. He had the role of distinguished down pat.

Wurth nodded to Maggie, his own sign for her to take the reins.

"We know you helped him get away."

"Excuse me?" There was maybe a flash of surprise. Nothing more.

"The Project Manager. You had a government-issued car pick him up. Tough to trace. A lot of security codes in place but we were able to do it."

He was shaking his head, a grin—or maybe a grimace—on his face.

"That's ridiculous. I had my government-issued jet fly you to Phoenix, but I don't know anything about a car. Do your superior officers know you two are here making these wild accusations?"

"We know about your secret organization." Wurth took his turn. "We're getting a list of all the businessmen and politicians."

"This is absurd. I'll have you both shoving paperwork next week. I'm calling security."

Senator Foster reached for his phone but stopped. His eyes widened as he stared between their shoulders. Maggie glanced back to see Henry Lee in the doorway.

He had shown up, after all. Kept his promise.

"It's over, Allan," he said. "It's time to come clean."

CHAPTER
82

Monday evening
Minneapolis-St. Paul International Airport

Patrick started to yawn, caught himself just as Maggie noticed.

"Maybe we should have waited for a morning flight. We haven't had much sleep. We're both exhausted," she told him.

"Hey, neither of us is piloting the plane. We'll be fine."

They'd been sitting at their gate for maybe twenty minutes. It felt like hours.

"And it's okay if you want to sleep the whole flight."

He raised an eyebrow at her.

"Sorry," she said. "I'm a bit of a nervous flyer."

"Really?"

She nodded.

"We're in first class. Maybe a glass of wine?"

He wanted to kick himself even before she shook her head. *Stupid.* He knew she didn't drink, couldn't drink.

Whatever. He had to admit he felt a bit fried. Still running on adrenaline. Looked like Maggie was, too.

"Do you ever get used to it?" he asked her. "I keep thinking about that guy being out there somewhere."

"Sometimes they get away." She shrugged but he saw her absentmindedly touch her jacket where her gun and shoulder holster usually sat just underneath the fabric. She had to check the gun for the flight. Looked like she missed it.

"Criminals don't change just because they got away," she told him. "Typically it emboldens them, makes them a little cocky, sometimes reckless. Maybe he'll get caught for speeding or a broken taillight. Timothy McVeigh was stopped outside of Perry, Oklahoma, by a state trooper, only hours after the bombing. All because his car was missing a tag."

Patrick listened but he wasn't sure he believed the Project Manager would ever put himself into a situation like that. He couldn't get the man's eyes out of his mind, that dark blue that seemed to pierce you and pin you down. He'd tried to sleep but couldn't do it without the guy showing up, grinning at him as he slipped the handcuffs onto Patrick's wrist. Sometimes the bomb actually went off and blasted Patrick awake.

He figured it was post-traumatic stress. It'd wear off in a couple of days, maybe a week.

That's when he saw him.

Patrick recognized the walk, shoulders back, chest out, that same military stature. His head swiveled from side to side. Patrick's heart started thumping. *Jesus! It wasn't possible. Was it?* His hair was still blond, that same bristle cut. He even wore the same golf shirt, navy jacket, khaki trousers and leather loafers. He dragged a black Pullman.

"It's him," he whispered to Maggie.

She looked up and he tried to point him out using only his chin and eyes. He could feel her stiffen beside him.

"Is it possible? Would he do that?"

"You stay here."

She stood slowly, digging her badge out of her jacket. She flipped it open, tucking one flap into her pocket and letting the badge show. Then she started in his direction.

Patrick couldn't keep his eyes off the man. He could only see a profile of his face. He wanted to get a glimpse of the eyes. He stood up and started to trail along only on the opposite side. Maggie kept glancing over at Patrick as if asking for reassurance. He only nodded. She was following behind him, three people in between.

The guy was making his way toward one of the ramps to another terminal. If he got into a crowd going the same way they'd lose him. Patrick remembered how slick the guy was in Phoenix. In front of him one minute and behind him the next.

Maggie closed the gap between them. Ten, maybe fifteen more feet and he'd turn onto the ramp, into a crowd of travelers. Patrick watched her say something to the man. He stopped but before he could turn around Maggie grabbed the back of his jacket collar and shoved him against the wall. She had one of his arms twisted up behind him and then she yelled for security.

Everything stopped. Two security officers had their weapons drawn. Both of them pointing directly at Maggie.

"I'm FBI." Patrick heard her yell at them, sticking out her hip with the badge flapping from the jacket pocket while one of her hands twisted the man's arm behind his back and her other hand hung onto his jacket collar.

In seconds more security officers converged on the area, holding back travelers. Three more joined the two. One

had grabbed Maggie's badge and was examining it. Two of
them pried the guy out of Maggie's hands. They had him
up against the wall and were patting him down. No one
touched the Pullman.

Maggie waved for Patrick to come over, pointing him
out to one of the security officers. He elbowed his way
through the crowd that had grown around him. His knees
felt a bit wobbly. His heart hadn't stopped banging. He
made his way to Maggie's side, just as they pulled the guy
away from the wall and turned him to face Patrick.

His heart dropped to his feet as he finally looked the guy
in the eyes.

"It's not him," Patrick said.

EPILOGUE

"Your decorations are incredible," Julia Racine said as Maggie led her into the kitchen. Racine stopped when she saw Gwen and Tully, especially Tully, his sleeves rolled up, a red "Grill Baby Grill" apron tied around him. He didn't look up from the sugar cookie shaped like a reindeer that he was frosting.

"Don't even say it," he warned, still not a glance up as he carefully swirled around the antlers. "Where did Patrick disappear? He's the one who got me into this."

"He's out back with Emma and Rebecca," Maggie said, glancing at her backyard from the kitchen window.

The three of them were throwing snowballs for Harvey to catch. For a minute she had an odd sense of déjà vu, another reminder of the day after Thanksgiving and being pulled away from a houseful of friends. She caught herself taking a deep breath.

"Maybe they can talk her into going to the University of New Haven," Tully said.

"Still no decisions as to where she wants to go?"

"Too many distractions."

Maggie decided to leave it alone. It hadn't been three months since Tully's daughter Emma had to deal with her father and her mother being the target of a madman. It would take time. Just like it would take time for Patrick.

He and Rebecca had driven down from Connecticut, arriving yesterday to spend the holidays with Maggie and Harvey. Last night he confessed to her—after Rebecca had gone to bed—that he still had nightmares about the Project Manager, handcuffing him to a bomb. She should have had an answer for him. She had gone through the same thing many times, different killers invading her sleep. All she could tell him was that it would take time. That's all she had to offer.

Despite her efforts, along with Charlie Wurth's and Henry Lee's, the so-called secret organization had managed to close ranks and board up doors around itself. It would take additional months to gather evidence and bring charges. Senator Foster was still being investigated, resigning his seat before being officially tossed out of the Senate. However, Senator Foster's cosponsor pushed through the Homeland Security bill with little opposition. In the wake of two bombings, it became the patriotic thing to do. And Henry Lee would spend Christmas with his wife and grandson, his testimony securing his freedom.

As for the Project Manager, how could Maggie tell Patrick not to worry? The man had vanished.

The doorbell rang again. Maggie left her guests in the kitchen and made her way down the hall to the entrance. She opened the door to find Benjamin Platt, his white West Highland terrier, Digger, up under one arm and his other arm raised, his hand holding a piece of mistletoe over his head.

"Merry Christmas!"

Without missing a beat, Maggie petted Digger and gave the dog a kiss on his head.

Ben laughed and shook his head. "This dog always gets more action than I do."

He stepped inside and put Digger down to scamper off in the direction of voices.

"Not quite the chick magnet you thought he'd be, huh?"

She helped him take his coat off and while she was behind him she whispered in his ear, "You don't need a dog or mistletoe."

The look in his eyes was enough to send a flutter through her.

Patrick interrupted. "We ready to go?"

"You're leaving?" Ben asked. "I just got here."

"We'll be back in about an hour," Maggie told him as Patrick took Ben's coat from Maggie and replaced it with her own.

"She's taking me tree hunting," Patrick told him.

"We're going to bring back the most magical Christmas tree in the field."

* * * * *

AUTHOR'S NOTE

After the Oklahoma City bombing there were at least twenty witnesses who insisted they saw a "third terrorist" or "John Doe #2" with Timothy McVeigh at different times and in different places, but they always described him with the same physical characteristics. Over half of those witnesses gave this description even before the now infamous sketch had been completed. All of the assertions I've made about a third terrorist conspiracy are not my own. Some people, including Timothy McVeigh's first attorney, still believe the mysterious John Doe #2 may have been the actual mastermind. No one, however, seems to know what happened to him.

ACKNOWLEDGMENTS

This past year and a half my family has been gathering way too often at hospitals, providing the writer in me with more than enough research material. Here's to the crew: Bob and Tracy Kava, Nancy and Jim Tworek, Kenny and Connie Kava and Patricia Kava.

Naming characters is often a unique process for most authors. Only on rare occasions have I used a real person's name for one of my characters. This novel is the exception. Thanks go to the following:

Joanne Ceimo for allowing me to use both her sons' names, David and Chris Ceimo. Chris actually does own an English pub called The Rose and Crown, only you'll find it in Phoenix, Arizona, not Minneapolis.

Ray Kunze—so you're not a headless, rotting corpse, after all. And no, I don't think you dress like a bouncer at a private nightclub.

Lee Dixon and his new grandson, Henry Lee Dixon. I haven't met the latter yet, but I'm sure he's as lovable and ornery as his grandfather.

Also special thanks to:

Leigh Ann Retelsdorf—all the questions helped...really they did...okay, maybe not in the beginning, but eventually they did.

Faith Cotton—for being my eyes by providing all the fantastic photos of Mall of America.

Frank Tripp at Alegent Health Wellness Center for answering questions about commercial dryers.

And of course, Sharon Car, Marlene Haney, Sandy Rockwood and Patti El-Kachouti—for your patience, your friendship and your reminders that there is life outside of writing books.

My unwavering respect and heartfelt gratitude to my incredible team:

Linda McFall, my editor and grace under pressure;

Amy Moore-Benson, my agent extraordinaire;

And Deb Carlin, my peace of mind, always.

A very special thank-you to the booksellers, book buyers and librarians across the country for mentioning my novels.

Last and most importantly, to all you faithful readers—I know there's plenty of competition for your time, your entertainment and for your dollars. I thank you for continuing to choose my novels.

REQUEST YOUR FREE BOOKS!

2 FREE NOVELS
FROM THE SUSPENSE COLLECTION
PLUS 2 FREE GIFTS!

ALEX KAVA

32640	EXPOSED	___ $7.99 U.S.	___ $8.99 CAN.
32703	WHITEWASH	___ $7.99 U.S.	___ $7.99 CAN.
32434	A NECESSARY EVIL	___ $7.99 U.S.	___ $9.50 CAN.
32055	AT THE STROKE OF MADNESS	___ $6.99 U.S.	___ $8.50 CAN.
32189	ONE FALSE MOVE	___ $7.50 U.S.	___ $8.99 CAN.
66701	THE SOUL CATCHER	___ $6.99 U.S.	___ $8.50 CAN.
66824	A PERFECT EVIL	___ $6.99 U.S.	___ $8.50 CAN.

(limited quantities available)

TOTAL AMOUNT	$ _____
POSTAGE & HANDLING	$ _____
($1.00 for 1 book, 50¢ for each additional)	
APPLICABLE TAXES*	$ _____
TOTAL PAYABLE	$ _____

(check or money order—please do not send cash)

To order, complete this form and send it, along with a check or money order for the total above, payable to MIRA Books, to: **In the U.S.:** 3010 Walden Avenue, P.O. Box 9077, Buffalo, NY 14269-9077; **In Canada:** P.O. Box 636, Fort Erie, Ontario, L2A 5X3.

Name: _____
Address: _____ City: _____
State/Prov.: _____ Zip/Postal Code: _____
Account Number (if applicable): _____

075 CSAS

*New York residents remit applicable sales taxes.
*Canadian residents remit applicable GST and provincial taxes.

MIRA®

www.MIRABooks.com

MAK0810BL